THE PENGUIN CLASSICS

FOUNDER EDITOR (1944–64): E. V. RIEU

IVAN SERGEYEVICH TURGENEV was born in 1818 in the Province of Orel, and suffered during his childhood from a tyrannical mother. After the family had moved to Moscow he entered in 1833 first Moscow, then Petersburg University where he studied history and philology. When he was nineteen, convinced that Europe contained the source of real knowledge, he went to the University of Berlin. After two years he returned to Russia and took his degree at the University of Petersburg. In 1843 he fell in love with Pauline Garcia-Viardot, a young Spanish singer, who influenced the rest of his life; he followed her on her singing tours in Europe and spent long periods in the French house of herself and her husband, both of whom accepted him as a family friend. His illegitimate daughter by a sempstress was for a time brought up among the Viardot children. After 1856 he lived mostly abroad, and he became the first Russian writer to gain a wide reputation in Europe; he was a well-known figure in Parisian literary circles, where his friends included Flaubert and the Goncourt brothers, and an honorary degree was conferred on him at Oxford. His series of six novels reflects a period of Russian life from the 1830s to the 1870s: they are *Rudin* (1855), *A House of Gentlefolk* (1858), *On the Eve* (1859; a Penguin Classic), *Fathers and Sons* (1861), *Smoke* (1867) and *Virgin Soil* (1876). He also wrote plays, which include the comedy *A Month in the Country*; short stories and *Sketches from a Hunter's Album* (a Penguin Classic); and literary essays and memoirs. He died in Bougival near Paris in 1883 after being ill for a year, and was buried in Russia.

LEONARD SCHAPIRO was born in Glasgow in 1908, and educated at St Paul's School and University College, London. He was called to the Bar in 1932 and practised until 1955, with interruption for war service. Since 1955 he has been at the London School of Economics and Political Science. He is now Emeritus Professor of Political Science with special reference to Russian Studies. Among his published works are *The Origin of the Communist Autocracy*, *The Communist Party of the Soviet Union*, *Totalitarianism* and *Turgenev: His Life and Times*. Professor Schapiro is a Fellow of the British Academy and a Fellow of University College, London.

Ivan Turgenev

SPRING TORRENTS

TRANSLATED BY
LEONARD SCHAPIRO
WITH NOTES
AND A CRITICAL ESSAY

PENGUIN BOOKS

Penguin Books Ltd, Harmondsworth, Middlesex, England
Penguin Books, 625 Madison Avenue, New York, New York 10022, U.S.A.
Penguin Books Australia Ltd, Ringwood, Victoria, Australia
Penguin Books Canada Ltd, 2801 John Street, Markham, Ontario, Canada L3R 1B4
Penguin Books (N.Z.) Ltd, 182–190 Wairau Road, Auckland 10, New Zealand

—

This translation first published by Eyre Methuen Ltd 1972
Published in Penguin Books 1980
Translation, Notes, Critical Essay copyright © Leonard Schapiro, 1972

—

—

Made and printed in Great Britain by
Richard Clay (The Chaucer Press) Ltd
Bungay, Suffolk
Set in Monotype Bembo

Contents

Foreword   7

Spring Torrents   11

Notes   177

Critical Essay – Spring Torrents:
   *Its Place and Significance in the Life and Work
   of Ivan Sergeyevich Turgenev*   183

Foreword

Spring Torrents is a late work of Turgenev: it was written during 1870 and 1871, when Turgenev was in his fifties. But its action takes place in 1840, when Turgenev was twenty-two, and the story is, to some slight extent, autobiographical.

To many readers the story will already be familiar. But there may be some who will be reading it for the first time. It is a story of quite extraordinary haunting beauty, constructed with consummate skill. It would be little short of vandalism to tempt any reader to start with a translator's preface, in which a bald summary would inevitably have to replace the Master's craftsmanship, and extracts and quotations would cloy the appetite for the main feast. So, I have avoided any introduction: my advice is, go to the story and enjoy it. For those who may be baffled by some passages or references I have appended a few notes at the back of the text. The existence of such a note by the translator is indicated by a superscript in the text: the reader can refer to the note as he proceeds or ignore the number, as he pleases. The few footnotes printed at the foot of the pages are the author's footnotes and have, of course, been retained in the form in which he cast them.

Its beauty as a work of art apart, *Spring Torrents* is, in many ways, particularly illuminating on Turgenev's craft. It is also of more than usual significance in revealing Turgenev's mind and thought and intimate emotions. For those who are interested in the suggestions that I have to make on these matters, an essay on these general questions is printed at the back of the book, after the text and after the notes.

Although the action of *Spring Torrents* takes place some thirty years before the date of composition and publication, the author's style is in no possible sense archaic or dated, but contemporary in character. I have therefore made no attempt, in turn, to suggest the style of the seventies of the past century, but have aimed at a contemporary style, which, to the best of my ability, reproduces the style and mood of the author. I hope that the usual difficulties which arise in translation from the Russian will not obtrude themselves too much. I have been sparing in the use of patronymics – but they are to a certain extent unavoidable, and I hope the reader will not find them too bizarre. The other difficulty – the use of 'you' and 'thou', so hard to reproduce in English – has not proved very serious. In some cases the form of address is not so material as to make it important for the reader to know which form is being used. In other cases, where it is important, the situation has been saved by the fact that the vital conversations take place in French, which is a language in which the different forms of address are easily indicated by the use of *tu* or *vous*.

But, it will be asked, why translate at all what has already been translated several times before? I suppose any translator (even so amateur a one as I am) persuades himself that he can do it better than it has been done before. (And I must confess here that I have never read any translation of *Spring Torrents* – perhaps if I did I would scrap this one. But it is too late.) I started to translate *Spring Torrents* for a friend who is a writer, and herself no mean stylist, because I felt that I could reveal Turgenev's art to her in this way better than others had done in the past. It is, of course, not possible for me to judge whether I have succeeded or failed: I merely record what set me upon the translator's path. As I proceeded with the translation I became increasingly aware, to an extent that I had never realized before (though I have read *Spring Torrents* many times since my boyhood), of the superb mastery of his craft that Turgenev exhibits. And so, the work of translation grew into a tribute, a small and humble tribute to a great master from one by whom the craft of writing has never been pursued for its own sake so much as for the utilitarian purposes of the record and analysis of facts.

I must record my gratitude to friends who have been kind enough to help me. Victor Frank generously went through the translation and saved me from a number of errors. Roma Thewes has critically worked through the text on several occasions, and made innumerable and valuable suggestions for improvement. To both these friends I owe a great debt of thanks. But I am an obstinate and headstrong man, and they are in no way to blame for the many errors or roughnesses which no doubt still remain.

Note to the Penguin edition

The text of 1972 is reprinted without alteration, except for the correction of several errors since discovered. In the death of Victor Frank in 1972 Russian letters suffered a grave loss. Roma Thewes, now my wife, has once again been of great assistance in going through the proofs.

Spring Torrents

Those happy years,
Those days so gay,
Like the rush of spring torrents
Have vanished away.

[*From a very old song*] [1]

*

. . . ABOUT two in the morning he returned to his study. He dismissed the servant who had come in and had lit the candles, then flung himself on to the armchair by the fireplace, and buried his face in his hands.

He had never before felt so tired – in body and in spirit. He had spent the whole evening in the company of agreeable women and educated men. There had been some beautiful women among them too, and nearly all the men had been witty and accomplished. His own conversation had come off very well, brilliantly even . . . and yet, and yet . . . never before had he felt such disgust for life, such *taedium vitae*, [2] which the Romans talked about in their time. It overwhelmed him like some irresistible force; he felt it choking him. Had he been somewhat younger he would have burst into tears of frustration, boredom and irritation. He felt as if his soul were filled with hot and acrid smoke, like the smoke of wormwood. Like a dark autumn night, a sense of disgust enveloped him; something repulsive and insufferable engulfed him. Try as he would he could not shake it off, could not dispel all this darkness and the pungent smoke. There was no escape for him in sleep; he knew it would not come. So he began to let his thoughts run – slowly, listlessly and rather angrily.

He reflected on the useless bustle, the vulgar falsity of

human existence. One after another he mentally reviewed each age of life (he himself had recently turned fifty-three). He had no good word for any of them. Everywhere he found the same squandering of time and effort, the same treading of water, the same self-deception, half unconscious and half deliberate – anything to keep the child quiet; and then – all of a sudden – like a fall of snow, old age is upon one – and with it the ever-growing fear of death, all-consuming, gnawing at one's very vitals – and then, the abyss. Come to that, it would not be so bad if that were the way life worked out. But there could also be disability and suffering, spreading like rust over iron, before the end came . . .

He did not picture life's ocean, as do the poets, all astir with stormy waves. No, he saw it in his mind's eye as smooth, without a ripple, motionless and translucent right down to the dark sea bed. He saw himself sitting in a small unsteady boat, staring at the dark silt of the sea bottom, where he could just discern shapeless monsters, like enormous fish. These were life's hazards – the illnesses, the griefs, madness, poverty, blindness . . . Here he is, looking at them – and then one of the monsters begins to emerge from the murk, rising higher and higher, becoming ever more clearly, more repellently clearly, discernible . . . Another minute and its impact will overturn the boat. And then, once again, its outlines grow dimmer, it recedes into the distance, to the sea bed, and there it lies motionless, but for a slight movement of its tail . . . But the destined day will come, and then the boat will capsize.[3]

He tossed his head, jumped up, paced up and down the room once or twice, and then sat at his desk. He began to pull open one drawer after another and to rummage around among his papers and old letters, which were mostly from women. He had no idea why he was doing this, he was not looking for anything in particular; his only desire was to find some occupation to drive away the thoughts which were exhausting him. He unfolded a few letters at random (one of them disclosed a pressed flower with a faded ribbon tied around it) and shrugged his shoulders. He threw them all aside, with a glance at the fireplace, probably intending to burn this useless rubbish.

Suddenly, as he was rapidly thrusting his hands into one drawer after another, his eyes started from his head. Slowly he pulled out a small octagonal box of old-fashioned design, and slowly lifted the lid. Inside the box, under a double layer of yellowed cotton-wool, lay a tiny garnet cross.

He examined the cross for a few moments without any sign of recognition, and then uttered a faint cry. His features showed something that was neither compassion nor joy, and yet had elements of each. It was the expression of a man suddenly confronted by someone he once loved tenderly, but has long lost sight of; someone who appears unexpectedly before him, looking exactly the same – and completely changed with the passage of time.

He got up and returned to the fireplace. Once again he sat down in the armchair, and once again buried his face in his hands ... Why today? Why today in particular? he kept wondering, and he remembered many things from the distant past ...

This is what he remembered ...

But first I must tell you his name, his patronymic and his surname. He was called Sanin – Dimitry Pavlovich Sanin.

This is what he remembered:

I

It was the summer of 1840. Sanin was just twenty-three years old, and was in Frankfurt on his way back to Russia from Italy. He was not a rich man, but he had a small private income and almost no family. He had inherited a few thousand roubles from a distant relation and had decided to spend the money on foreign travel before entering the public service – before putting on the harness of employment in a government department, without which it was impossible for him to envisage any kind of assured existence. Sanin had carried out to the letter his plan of spending his legacy, and had managed his affairs so skilfully that on the day of his arrival in Frankfurt, he had precisely enough money left to pay for his journey back to St Petersburg.

In 1840, railways scarcely existed: your gentleman on his tour had to be content with the stagecoach. Sanin had reserved his seat in the extra coach (*Beiwagen*) which was not due to leave until after ten o'clock that night. There was still plenty of time. Fortunately, the weather was superb, and so Sanin, after lunching at the White Swan Inn (which was renowned at that date) set off to explore the town. He took a look at Danneker's Ariadne, which he did not much like, and visited Goethe's house – he had, incidentally, read nothing of Goethe except for *Werther*, and in a French translation at that. Then he went for a walk along the bank of the Main, and felt a bit bored, as every self-respecting traveller should. At last, some time after five, tired out and with his boots covered with dust, he found himself in one of Frankfurt's most insignificant streets. It was a street that he was destined not to forget for a long time.

On one of the few houses in the street he observed a signboard: Giovanni Roselli's Italian Patisserie made its existence known to passers-by. Sanin went into this establishment intending to drink a glass of lemonade. But when he entered the front shop, there was not a soul inside. It looked a little like a chemist's. Behind the simple counter stood a painted cupboard, with a few gold-labelled bottles on its shelves, and some glass jars, containing rusks, chocolate drops and boiled sweets. A grey tomcat was blinking and purring, kneading with its paws the seat of a high cane chair which stood near the window. A large ball of red wool, glowing brilliantly in the slanting rays of the evening sun, lay on the floor beside an overturned carved wooden basket. A confused noise could be heard coming from the adjoining inner room. Sanin stood for a moment, waiting for the little bell attached to the shop door to stop jangling. Then he raised his voice and called out 'Is anyone there?' At that very moment the door leading to the inner room opened – and Sanin was taken completely by surprise.

II

A GIRL of about nineteen, her dark hair falling about her bare shoulders, her bare arms outstretched, burst into the shop. Seeing Sanin, she rushed straight at him, seized his hand, and tugged at him, exclaiming breathlessly: 'Hurry, come here, save him!' Sanin did not follow the girl at once – it was not that he did not wish to obey her, but that he was simply too amazed to move. He was almost rooted to the spot: he had never seen so beautiful a girl in his life. But she turned towards him, with a tone of such despair in her voice, in her look, in the motion of her clenched hand as she lifted it, trembling, to her pale cheek and murmured, 'Oh come on, why don't you come?' that he rushed after her through the open door.

In the inner room, on an old-fashioned horsehair divan, lay a boy of about fourteen, his white face tinged with yellow, like wax or ancient marble. He was strikingly like the girl, and was evidently her brother. His eyes were closed. His hair, which was black and thick, cast a shadow like a stain on his forehead, which seemed frozen to stone, and on his thin and motionless eyebrows. His clenched teeth were visible under his bluish lips. He did not appear to be breathing. One arm had dropped to the floor, the other was flung above his head. The boy was fully dressed and buttoned up. His throat was constrained by a tight necktie.

The girl flung herself at him with a cry of despair.

'He's dead, he's dead! Only a moment ago he was sitting here talking to me – and then suddenly he fell down and went completely rigid. Oh God, can nobody help him? And

Mother isn't here! Pantaleone, Pantaleone, what about the doctor?' she added, suddenly switching to Italian. 'Have you been to fetch the doctor?'

'Signora, I haven't been to the doctor, I sent Luisa,' a hoarse voice replied from behind the door, and a little old man came into the room, hobbling on a pair of short bandy legs. He was attired in a lilac-coloured dress coat, with black buttons and a high white stock, short nankeen breeches and blue woollen stockings. His tiny face was all but invisible beneath an enormous shock of iron-grey hair, which sprouted upwards round his head and then fell down in untidy little wisps. This made the old man look rather like a broody hen, and the likeness was made more striking still by the fact that all that could be discerned under the dark grey mass of hair were a pointed nose and a pair of round yellow eyes.

'Luisa will get there faster, and in any case I can't run,' the old man went on in Italian, lifting alternately each of his flat, gouty feet which were encased in high-cut shoes with bows. 'But I have brought some water.'

His dried-up, gnarled fingers were grasping the long, thin neck of a bottle.

'But Emil will die meanwhile,' cried the girl and stretched out her hands to Sanin. 'Oh sir, please, *Oh mein Herr*, is there nothing you can do to help?'

'It's a stroke, he must be bled,' observed the old man who answered to the name of Pantaleone.

Although Sanin knew absolutely nothing about medical matters, he was quite certain of one thing: fourteen-year-old boys do not have strokes.

'It's a fainting fit, and not a stroke,' he said, turning to Pantaleone. 'Have you some brushes?'

The old man raised his little face.

'What?'

'Brushes, brushes,' Sanin repeated in German and in French. 'Brushes,' he added, going through the motions of cleaning his clothes.

The old man understood at last.

'Ah, brushes! *Spazzette!* Of course we have brushes!'

'Bring them here. We will take off his coat and start rubbing him.'

'Good ... *Benone!* But shouldn't I pour water over his head?'

'No ... Later. Hurry up now and fetch the brushes.'

Pantaleone put the bottle on the floor, ran off and returned at once with a hair-brush and a clothes-brush. He was accompanied by a curly-haired poodle who wagged his tail vigorously, and stared inquisitively at the old man, the girl and even Sanin, as if anxious to discover what all the excitement was about.

Sanin quickly removed the boy's coat, undid the collar of his shirt, rolled up the shirt-sleeves and, seizing one of the brushes, began to rub the boy's chest and arms with all his might. At the same time, Pantaleone wielded the other brush – the hair-brush – over the boy's boots and trousers. The girl threw herself down on her knees by the divan, seized her brother's head with both hands and gazed at him so intensely that she did not even blink her eyes.

Sanin rubbed away, and at the same time kept stealing a glance at her. Dear God! What a lovely girl she was!

III

HER nose was slightly large, but of a beautiful aquiline shape. There was a faint trace of down on her upper lip. Her skin was smooth and without lustre, for all the world as if she were made of ivory or of meerschaum, and her hair fell in a wave like that of Allori's Judith in the Palazzo Pitti. Most striking of all were her eyes – dark grey, with a black border round the iris – superb, triumphant eyes, even now when their light was dimmed by fear and grief . . . Sanin could not help thinking of the wonderful land from which he was returning home . . . But even in Italy he had never seen anything to equal this! The girl's breathing was interrupted and uneven: it seemed as if every time she drew breath she was waiting for her brother to start breathing too.

Sanin continued to brush the boy, but his eyes were not for the girl alone. The remarkable figure of Pantaleone also attracted his attention. The old man was quite weak from the effort, and was panting: every time he applied the brush, he gave a little jump and emitted something between a groan and a squeak. His enormous mane of hair was damp with sweat, and swayed heavily from side to side, like the roots of some large plant washed by a rising flood.

Sanin was just about to say to him, 'You might at least take off his boots . . .' when the poodle, no doubt excited by the unusual nature of what was going on, dug in his front paws and began to bark.

'Tartaglia! Canaglia!' the old man hissed at him.

But at this moment, the girl's face was transfigured. Her eyebrows lifted, her eyes became even larger and suddenly alight with joy . . . Sanin looked round . . . The colour had reappeared in the young man's face . . . There was a movement of his eyelids . . . His nostrils quivered. He drew the air in through his teeth which were still clenched, and gave a sigh . . .

'Emil!' cried the girl. '*Emilio mio!*'

The boy's large, black eyes opened slowly. They were still dull, but they were smiling weakly. The same weak smile spread downwards to his pale lips. Then he moved the arm which was hanging by his side and suddenly and swiftly raised it to his chest.

'Emilio!' repeated the girl and rose to her feet. The expression on her face was so strong and vivid that she looked as if she was near to tears or about to burst out laughing.

'Emil! What is all this? Emil!' came a voice from behind the door. A neatly dressed woman with silver-grey hair and a dark complexion walked briskly into the room. An elderly man followed close behind her. Sanin caught a glimpse of the head of a maidservant behind the man's shoulders.

The girl ran towards them.

'He has been saved, Mother; he's alive!' she exclaimed, trembling as she embraced the woman who had just come in.

'But what is it all about?' repeated the woman. 'I come back to the house . . . and suddenly I meet the doctor, and Luisa.'

The girl began to recount what had happened. The doctor went up to the invalid who was rapidly becoming more conscious and still continued to smile. He looked as if he was beginning to feel ashamed of the alarm which he had caused.

'I see you have been rubbing him with brushes,' said the doctor, turning to Sanin and Pantaleone, 'and you did very well. A most excellent idea . . . Now let us see what else we can think of . . .' He felt the young man's pulse. 'Hm! Now, let's see your tongue!'

The woman bent over the boy with an expression of concern. He smiled even more openly – and then turned his eyes on her and blushed . . .

It occurred to Sanin that he was in the way. He went out into the shop. He had hardly had time to grasp the handle of the street door, when the girl appeared in front of him and stopped him.

'I see you are going,' she said, with a friendly look. 'I won't detain you, but you simply must come and see us this evening. We owe you so much – you may have saved my brother's life. We want to thank you – my mother too. You must tell us who you are, you must join us in our happiness.'

'But I am leaving for Berlin tonight . . .' Sanin said hesitantly.

'There is plenty of time,' the girl replied with alacrity. 'Come here in an hour's time for a cup of chocolate. Do you promise? I must get back to him. You will come, won't you?'

What was Sanin to do?

'I'll come,' he promised.

The lovely creature quickly shook him by the hand and was gone like a bird, and he found himself in the street.

IV

AN hour and a half later, when Sanin returned to the Patisserie Roselli, he was received like a member of the family. Emilio was sitting on the very same divan where the rubbing with the brushes had taken place. The doctor had prescribed some medicine and had advised great care in avoiding stress, since the patient was of a nervous disposition and prone to heart trouble. He had had fainting fits before: but never so prolonged or so deep as on this occasion. However, the doctor declared that all danger was now passed. Emil was dressed, as befitted a convalescent, in an ample dressing-gown, and his mother had wound a pale blue woollen scarf around his neck. But he looked gay, almost festive – indeed the whole scene had a festive air. In front of the divan stood a round table covered with a clean cloth. An enormous china coffee-pot filled with fragrant chocolate dominated the table. It was surrounded by cups, little decanters of syrup, sponge cakes, buns, even flowers. Six thin wax candles were burning in a pair of antique silver candelabras. On one side of the door a great wing chair offered its soft and comfortable embrace – Sanin was made to sit there. All the inmates of the Patisserie with whom he had had occasion to become acquainted that day were present, including the poodle Tartaglia, and the tomcat. There was an atmosphere of untold happiness. The poodle was actually sneezing from sheer delight – only the tomcat was still blinking his eyes and screwing up his face.

Sanin was made to explain who he was, where he came from and what he was called. When he told them that he was a Russian, the two ladies were somewhat surprised, and even exclaimed a little. Both declared in unison that his German accent was excellent, but that if he preferred to speak French, he was welcome to do so, since both of them understood French well and could express themselves freely in that language. Sanin immediately took advantage of this suggestion. 'Sanin, Sanin?' The ladies had never imagined that a Russian surname could be so simple to pronounce. His Christian name, Dimitry, was also much admired. The older lady observed that she had heard in her youth a beautiful opera '*Demetrio e Polibio*' but that 'Dimitry' sounded much better than 'Demetrio'. This kind of conversation continued for about an hour. The ladies, for their part, initiated him into all the details of their own lives.

The mother, the woman with the grey hair, did most of the talking. Sanin learned that her name was Leonora Roselli and that she had been left a widow after the death of her husband, Giovanni Battista Roselli, who had settled in Frankfurt as a pastry-cook about twenty-five years ago. Giovanni Battista had come from Vicenza, and had been a very good man, although rather hot-tempered and overbearing, and a republican at that. As she said this, Madame Roselli pointed to his portrait in oils which hung above the divan. Sanin could only suppose that the painter – 'also a republican', as Madame Roselli observed with a sigh – had failed to catch the likeness of his sitter, since, to judge by the portrait, the late Giovanni Battista had resembled a grim and severe brigand, for all the world like Rinaldo Rinaldini!

Signora Roselli herself had been born in the 'ancient and beautiful city of Parma, where there is such a superb cupola painted by the immortal Correggio'. But she had become quite a German through long sojourn in the country. Then, shaking her head sadly, she added that all that remained for her now were *this* daughter and *this* son (she pointed to each in turn), that the daughter was called Gemma and the son Emilio, and that both were good and obedient children, especially Emilio ('Am I not obedient, then?' interposed the daughter at this point. 'Oh, you're a republican too,' replied her mother); that business was, of course, much worse now than it had been while her husband was alive, for he had been a great artist in the pastry-cook line. ('*Un grand'uomo*,' Pantaleone remarked at this point, looking stern); but that, thank God, it was still possible to manage.

<h2 style="text-align:center">V</h2>

GEMMA listened to her mother. She was laughing one moment, sighing the next, now stroking her mother's shoulder, now wagging an admonitory finger at her, and sometimes glancing at Sanin. At last she stood up, put her arms around her mother and kissed her in the hollow of the throat – all of which produced a great deal of laughter from Signora Roselli, and even a few squeals.

Pantaleone was also presented to Sanin. It appeared that he had once sung baritone parts in opera, but had long given up his theatrical life and occupied a position in the Roselli household that was something between that of a family friend and a servant. Although he had lived in Germany for a considerable number of years, he had succeeded in acquiring only a very little of the language, and could really do no more than curse in German, and that mainly by dint of unmercifully murdering the words of abuse. Almost any German was a '*ferroflucto spizzebubbio*' to Pantaleone.[1] But his accent in Italian was perfect, because he came from Sinigaglia where one can hear '*lingua toscana in bocca romana*'.[2]

Emilio was clearly enjoying himself and basking in the pleasurable mood which comes upon one who has escaped imminent danger or is convalescing from an illness. Besides, everything pointed to the fact that the whole family was in the habit of spoiling him. He uttered some shy words of thanks to Sanin, but mostly concentrated on the syrups and sweets. Sanin was forced to drink two large cups of excellent chocolate and to devour a remarkable number of cakes: no sooner had he swallowed one, than Gemma would be offering another – and it was impossible to refuse.

He very soon began to feel quite at home. It was incredible how swiftly the time passed. There were so many things he had to tell them: about Russia in general, about the Russian climate, Russian society, about the Russian peasants and especially about the Cossacks; about the war of 1812 and Peter the Great, about the Kremlin, about Russian songs and Russian church bells. Both the ladies had only the vaguest notion of our far-flung and remote country: Signora Roselli, or, as she was more usually called, Frau Lenore, even astounded Sanin by asking him if the famous Ice Palace, built in St Petersburg in the previous century, was still standing: she had recently read such an interesting article about it in a book that had belonged to her late husband, *Bellezze delle arti*. When Sanin exclaimed, 'Do you really think that we never have any summer in Russia?' Frau Lenore replied that hitherto her picture of Russia had been of a country where the snow lay permanently and everyone went around in a fur coat and served in the army – but that the hospitality was quite extraordinary, and all the peasants were very obedient. Sanin did his best to provide her and her daughter with some rather more exact intelligence.

When the conversation touched on Russian music, he was at once requested to sing some Russian air and was shown to a small pianoforte which stood in the room, and which had black keys instead of white, and white ones instead of black. Sanin immediately complied with their wishes without making excuses, and sang, in a small, nasal tenor voice, first 'The Red Sarafan' and then 'Along the Highway', accompanying himself with two fingers of the right hand and three of the left – the thumb, the middle and the little fingers. The ladies praised both his voice and the tunes, but were even more enthusiastic about the soft melodiousness of the Russian language and demanded a translation of the words. Sanin acceded to their wishes, but in view of the fact that the words of 'The Red Sarafan' and 'Along the Highway' (*Sur une rue pavée une jeune fille allait à l'eau*, in his rendering of the original) could scarcely provide his listeners with any very exalted idea of Russian poetry, he turned to Pushkin. He first recited, then translated and then sang, Pushkin's 'I Recall a Wondrous Moment' in Glinka's setting, getting some of the melancholy couplets slightly wrong in the process. The ladies were now absolutely delighted – Frau Lenore even discovered a remarkable similarity between the Russian and Italian languages – the Russian for 'moment', *mgnovenie*, was just like '*o vieni*', 'with me', *so mnoi*, like '*siam noi*', and so on. Even the names Pushkin (which she pronounced Pussekin) and Glinka somehow seemed natural to her. Sanin in his turn asked the ladies to sing something and they did not stand on ceremony either. Frau Lenore sat down at the pianoforte and sang a few *duettini* and *stornelli*[3] with Gemma. The mother had once had a good contralto voice: the daughter's voice was slight but agreeable.

VI

BUT Sanin was admiring Gemma herself, not her voice. He was sitting a little behind and to one side of her and thinking to himself that no palm tree – not even in the verses of Benediktov,[1] who was at that time the fashionable poet – could rival the elegant grace of her figure. And when she came to some particularly emotional point in the song and raised her eyes to the heavens, it seemed impossible to imagine any skies that would not open before so beautiful a glance. Even old Pantaleone, leaning against the doorpost, with his chin and mouth tucked into his ample cravat and listening gravely with the look of an expert, even Pantaleone was admiring the face of this lovely girl and marvelling at it – and, after all, he should have become used to it by now. When the *duettino* was finished, Frau Lenore remarked that Emilio *also* sang excellently – a real silver-toned voice. But he had just reached the age when the voice begins to change (he did, in fact, talk in a kind of bass that was constantly breaking) and for this reason he was forbidden to sing. However, Pantaleone – now he might, for old times' sake, honour the guest with a song. Pantaleone immediately looked very displeased. He frowned, ruffled his hair and declared that he had given up all that long ago. Certainly, as a young man, he had been able to give a good account of himself. Indeed, he belonged to that great age when there were real, classical singers – not like the present screechers – and a real school of *bel canto*. He, Pantaleone Cippatola of Varese, was once presented with a laurel wreath in Modena, and on that occasion several white doves were released in the theatre, and incidentally, a certain Russian Prince, Il Principe Tarbusski, with whom he had been on terms of most intimate friendship, was always urging him at supper-time to come to Russia and promised him mountains of gold, literally mountains! But that he, Pantaleone, would not be parted from Italy, the country of Dante, *il paese del Dante*. After that, of course, certain unfortunate things happened, he had himself been somewhat incautious . . . Here the old man stopped abruptly, gave a deep sigh, then sighed again and looked at the floor . . . Then he began once again to talk of the classical age of singing, about the famous tenor Garcia for whom he had boundless veneration and respect.

'There was a man!' he exclaimed. 'The great Garcia[2] – *il gran Garcia* – never demeaned himself so far as to sing *falzetto* like the present-day miserable little tenors – *tenoracci*. No sir, he sang with a full chest, the full chest, *voce di petto, si*!'

The old man struck his shirt-front hard with his little withered fist.

'And what an actor! A volcano, *signori miei*, a volcano, *un Vesuvio*! I had the honour and good fortune to appear with

27

him in an opera *dell' illustrissimo maestro Rossini* – in *Otello*.
Garcia was Othello, I was Iago, and when he pronounced the
phrase . . .'

Here Pantaleone took up a theatrical stance and sang in a
voice which was tremulous and hoarse, but still full of passion.

> *'L'i . . . ra da ver . . . so da ver . . . so il fato*
> *Io più no . . . no . . . no . . . non temerò*

'The whole theatre was in a fever, *signori miei*. But I was not
too bad either, and followed on with,

> *'L'i . . . ra da ver . . . so da ver . . . so il fato*
> *Temer più non dovrò!*

'And then he came in suddenly, like a flash of lightning, like
a tiger,

> *'Morrò! . . . ma vendicato . . .*

'Or again, listen to this. When he sang . . . when he sang the
famous aria from 'Matrimonio Segreto': *Pria che Spunti . . .*
now here *il gran Garcia*, after the words *I cavalli di galoppo*,
used to do this when he came to the words *senza posa caccerà* –
just listen how wonderful this is, *com'è stupendo*! This is what
he used to do . . .'

The old man began to sing some kind of extraordinary
fioritura, but on the tenth note he broke down, and was seized
with a coughing fit. He turned away with a gesture of his
hands, muttering, 'Why do you torment me?' Gemma immediately jumped up from her chair, clapped her hands loudly,
crying 'Bravo! . . . Bravo! . . .' ran up to poor retired Iago
and gave him a few affectionate pats on both shoulders. Only
Emil was laughing without any trace of pity. *Cet âge est sans
pitié* – this age knows no compassion – as Lafontaine remarked
in his time.

Sanin tried to comfort the old baritone and began to talk
Italian to him (he had picked up a little of the language on his

recent trip). He spoke of '*paese del Dante dove il sì suona*'.[3] This phrase, together with '*lasciate ogni speranza*'[4] made up the entire Italian poetic equipment of our young tourist. But Pantaleone was not to be distracted by these efforts. With his chin tucked deeper than ever into his cravat, and his eyes staring grimly out of his head, he once again looked like a bird, and an angry bird at that – a raven, or a kite, perhaps. Then Emil, blushing momentarily, as spoiled children usually do, turned to his sister, and said that if she wished to entertain their guest, she could do nothing better than read aloud one of the comedy sketches by Malz, which she did so well. Gemma laughed and rapped her brother's hand, exclaiming, 'He would think of something like that!' However, she went straight to her room and returned, carrying a small book. She sat down at the table beside the lamp, glanced around her, raised her forefinger – meaning 'Quiet, please', a pure Italian gesture – and began to read.

VII

MALZ was a Frankfurt littérateur of the 'thirties. His short, slight comedy sketches, written in the local dialect, portrayed Frankfurt types without any profound wit, but brightly and amusingly. It turned out that Gemma did indeed read superbly well, quite like an actress. She would bring the character to life and sustain it throughout, making good use of the gift for mimicry which she had inherited with her Italian blood. She spared neither her gentle voice nor her lovely face. When it was necessary to portray an old woman who had lost her wits, or a stupid town mayor, she twisted her features into the funniest of grimaces, screwed up her eyes, wrinkled her nose, her voice meanwhile ranging from a high-pitched squeak to a guttural bass . . . She did not laugh herself during the reading. But whenever her audience (with the exception, it is true, of Pantaleone, who had left with a show of indignation the moment the subject of *quel ferroflucto tedesco* had been raised) interrupted her with a roar of happy laughter, she would let the book fall on her lap and burst out laughing, throwing back her head, while her black curls cascaded softly about her neck and shaking shoulders. Then the laughter would cease. Gemma would immediately raise the book from her lap, compose her features appropriately and once again resume the serious business of reading.

Sanin could hardly contain his admiration. Most especially striking was the miraculous way in which a face of such ideal beauty could suddenly take on so comical, even common, a look. Gemma was much less successful in the parts of young women, *les jeunes premières* as they were called, and her portrayal of love scenes was not successful. She felt this herself, and tended to read them with a slight trace of mockery, as if to underline her lack of conviction in the enthusiastic protestations of love and fidelity, and the stilted speeches – actually, the author himself avoided such passages so far as possible.

Sanin did not notice how swiftly the evening passed, and only remembered about his imminent journey when the clock struck ten. He jumped up from his chair as if he had been stung.

'What is the matter?' asked Frau Lenore.

'I was supposed to be leaving for Berlin tonight: I had my seat reserved on the stagecoach.'

'When does it leave?'

'At half past ten.'

'Well,' said Gemma, 'that means you have missed it anyway . . . You had better stay and I will read some more.'

'Have you paid the full price for the ticket, or just a deposit?' asked Frau Lenore.

'The lot!' Sanin lamented with a gesture of mock despair.

Gemma looked at him with narrowed eyes – and burst out laughing. Her mother scolded her.

'This poor young man has wasted his money, and here you are laughing!'

'That's all right,' said Gemma. 'It won't ruin him, and we must try to console him. Would you like some lemonade?'

Sanin drank a glass of lemonade. Gemma continued with Malz and everything went with a swing.

The clock struck twelve. Sanin began to take his leave.

'You will have to stay a few more days in Frankfurt now,' Gemma told him. 'What is the hurry? You won't find a more entertaining town.' She was silent for a moment. 'Really, that is so,' she added with a smile.

Sanin did not reply, and reflected that in view of the empty state of his purse he would have to stay in Frankfurt, whether he wished or no, until he had received a reply from a friend in Berlin to whom he now intended to write and ask for a loan.

'Yes, do stay,' Frau Lenore said in her turn. 'We will introduce you to Gemma's future husband, Herr Karl Klueber. He could not come this evening because he was very busy in his shop. I expect you noticed when you were in the Zeile, the largest store for silks and woollen cloth? Well, he is the chief man there. But he will be delighted to pay his respects to you.'

Heaven alone knows why, but Sanin was slightly taken aback by this piece of information. What a lucky fellow he is, flashed through his mind. He glanced at Gemma – and he thought he noticed a slight look of mockery in her eyes. He began to say good-bye.

'So it is till tomorrow? Is that so – until tomorrow?' asked Frau Lenore.

'Till tomorrow,' Gemma pronounced, but as a statement, not a question, taking for granted that it could not be otherwise.

'Till tomorrow,' Sanin replied.

Emil, Pantaleone and the poodle Tartaglia accompanied him to the street corner. Pantaleone could not resist expressing his displeasure on the subject of Gemma's reading.

'She ought to be ashamed of herself! All those grimaces and that squawking! *Una carricatura*. She ought to act noble parts,

Merope or Clytemnaestra, some great tragic role. And here she is screwing herself up to sound like some dreadful German woman. Why, I can do that – *mertz, kertz, smertz*,' added the old man in his hoarse voice, poking his face forward and splaying his fingers. Tartaglia started barking at him, and Emil burst out laughing. The old man turned sharply on his heels, and strode back.

Sanin returned to the White Swan Inn (where he had left his belongings in the hall) in a state of some confusion. All those conversations in German, French and Italian were ringing in his ears.

'Engaged,' he whispered to himself, lying in bed in the modest room which had been allotted to him. 'And what a beautiful girl she is! But why on earth have I stayed here?'

However, next day he sent off the letter to his friend in Berlin.

VIII

He had not yet had time to dress when a waiter came in to announce the arrival of two gentlemen. One of them turned out to be Emil. The other, a tall and impressive young man with a most handsome face, was Herr Karl Klueber, to whom the lovely Gemma was engaged.

It may well be supposed that, at that time, in all the shops in all Frankfurt there was not to be found another such courteous, well-mannered, grave and polite chief assistant as Herr Klueber. His immaculate dress was of the same high level as the dignity of his demeanour and the elegance of his manners – a little prim and stiff, it is true, in the English fashion (he had spent two years in England) – but beguiling elegance for all that. It was evident at a glance that this good-looking, somewhat stern, exceedingly well brought-up and superlatively well-washed young man was in the habit of obeying his superiors and of issuing orders to his inferiors. The sight of such a man behind his counter was indeed bound to inspire respect even in the customers. There could not be the slightest doubt that his honesty surpassed all natural limits – why, one only had to look at the points of his stiffly starched collar. His voice too turned out to be exactly what one was led to expect – deep, self-confident and rather rich in tone; yet not too loud, and even with some notes of a certain kindliness. This is the sort of voice which is particularly well-adapted to giving orders to subordinate shop assistants. 'Bring that length of purple Lyons velvet, will you?' or, 'A chair for the lady!'

Herr Klueber began by introducing himself. In the process, he bowed from the waist with such nobility of manner, while at the same time bringing one leg close to the other in so agreeable a fashion, and touching his heels together with such courtesy, that everyone was bound to think: 'This man's linen and spiritual virtues are both of the first quality.' The grooming of his exposed right hand, which he offered to Sanin modestly but firmly, exceeded the bounds of all probability: each single fingernail was a model of perfection. (In his left hand, which was clad in a suède glove, he held his hat which shone like a looking-glass: in the depths of the hat lay the other glove.) He then declared, in the choicest German phrases, that he desired to express his respect and his gratitude to the *Herr Auslaender* who had rendered so important a service to his future kinsman, the brother of his betrothed. At this point, he gestured with his left hand, which held the hat, in the direction of Emil. The boy was evidently embarrassed, and turned away towards the window, putting his finger in his mouth. Herr Klueber added that he would count himself happy if he ever found it in his power to do something on his part that might be agreeable to the *Herr Auslaender*.

Sanin replied, in German, not without some difficulty, that he was most gratified . . . that his services had been of the most trivial nature . . . and invited his guests to be seated. Herr Klueber thanked him, and in an instant flung asunder his coattails and let himself down in a chair, but let himself down so lightly, and adhered to the chair so insecurely, that the inference was clear to all: this man has only sat down out of politeness, and will immediately take wing once again. And indeed he leapt up instantly and executed a few modest movements with his legs, rather like some dance sequence. He then declared that, much to his regret, he could stay no longer since he was in a hurry to return to his shop – business before pleasure! But tomorrow was Sunday, and with the consent of Frau Lenore and Fräulein Gemma he had arranged a pleasurable excursion to Soden, to which he had the honour of inviting the *Herr Auslaender*. He expressed the hope that the distinguished foreigner would not refuse to grace the party with his presence. Sanin consented to grace the excursion with his presence. Thereupon Herr Klueber once again took his leave and departed – displaying a most agreeable glimpse of pea-green trousers of a most delicate hue, and emitting an equally delectable squeak from the soles of his brand-new boots.

IX

EMIL, who had remained standing, looking out of the window, even after Sanin had issued the invitation to his guests to be seated, made a left turn as soon as his future kinsman had departed. Blushing and grimacing in a somewhat childish way, he asked Sanin if it was in order for him to stay a little longer. 'I am much better today,' he added, 'but the doctor has told me not to do any work.'

'Yes, please stay, you are not in the least in the way,' Sanin exclaimed at once: like every true Russian, he was delighted to seize on the first excuse which would relieve him of the obligation to do anything whatsoever.

Emil thanked him, and in no time had made himself at home in Sanin's quarters. He examined all his belongings and questioned him closely about nearly every article – where he had bought it and what its particular qualities were. Then he helped him to shave, observing in passing that he ought to grow a moustache. He told him in the end innumerable details about his mother, his sister, about Pantaleone and even about the poodle Tartaglia, going into minute particulars of their daily life. Emil had lost every trace of shyness. He suddenly felt extraordinarily attracted to Sanin, and not because he thought Sanin had saved his life the day before, but simply because he was such a nice man.

Emil lost no time in confiding all his secret thoughts. He spoke with most heat about the fact that his mother was determined that he should go into business, while he himself *knew*, knew beyond doubt, that he was born to be an artist, a musician, a singer. He knew that the theatre was his true calling. Even Pantaleone encouraged him in this, but Herr Klueber supported his mother, over whom he had a great deal of influence. Indeed, the idea that he should become a tradesman had originated with Herr Klueber, according to whose ideas nothing in the world could compare with the businessman's calling. To sell cloth and velvet and cheat the public by making them pay *Narren-oder Russenpreise** (fools' or Russian prices) – that was his loftiest aspiration.

'Well, then. Now we must go home,' the boy exclaimed as soon as Sanin had finished dressing and had written his letter to Berlin.

'It's too early yet,' remarked Sanin.

'That doesn't matter,' said Emil, coming up to him affectionately. 'Let's go! We'll call in at the post office and then go on to our house. Gemma will be so pleased to see you. You

*In times gone by – and it may perhaps still be going on – when from May onwards a multitude of Russians began to appear in Frankfurt, prices went up in all the shops and acquired the name of 'Russen', or alas! 'Narrenpreise'.

must have breakfast with us . . . You can say something to my mother about me, about my future career . . .'

'Well, come along then,' Sanin said, and they set off.

X

GEMMA was indeed pleased to see him and Frau Lenore greeted him in the friendliest manner. It was apparent that he had made a good impression on them both the night before. Emil ran off to make the arrangements for breakfast, having first whispered in Sanin's ear, 'Don't forget!' 'I won't,' Sanin promised.

Frau Lenore was a trifle indisposed. She was suffering from migraine, and reclining in an armchair, trying not to move. Gemma was wearing a wide-cut yellow blouse, gathered in with a black leather belt. She also seemed exhausted and somewhat pale. There were dark circles round her eyes, but this did not make them shine the less and her pallor added a mysterious appeal to her strictly classical features. That day Sanin was particularly impressed by the elegant beauty of her hands. Every time she raised them to smooth or rearrange the dark, gleaming waves of her hair he could not take his eyes off these long, pliant, well-separated fingers, like those of Raphael's Fornarina.

It was very hot out of doors. Sanin was of a mind to leave after breakfast, but when it was pointed out that the best plan on such a day was to stay quietly in one spot, he agreed – and so he stayed on. It was cool in the back room where he sat with his hostesses: the windows gave out on to a small garden, overgrown with acacia trees. A multitude of bees, wasps and bumble-bees droned eagerly and good-humouredly in the thick branches which were strewn with golden flowers. The never-ceasing sound penetrated the room through the half-open shutters and the lowered blinds. It was a sound which sang of the scorching heat which charged the outside air, and made the cool atmosphere of the enclosing, comfortable room seem all the sweeter.

Sanin talked much as he had done the previous day. But not about Russia or Russian life. He wanted to be of help to his young friend, who had been sent off immediately after breakfast to Herr Klueber to get some practice with the account books. So he brought the conversation round to the comparative advantages and disadvantages of art and commerce. He was not surprised to discover that Frau Lenore was on the side of commerce – he had expected that. But Gemma too shared her mother's opinion.

'If one is an artist, and especially a singer,' she asserted, with a vigorous up-and-down movement of her hand, 'one must be at the top. Anything less than that is worth nothing. And who can say if one is capable of reaching the top?'

Pantaleone also joined in this debate. As he had served them for many years and was an old man, he was even permitted to sit in the presence of his employers: the Italians in general are not strict in matters of etiquette.

Naturally the old man was resolutely on the side of art. To tell the truth, his arguments were a little weak. He was mainly concerned to insist that the first requirement for the artist was *un certo estro d'ispirazione*, a certain dash of inspiration. Frau Lenore observed that he certainly had possessed this *estro* and yet . . .

'I had enemies,' remarked Pantaleone gloomily.

'And how do you know,' (she addressed him in the familiar *tu* since Italians use this form very readily), 'that Emil will not have enemies, even if some of this *estro* should become apparent in him?'

'All right,' said Pantaleone angrily, 'make a tradesman of the boy – but Giovan' Battista would not have done it, even though he was a pastry-cook himself.'

'My husband, Giovan' Battista, was a very sensible man . . . and if he *did* get carried away in his youth . . .'

But the old man did not wish to hear any more and went off muttering once again reproachfully, 'Ah! Giovan' Battista . . .!'

Then Gemma declared that if Emil turned out to be a patriot, and wished to devote all his energies to the liberation of Italy, that would be another matter: it was right to sacrifice one's future security to such a noble and sacred cause – but not for the theatre! At this Frau Lenore became excited and began to implore her daughter at least to refrain from putting dangerous ideas into her brother's head. Wasn't it enough for her that she was a desperate republican herself? With these words, Frau Lenore began to groan and to complain of her aching head which was 'ready to burst' (Frau Lenore, out of consideration for their guest, spoke French with her daughter).

Gemma immediately began to minister to her mother. She moistened her forehead with eau de Cologne, and then blew on it very gently. She kissed her lightly on the cheeks, arranged her head on a pillow, ordered her to keep quiet and began kissing her again. She then turned to Sanin and began to tell him, in a voice which showed both humour and emotion, what an excellent mother she had, and what a beauty she had been. 'What am I saying? *Was* a beauty! She is one now, an absolute delight! Look at her eyes, just look at her eyes!'

Gemma whipped a white handkerchief out of her pocket and covered her mother's face. Then, very slowly, she lowered the top hem of the handkerchief, gradually disclosing Frau Lenore's forehead, eyebrows and eyes. She waited a little and then demanded that Frau Lenore should open her eyes. Her mother obeyed. Gemma exclaimed with delight (Frau Lenore's eyes really were very beautiful), then quickly drew the handkerchief right down to reveal the lower and less regular features of her mother's face, and once again began covering her with kisses. Frau Lenore laughed, turned aside slightly, and pretended to push her daughter away. The girl also made some pretence of struggle with her mother, and kissed and fondled her – not like a cat, in the French manner, but with that Italian grace which always makes one feel the presence of vigour.

At last Frau Lenore declared that she was tired . . . Gemma at once advised her to sleep for a little, here in the chair, 'while I and the Russian gentleman, *le Monsieur Russe*, will be as quiet . . . as quiet as little mice, *comme des petites souris* . . .' Frau Lenore smiled by way of an answer, closed her eyes, sighed once or twice and dozed off.

Gemma sat down on a stool by her side and stayed there without moving – except that occasionally she raised a finger of one hand to her lips (the other hand was supporting the pillow under her mother s head) and quietly shushed at Sanin, looking askance at him when he permitted himself to make the slightest movement. It ended with Sanin as motionless as if he were frozen in his seat, spellbound, totally absorbed in admiring the picture before his eyes: the half-darkened room, in which bunches of magnificent fresh roses, standing in antique vases of green glass glowed here and there like bright points of light; the sleeping woman, her hands folded simply before her and her tired, kindly face framed in the snow-white pillow; and this young creature, alert and also kindly, clever and pure, and beautiful beyond description, the black depths of her eyes suffused with shadows and yet luminous at the same time . . . What was it all? A dream? A fairy-tale? And how did *he* come to be there?

XI

THE bell on the entrance door to the shop suddenly jangled. A young peasant lad in a fur cap and a red waistcoat came into the patisserie from the street. Not a single customer had entered the shop throughout the entire morning . . . 'This is the kind of business we do,' Frau Lenore had remarked to Sanin during breakfast. Now she continued to doze, and

Gemma, who was afraid of removing her arm from under the pillow, whispered to Sanin: 'You go and deal with the shop for me.' Sanin immediately tiptoed into the shop. The lad was asking for a quarter of a pound of mint lozenges.

'How much is it?' Sanin whispered to Gemma through the door.

'Six kreutzers,' she replied, again in a whisper.

Sanin weighed out a quarter of a pound, found a piece of paper, screwed it into a poke, wrapped up the sweets, spilled them, wrapped them up again, spilled them again, then at last delivered them to the customer and received the money. The lad was meanwhile staring at him with amazement, fumbling with his cap against his stomach, while Gemma next door, her hand held to her mouth, was dying of laughter. This customer had hardly time to depart before another appeared, and then a third ... 'I seem to be bringing them luck,' Sanin thought. The second customer called for a glass of *orgeade*, and the third for half a pound of sweets. Sanin served them, enthusiastically rattling spoons, moving the saucers around and delving deftly into tins and drawers. In the final reckoning, it was discovered that he had undercharged for the *orgeade*, and had collected two kreutzers too many for the sweets. Gemma continued to laugh quietly to herself. As for Sanin, he felt unusually gay, and some special mood of happiness was upon him. He felt as if he was ready to stand behind the counter for all time dealing in sweets and *orgeade* under the friendly and slightly mocking eyes of that charming creature, while the midsummer sun beat down through the massive foliage of the chestnut trees which rose in front of the windows. He would stand for all time while the whole room was filled with the green and gold of the sun's mid-day rays and mid-day shadows, and his heart overflowed with the sweet langour of idleness and of carefree youth – carefree first youth.

The fourth customer demanded a cup of coffee, so Pantaleone's help had to be invoked. (Emil had still not returned from Herr Klueber's store.) Sanin once again sat down at Gemma's side. Frau Lenore continued to doze, to the great delight of her daughter.

'Mother's migraine always passes when she sleeps,' she observed.

Sanin began to talk – still in whispers, of course – about his transactions in the shop. He inquired gravely about the prices of various commodities on sale in the patisserie. Gemma answered in the same grave tones, reciting the prices. At the same time, both of them were inwardly consumed with companionable laughter, as if aware that they were enacting an amusing farce. Suddenly a street organ in the road outside broke into the strains of the 'Freischütz' aria *Durch die Felder, durch die Auen* . . . Its whimpering notes, tremulous and with an occasional whistle, came wailing through the still air. Gemma started . . . 'He will wake Mother!'

Sanin promptly dashed into the street, thrust a few kreutzers into the organ-grinder's hand and persuaded him to stop and to move on elsewhere. When Sanin returned Gemma thanked him with a slight nod, and, with a meditative smile, began to hum, almost inaudibly, under her breath, Weber's beautiful air in which Max expresses all the perplexities of first love. She then asked Sanin if he knew the 'Freischütz', if he liked Weber, and added that, although she was Italian, this was the kind of music she loved above all. From the subject of Weber, the conversation slipped to poetry and romanticism, and to Hoffmann, whom at that date everyone was still reading.

Meanwhile Frau Lenore slept on, even snoring just a little, while all the time the rays of sunlight, breaking through the shutters, in little narrow strips, imperceptibly but ceaselessly travelled across the floor, the furniture, Gemma's clothes and over the leaves and petals of the flowers.

XII

IT appeared that Gemma was not too well disposed towards Hoffmann, and even found him – of all things – rather dull. The northern world of fantasy and mist in his tales meant little to her southern and luminous temperament. 'He writes nothing but fairy-tales, nothing but children's stories,' she kept on asserting with slight contempt. She was also dimly aware of the lack of poetry in Hoffmann – but there was one of his tales, of which she had incidentally forgotten the title, which she liked very much. At least, to be exact, she only liked the beginning of the story – she had either not read the end of it, or else had also forgotten it. It was about a young man who meets a girl of astonishing beauty, a Greek girl, somewhere or other – it might have been in a tea-room. The girl is in the company of a strange and mysterious, evil old man. The young man falls in love with the girl at first sight. She looks at him most piteously, as if imploring him to rescue her. He leaves the shop for a moment – and on his return neither the girl nor the old man is there. He hastens off in search of them, repeatedly lights upon the most recent traces of them, flies off in hot pursuit – and never at any time succeeds in finding them anywhere. The beauty vanishes from him for ever – and he is unable to forget her imploring look, and is tortured by the thought that perhaps all his life's happiness had slipped from his grasp.

This is hardly the way Hoffman ends his tale. But this was the form in which it had remained imprinted on Gemma's memory.[1]

'It seems to me,' she said softly, 'that such meetings and partings happen in the world more often than we think.'

Sanin did not reply. Then, after a pause, he began to speak – of Herr Klueber. It was the first time that he had mentioned him. Until that moment he had not once remembered the man's existence.

It was Gemma's turn to remain silent. She was plunged in

thought, her eyes were averted and she was biting at the nail of her forefinger. Then she praised her husband-to-be, mentioned the excursion which he had arranged for the following day, threw a quick glance at Sanin, and fell silent once more.

Sanin could not think of a subject for conversation.

Emil came running in noisily, and woke Frau Lenore. Sanin was glad that he had come. Frau Lenore rose from her armchair. Pantaleone appeared and announced that lunch was ready. The friend of the household, the retired singer and the servant also carried out the duties of cook.

XIII

SANIN stayed on after lunch, too. They would not let him go on the same pretext – the terrible heat – and when it became cooler, they suggested taking coffee in the garden in the shade of the acacias. Sanin agreed. His sense of well-being was complete. There are great delights hidden in the uneventful, still and placid stream of life, and he abandoned himself to them with rapture – demanding nothing specific of this day and neither thinking of the morrow nor recalling yesterday. How he treasured the very proximity of a creature such as Gemma! He would soon part from her, probably for ever. But for the moment, they were drifting together in the same barque along the safe and gentle course of life's river, just like the travellers in Uhland's poem.[1] Rejoice, wanderer! Be happy! And everything seemed agreeable and dear to our lucky traveller! Frau Lenore suggested that he should join her and Pantaleone in a game of *tresette*.[2] She instructed him in this uncomplicated Italian card game, won a few kreutzers off him – and he was most delighted.

At Emil's request, Pantaleone made the poodle Tartaglia go through all his tricks – and Tartaglia jumped over a stick, 'spoke' – that is to say barked – sneezed, shut the door with his nose, dragged along his master's well-worn slipper and at last, with an old shako on his head, enacted the part of Marshall Bernadotte being subjected to a severe reprimand from the Emperor Napoleon – for treason. Napoleon was naturally portrayed by Pantaleone, and very faithfully portrayed. With his arms crossed on his chest, and a three-cornered hat pushed down over his eyes, he spoke coarsely and very sharply in French – and, heavens, what French! Tartaglia sat all huddled up before his sovereign, his tail between his legs, blinking from shame, and screwing up his eyes under the peak of the shako which sat askew on his head. From time to time, as Napoleon raised his voice, Bernadotte would stand on his hind legs. '*Fuori, traditore!*' exclaimed Napoleon at last, having quite forgotten, in his excessive fury, that he should maintain his part of a Frenchman to the very end. Bernadotte dashed headlong under the divan, and immediately jumped out again, barking delightedly, as if to indicate that the performance was over. The spectators laughed a great deal, and Sanin more than anyone.

Gemma had a very special and lovable way of laughing. It was a quiet laugh which hardly stopped, but was punctuated by the most amusing little squeals. Sanin was completely captivated by her laughter – he wanted to cover her with kisses for those little squeals!

Night fell at last. Now it really was time to go, and so Sanin said goodbye to everyone several times over, repeatedly saying, 'Till tomorrow,' to each of them (Emil he actually embraced), and went on his way. The image of the young girl went with him – now laughing, now pensive, sometimes calm, even indifferent, yet always attractive. And all the time he seemed to see her eyes before him – sometimes open wide, luminous and full of joy like the light of day, and then half-shaded by their lashes, and deep and dark as night. These eyes penetrated all other images and perceptions in his mind, and suffused them with a strange sweetness.

44

Not once did he think of Herr Klueber, of the reason which had induced him to stay on in Frankfurt – in short, of all the things which had perturbed him the day before.

XIV

HOWEVER, we must devote a few words to Sanin himself. In the first place he was very far from bad-looking – very far indeed. He was well built and tall, his features, if somewhat formless, were agreeable. His eyes, small and of a faded blue, were kindly, his hair was fair with some gold in it, his complexion was all pink and white. But the chief thing about him was his expression of unsophisticated gaiety – trusting, open, and at first impact slightly silly. In the old days, one could immediately spot the sons of the sedate provincial gentry by this expression – those 'father's boys', the 'good young masters', born and fattened up in those wide and open parts of our country which are half steppe. He had a mincing, slightly hesitant way of walking, a trace of a lisp in his voice, a smile like a child's, which appeared as soon as he caught your glance, and finally freshness and good health – yes, and softness, softness, softness – there was all Sanin for you.

And secondly he was no fool, having picked up a bit of experience. But he had remained fresh in outlook, in spite of his travels abroad: he knew little of the disturbing emotions which had raised a storm in the breasts of the best of the younger generation of that epoch.

It has become fashionable of late in our literature, after long and vain attempts to discover 'new men', to portray youths who have determined, come what may, to be fresh – as fresh as the oysters which are imported into St Petersburg from Flensburg . . . Sanin was not a bit like these youths. If comparisons are necessary, he was rather like a young, newly grafted, curly-headed apple tree in one of Russia's southern orchards in the black earth country . . . or better still, one of those sleek, well-groomed, tender and fat-legged three-year-olds that one used to see on the master's stud-farm, just beginning to be broken in ... Those who came across Sanin in later years, when life had buffeted him around, and after he had long shed his youthful puppy-fat, saw quite a different kind of man.

On the following day, Sanin was still in bed when Emil, wearing his Sunday best, carrying a cane and with his hair heavily pomaded, burst into the room and announced that Herr Klueber would be arriving at any moment with the carriage, that the weather promised to be wonderful, that they had everything ready, but that Mother would not be joining them because her headache had come on again.

He began to hurry Sanin, assuring him that there was not a minute to lose ... and indeed, Herr Klueber arrived to find Sanin still at his toilet. He knocked on the door, entered, delivered a bow from the waist, expressed his willingness to wait for any length of time that was desired – and then sat down, resting his hat elegantly upon his knee.

The exquisite shop walker had dressed himself up to the eyes and was drenched in scent: his every movement was accompanied by great waves of the most delicate fragrance. He arrived in a commodious open carriage of the kind known as a landau, drawn by two strong and well-developed, if rather ugly, horses. A quarter of an hour later, Sanin, Klueber and Emil, seated in this carriage, ceremoniously drew up at the porch of the patisserie. Signora Roselli definitely refused to take any part in the excursion; Gemma wanted to stay behind with her mother, but the latter drove her out, as the saying goes.

'I need no one,' she said. 'I am going to sleep. I would send Pantaleone with you as well, but someone must look after the customers.'

'May we take Tartaglia?' Emil asked.

'Of course.'

Tartaglia immediately, with some effort, but with obvious delight, clambered up on to the box. He sat there licking his chops – it was plain that all this was customary procedure for him.

Gemma had put on a large straw hat with brown ribbons. The brim of the hat dipped down in front and shielded almost all her face from the sun. The shadow line stopped just short of her lips, which glowed soft and virginal like the petals of a Provence rose. Her teeth glistened almost stealthily and with the innocence of a child. Gemma sat down on the back seat next to Sanin: Klueber and Emil sat opposite. The pale figure of Frau Lenore appeared at the window. Gemma waved to her with her handkerchief, and the horses started.

XV

SODEN is a small town about half an hour's distance from Frankfurt. It lies in pretty countryside on a spur of the Taunus mountains and is well known among us in Russia for its waters, which are reputed to be beneficial for weak chests. The inhabitants of Frankfurt mostly visit it for recreation, since Soden contains a magnificent park and a number of *Wirtschaften* where one can drink beer or coffee in the shade of tall lime or maple trees.

The road from Frankfurt to Soden follows the right bank of the Main and is lined with fruit trees. While the carriage rolled quietly along the excellent metalled road, Sanin was unobtrusively observing how Gemma conducted herself in the company of her betrothed: it was the first time that he had seen the two of them together. *She* remained calm and unaffected, although somewhat more restrained and serious than usual. *He* presented the appearance of a condescending tutor who was conferring both upon himself and his charges modest and polite enjoyment. Sanin did not observe that he paid

Gemma any of the particular attentions which the French call *empressement*. It was evident that Herr Klueber considered the business as settled, and therefore had no occasion to put himself out or to fuss. Condescension never left him for a moment – not even during the long walk before lunch over the wooded hills and dales beyond Soden. Even while he was enjoying the countryside, his attitude to natural beauty remained one of patronage, occasionally marked by his usual stern tones of the man in authority. Thus, for example, he remarked on the subject of a certain stream that it flowed in too straight a line along the vale, instead of forming a few picturesque curves. He was also disapproving on the subject of a bird – a chaffinch – which had failed to display sufficient variety in the notes of its song.

Gemma was not bored and even seemed to be enjoying herself. But Sanin could not recognize the former Gemma. It was not that her beauty was dimmed – never, indeed, had it been so radiant – but her spirit had withdrawn. She had opened her parasol and, without unbuttoning her gloves, she walked in a staid and unhurried manner, like a well brought-up young lady, and spoke little. Emil did not feel at ease either, and Sanin even less. He was, incidentally, somewhat put out by the fact that the conversation was all conducted in German. Tartaglia alone was in high spirits. He would dash off in pursuit of any blackbird he encountered, barking like mad, jump over ditches, tree-stumps and puddles, throw himself into the water, hurriedly lap up a few mouthfuls, shake himself and then, with a yelp, make off again like an arrow, his red tongue curling round almost to his shoulder.

Herr Klueber for his part did everything that he considered necessary for entertaining the company. He requested everyone to be seated in the shade of a spreading oak tree, produced from his side pocket a small volume entitled *Knallerbsen oder Du Sollst und Wirst Lachen* (Merry Quips or You Must and Will Laugh)[1] and proceeded to read aloud the mirth-provoking anecdotes which the work contained. He read about a dozen without, however, provoking very much merriment. Only Sanin bared his teeth politely and Herr Klueber himself after every anecdote executed a short, businesslike and, at the same time, condescending laugh. Around noon the whole company returned to Soden to the best inn that the town could offer.

It was necessary to make arrangements for luncheon.

Herr Klueber proposed that luncheon should be partaken in a summer house which was enclosed on all sides, '*im Garten-salon*'; but at this point Gemma suddenly rebelled and declared that she refused to eat anywhere but in the open air, in the garden, at one of the small tables that stood in front of the inn. She announced that she was bored with seeing the same faces all the time, and wanted to see some new ones. There were already groups of newly-arrived patrons seated at some of the tables.

While Herr Klueber, who had graciously yielded to the 'caprice of my fiancée', departed to consult the head waiter, Gemma stood motionless, her eyes lowered, her lips firmly pursed. She sensed that Sanin was looking at her fixedly and a little interrogatively, and this seemed to make her angry. At last Herr Klueber returned, announced that luncheon would be ready in half an hour and proposed to pass the time with a game of skittles, adding that this was very good for the appetite, hee, hee, hee! He was a masterly skittles player. When he bowled, he adopted a number of remarkably energetic stances, made great play with his muscles and executed the most elegant motions in the air with his leg. In his own way, he was an athlete, and superbly well-built. And his hands were so white and beautiful, and he kept on wiping them with such a luxurious Indian foulard handkerchief, rich in gold and bright colours.

The moment for luncheon arrived, and the company sat down at the table.

XVI

WHO is not acquainted with a German meal? A watery soup with bullet-like dumplings flavoured with cinnamon, boiled beef, dry as cork, with some white fat adhering to it, garnished with soapy potatoes, puffy beetroot and some chewed-up looking horse-radish, followed by a bluish eel, with capers and vinegar, a roast of meat with some jam, and the inevitable '*Mehlspeise*' – a sort of pudding with a sourish red sauce. However, the wine and beer are excellent. This was exactly the kind of meal that the Soden innkeeper now provided for his patrons. Actually the luncheon went off quite successfully. True, it was not marked by any special gaiety – not even when Herr Klueber proposed a toast to 'whatever we love' (*was wir lieben*). Everything was most decorous and most refined. Coffee was served after luncheon – weak and amber-coloured, real German coffee. Herr Klueber, always the perfect gentleman, asked Gemma's permission to light a cigar . . . And, at this point, something suddenly happened, something quite unforeseen and certainly most unpleasant – even indecent.

A few officers from the Mainz garrison were ensconced at one of the neighbouring tables. From their glances and whispering, it was easy to guess that Gemma's looks had made a great impression on them. One of them, who had probably already had time to go into Frankfort, kept eyeing her, rather as if she were someone with whom he was well acquainted. Evidently he knew who she was. All of a sudden, he rose and, with his glass in his hand (the gallant officers had consumed a fair amount of drink and the tablecloth in front of them was crowded with bottles) approached the table at which Gemma was sitting. He was a flaxen-haired and very young man. His features were agreeable enough and not unattractive, but the wine which he had taken had distorted them. There was a tremor in his cheeks and his roving eyes were swollen, and had assumed an expression of insolence. His companions at first tried to restrain him, but then let him go – 'Well, what's the odds? Let's see what happens.'

Swaying slightly, the officer halted in front of Gemma and declaimed, in an artificially shrill voice which betrayed his inner conflict, 'I drink the health of the most beautiful coffee-house lady in all Frankfurt and in all the world' (at this point he drained his glass in a gulp), 'and, as a reward, I claim this flower, plucked by her own divine little fingers.' He picked up a rose which was lying by Gemma's place on the table.

She was at first startled and frightened, and went deathly pale. Then her fright gave way to indignation. She flushed to the roots of her hair and looked steadily at the man who had insulted her. Her eyes went dark and at the same time seemed to blaze, as a flame of uncontrollable fury burned through the deep shadows. The officer was apparently embarrassed by her look. He murmured something unintelligible, bowed and went back to his friends, who greeted him with laughter and some light applause.

Herr Klueber rose abruptly from the table, drew himself up to his full height, put on his hat and pronounced, with dignity but not too loudly. 'This is unheard of! Unheard-of insolence!' (*Unerhoert! Unerhoerte Frechheit!*) He then immediately summoned the waiter in a voice of great severity and demanded the bill without delay. More than that, he ordered the carriage to be made ready, and added that decent people could not be seen in this establishment in view of the fact that they were liable to be subjected to insults. At these words Gemma, who had remained motionless in her place, her breast heaving violently, transferred her look to Herr Klueber with a gaze of the same intensity and with exactly the same expression as she had bestowed on the officer. Emil was literally trembling with rage.

'Please rise, *mein Fräulein*,' Herr Klueber said in the same severe voice, 'this is no fit place for you to remain. We will accommodate ourselves there, inside the inn.'

Gemma rose silently. He offered her his arm, she took it, and he proceeded towards the inn, with a majestic gait which, like his whole bearing, became the more majestic and haughty the farther he retreated from the spot where luncheon had taken place. Poor Emil shuffled along behind them.

But while Herr Klueber was settling with the waiter, whom as a punishment he did not tip a single kreutzer, Sanin briskly walked up to the table at which the officers were sitting. Addressing himself to the one who had insulted Gemma (and who at that moment was inviting each of his friends in turn to sniff at her rose), he said in a clear voice and in French:

'Your conduct just now, sir, was unbecoming to a gentleman and unworthy of the uniform you wear, and I have come to tell you that you are an ill-bred bounder.'

The young man jumped to his feet, but another slightly older officer barred him with a motion of his arm, and made him sit down again. Turning to Sanin, he asked him, also in French:

'Are you related to this young lady – a brother, or engaged to be married to her?'

'I am a complete stranger to her!' exclaimed Sanin. 'I am a Russian, but I cannot be an indifferent witness to such insolence. Here, incidentally, is my card, with my address. This officer can find me there.'

With these words, Sanin flung his visiting card on the table and at the same time deftly seized Gemma's rose which one of the officers had dropped onto his plate. The young officer once more made as if to jump to his feet, but the older man stopped him with the words, 'Quiet, Doenhof!' (*Doenhof, sei still!*) He then rose to his feet himself, saluted and, with a certain degree of respect in his voice and manner, informed Sanin that an officer of their regiment would have the honour of waiting on him the following morning at his lodgings. Sanin replied with a curt bow and quickly returned to his party.

*

Herr Klueber made pretence that he had completely failed to notice either Sanin's absence or his conversation with the officers. He was engaged in urging on the coachman who was harnessing the horses, and was indignant with him for his dilatoriness. Gemma said nothing to Sanin either, and did not even glance at him. It was clear from her frown, from her pale, clenched lips, from her very stillness, that her heart was heavy. Only Emil was obviously longing to speak to Sanin and to question him. He had seen Sanin go up to the officers and had seen him hand them something white – a scrap of paper, a note, a card ... The poor boy's heart was thumping, his cheeks were burning; he was ready to throw his arms around Sanin, to burst into tears, or to set off with him straight away and beat the life out of all those odious officers! However, he restrained himself and contented himself with following attentively every movement of his noble Russian friend.

The carriage at last was got ready and the company took their seats. Emil clambered up on to the box after Tartaglia. He felt more at ease there. Besides, he did not have Klueber, whom he could not look at calmly, sticking up in front of him.

During the entire journey, Herr Klueber pontificated ... and pontificated on his own. No one disagreed with him, but then no one agreed with him either. He stressed with particular insistence how wrong everyone had been to reject his proposal that they should take luncheon in the enclosed summerhouse. There would have been no unpleasantness then! He then vouchsafed several quite sharp and even radical judgements on the subject of the Government's unpardonable policy of pandering to the officers, failing to pay adequate attention to their discipline and failing in its respect for the civilian element of society (*Das bürgerliche Element in der Societät*). Such a policy gave rise to feelings of dissatisfaction from which it was only a step to revolution – a fact regarding which France served as a sad example. At this point he gave a sigh of sympathy, but of sympathy tinged with censure. However, he immediately added the observation that he himself had a veneration for authority and would never ... no, never ... become a revolutionary. But he could not refrain from expressing his ... how should he put it? ... disapproval at the sight of such laxity! He then offered a few more observations on morality and on immorality, on decency and on the sense of dignity.

During all this 'pontification', Gemma quite obviously began to be ashamed of her husband-to-be. She had already seemed a little unhappy about Herr Klueber during the morning walk – that was why she had kept some distance from Sanin and had appeared somewhat embarrassed by his presence. Towards the end of the drive, she was positively wretched, and although, as before, she did not say a word to Sanin, she suddenly threw him a glance of entreaty ... as far as he was concerned, he felt much more pity for her than indignation towards Herr Klueber ... Secretly and half-unconsciously, he was even rejoicing at everything that had happened in the course of the day, although he could expect a challenge the following morning.

At last this painful *partie de plaisir* came to an end. When he handed Gemma out of the carriage in front of the patisserie, Sanin, without saying a word, placed in her hand the rose which he had recaptured. She coloured violently, pressed his hand and immediately hid the rose away. Although the evening was only just beginning, he did not wish to enter the house. She did not invite him in. Besides, Pantaleone, who had appeared at the porch, announced that Frau Lenore was resting. Emil said goodbye to Sanin in a state of some confusion. The boy seemed to shy away from him now – so much did the Russian astonish him. Klueber conveyed Sanin to his hotel and bowed a stiff farewell. For all his self-assurance, the well-regulated German was ill at ease. But indeed, everyone was ill at ease.

However, this unease soon disappeared so far Sanin was concerned. It was replaced by another mood, difficult to define, though agreeable, even exalted. He strode up and down the room, did not want to think about anything, whistled from time to time – and felt very pleased with himself.

XVII

NEXT morning as he was dressing, he said to himself, 'I will wait for this officer until ten o'clock, and after that I will leave it to him to find me.' But the Germans are early risers. It had not yet struck nine when the waiter came in to announce that Second Lieutenant (*der Herr Seconde Leutnant*) von Richter wished to see him. Sanin quickly threw on his coat and told the waiter to show him in. Contrary to Sanin's expectations, Herr Richter turned out to be a very young man indeed, little more than a boy. He did his best to give his beardless face an expression of importance, but was extremely unsuccessful. He could not even conceal his embarrassment – as he sat down, he nearly fell over his sword which had got caught in the chair. With much stumbling and stammering he declared to Sanin, in atrocious French, that he had come at the instance of his friend, Baron von Doenhof; that his mission was to demand of Herr von Zanin an apology for the insulting expressions which he had used the day before; and that in the event of Herr von Zanin refusing such an apology, Baron von Doenhof required satisfaction.

Sanin replied that he had no intention of apologizing, but was prepared to give satisfaction. Thereupon, Herr von Richter, still stammering, inquired the time when, and the place where, and the person with whom the necessary discussions could take place. Sanin replied that he could return in about two hours' time, and that in the meantime, he, Sanin, would endeavour to find a second. (Who the devil shall I have as my second? he was thinking to himself meanwhile.)

Herr von Richter rose and began to make his farewell bows ... but stopped as he reached the door, as if his conscience had smitten him, and turning towards Sanin, muttered that his friend, Baron von Doenhof, did not conceal from himself ... some degree of blame on his own part ... for what occurred yesterday, and would therefore be satisfied with a very mild apology – '*des exghizes léchères*'. To this, Sanin replied he had no intention of making any apology whether deep or mild, since he did not consider himself to be in the wrong.

'In that case,' replied Herr von Richter, blushing even more, 'it will be necessary to exchange some amicable pistol shots – *des goups de bisdolet à l'amiaple.*'

'I don't understand this at all,' remarked Sanin. 'Are we to fire in the air, or what?'

'Oh no, not at all,' babbled the subaltern, now in a state of complete confusion. 'I only thought that since this was an affair between gentlemen ... I will talk to your second,' he interrupted himself, and was gone.

As soon as von Richter had left the room, Sanin sank on to a chair and stared at the floor. 'What on earth is all this? How has life all of a sudden taken this turn? Everything past and future has vanished, is lost, and all that remains is that here I am in Frankfurt, about to have a fight with someone about something or other.' He remembered a mad aunt, who was in the habit of singing a little doggerel to herself, and dancing to it:

> Fiddle-de-dee,
> Fiddle-de-doh
> My subaltern, my boy – O
> Come dance with me
> Come prance with me
> My subaltern, my joy – O!

And he burst out laughing and sang like her:

Come dance with me,
Come prance with me,
My subaltern, my joy – O![1]

All at once, he exclaimed aloud: 'However, I must act and not lose any time,' jumped up and saw Pantaleone in front of him with a note in his hand.

'I knocked several times, but you did not answer. I thought you were not in,' murmured the old man and handed him the note. 'From Signorina Gemma.'

Sanin took it – mechanically, as the saying goes – opened it and read it. Gemma wrote that she was very much perturbed on account of a certain matter of which he was aware, and would like to see him at once.

'The Signorina is worried,' remarked Pantaleone, who was evidently aware of the contents of the note. 'She told me to find out what you were doing and to bring you to her.'

Sanin glanced at the old Italian – and plunged into thought. An idea flashed through his mind. It seemed at first so strange as to be impossible. And yet – why not? he said to himself, and then out loud, 'Signor Pantaleone!'

The old man pulled himself together, tucked his chin into his cravat and fixed his eyes on Sanin.

'Do you know,' continued Sanin, 'what happened yesterday?'

Pantaleone went through some chewing motions and jerked his enormous mane.

'I do.' (Emil had told him everything as soon as he got back.)

'You do, do you? Then listen to me. An officer has just left this room. That bounder has challenged me to a duel. I have accepted his challenge. But I have no second. Would *you* like to be my second?'

Pantaleone gave a start and raised his eyebrows so high that they disappeared under the overhanging hair.

'It is absolutely necessary for you to fight?' he asked at last in Italian. Until then he had been expressing himself in French.

'Absolutely. To act otherwise would mean dishonour for the rest of my life.'

'Hm. If I do not agree to act as your second, will you then look for someone else?'

'Certainly. Of course I will.'

Pantaleone dropped his gaze.

'But may I ask you, Signor de Zannini, do you not think that your duel may cast a certain unfavourable shadow on the reputation of a certain personage?'

'I don't think so. But, in any case, there is nothing to be done about it.'

'Hm.' Pantaleone had by now completely disappeared into his cravat. 'Well, and that *ferroflucto* Kluberio, what about him?' he exclaimed, suddenly jerking his face upwards.

'He? Oh, nothing.'

'*Che!*'*

Pantaleone shrugged his shoulders contemptuously. 'In any event, I have to thank you,' he pronounced at length in an unsteady voice, 'for the fact that you are able to recognize a gentleman – *un galant'uomo* – even in my present degraded state. By acting in this manner, you have demonstrated that you are a real *galant'uomo*. But I must think over your proposal.'

'Time will not wait, dear Signor Ci . . . Cippa . . .'

'Tola,' prompted the old man. 'I am only asking for one hour's time for reflection. The daughter of my benefactors is involved in this, and therefore I must, I am in duty bound, to give the question some thought. In an hour's time, in three-quarters of an hour's time, you will learn my decision.'

'Very well. I will wait.'

'And now, what answer am I to give Signorina Gemma?'

Sanin took a sheet of paper and wrote: 'Do not worry, my

* An untranslatable Italian exclamation rather like our Russian *nu* (Oh, well! *Tr.*).

58

dear friend, I will come to see you in about three hours' time and all will be explained. Thank you with all my heart for your concern.' He entrusted the note to Pantaleone, who put it carefully in a side pocket, repeated, 'In an hour's time', and made for the door. But suddenly he turned back sharply, ran up to Sanin, seized his hand, pressed it to his frilled shirt-front and, raising his eyes to Heaven, exclaimed, 'Noble youth! Great heart! (*Nobil giovanotto! Gran cuore!*) Suffer a feeble old man (*a un vechiotto*) to press your valiant hand! (*la vostra valorosa destra!*).' He then leapt back a little, waved both arms in the air . . . and was gone.

Sanin followed him with his eyes . . . then picked up a newspaper and began to read. But he scanned the printed lines in vain: he could take in nothing.

XVIII

AN hour later, the waiter came up once more and handed Sanin an old and dirty visiting card on which the following words were engraved: *Pantaleone Cippatola of Varese, Court Singer (Cantante di Camera) to his Royal Highness the Duke of Modena.* The waiter was closely followed by Pantaleone himself. He had changed all his clothes from top to toe. He was wearing a black frock coat which had gone brown with age, and a white piqué waistcoat, across which a pinchbeck watch-chain was elaborately draped. A heavy cornelian seal hung low over the flap of his narrow black breeches pocket. In his right hand, he held a black hat made of hare's wool, and in his left two thick chamois leather gloves. His cravat was tied even wider and higher than usual, and a tiepin with a stone which is called a 'cat's eye' (*oeil de chat*) was stuck in his starched shirt-front. The index finger of his right hand was embellished with a ring representing two clasped hands with a flaming heart between them. A heavy smell of storage, of mothballs and of musk came wafting across from the old man. But the most indifferent spectator would have been struck by his appearance of perplexed solemnity. Sanin rose to greet him.

'I am your second,' murmured Pantaleone in French, and bowed with the whole of his trunk, at the same time placing his heels together and his toes apart like a ballet dancer. 'I have come for my instructions. Do you wish to fight without mercy?'

'Why without mercy, dear Signor Cippatola? Nothing in the world would make me withdraw the words which I used yesterday – but I am not bloodthirsty! But wait, my opponent's second will be here any moment. I will go into the next room, and you two can agree conditions. Believe me, I will never forget your services to me, and I thank you with all my heart.'

'Honour must come first,' replied Pantaleone, and sank into an armchair without waiting for Sanin to invite him to be seated.

'If this *ferroflucto spicebubio*,' he continued, mixing French and Italian, 'if this shop-walker Kluberio was incapable of perceiving where his plain duty lay, and was too cowardly – so much the worse for him! A tuppeny ha'penny good-for-nothing – and there's an end of it. As for the conditions of the duel, I am your second and your interests are to me sacred! When I lived in Padua, a regiment of White Dragoons was stationed there – and I was very close to many of the officers. I know their code intimately. Of course I also frequently discussed these matters with your Principe Tarbussky . . . Is that second due here soon?'

'I expect him any minute – and indeed here he comes,' Sanin added, glancing into the street.

Pantaleone rose, looked at his watch, adjusted his great lock of hair and quickly pushed back into his shoe an errant tape which was dangling from under his breeches. The young subaltern came into the room, still as red-faced and confused as before.

Sanin presented the two seconds to each other.

'Monsieur Richter, *sous lieutenant* – Monsieur Cippatola, *artiste*.'

The subaltern was a little taken aback at the sight of the old man . . . What would he have said if someone had whispered to him at this moment that the '*artiste*' who had just been introduced to him was also occupied in the culinary arts! But Pantaleone assumed the air of one for whom arranging duels was an everyday affair. He was helped on this occasion by the memories of his theatrical career, and he played the part of a second precisely as if it were a stage role. Both he and the young officer were silent for a few moments.

'Well, shall we begin?' Pantaleone, playing with his cornelian seal, was the first to speak.

'Yes, let us begin,' replied the subaltern. 'But . . . the presence of one of the adversaries . . .'

'I will leave you immediately, gentlemen,' Sanin exclaimed. He bowed and went into the bedroom, locking the door behind him.

He flung himself on the bed and began to think about Gemma . . . but the conversation of the seconds reached him through the closed door. It was being conducted in French, and each was massacring that language mercilessly after his own fashion . . . Pantaleone once again mentioned the Dragoons of Padua and the Principe Tarbussky, and the subaltern spoke of '*exghizes léchères!*' and of '*goups à l' amiaple*'. But the old man refused to listen to any talk of '*exghizes*'. To Sanin's horror, he suddenly launched into a lecture on the subject of a certain young and innocent maiden, whose little finger alone was worth more than all the officers in the world (*oune zeune damigella innoucenta qu'a ella sola dans soun peti doa vale più que toutt le zouffissié del mondo!*), and repeated several times with heat, 'It is shameful, shameful (*E ouna onta, ouna onta!*).'

The subaltern did not at first react, but before long a tremor of anger appeared in the young man's voice, and he remarked that he had not come for the purpose of listening to moral sermons.

'At your age, it is always salutary to listen to the truth,' exclaimed Pantaleone.

The argument between the two seconds grew stormy at several stages. It lasted for over an hour, and resulted at length in agreement on the following conditions: 'Baron von Doenhof and Monsieur de Sanin to duel with pistols on the following day at ten o'clock in the morning, in a small wood near Hanau, at twenty paces' distance. Each to have the right to fire twice on a signal to be given by the seconds. Pistols to have unrifled barrels and the triggers not to be fitted with hair-springs.'

Herr von Richter departed, and Pantaleone ceremoniously opened the bedroom door, announced the result of the conference and once again exclaimed, '*Bravo Russo! Bravo giovanotto!* Thou wilt be victorious!'

A few minutes later, the two of them set off for the Roselli patisserie. Before setting out, Sanin had exacted a promise from Pantaleone to keep the whole matter of the duel a deep secret. In reply, the old man merely raised a finger, screwed up one eye, and whispered twice '*Segredezza!*' He was visibly younger and even seemed to walk more jauntily. All these extraordinary, if unpleasant, events vividly transported him to that epoch when he himself had issued and accepted challenges – on the stage, it is true. Baritones, as is well known, are very full of sound and fury in their stage roles.

XIX

EMIL ran out to meet Sanin – he had been keeping a look-out for over an hour – and hurriedly whispered in his ear that his mother knew nothing about the unpleasant incident of the day before, and that it must not even be hinted at, that he was once again being sent off to Herr Klueber's store, but that he would not go, and would hide somewhere. Having imparted all this information in a few seconds, the boy suddenly fell on Sanin's shoulder, kissed him impetuously and dashed off down the street.

Gemma met Sanin in the shop, tried to say something – and could not do so. Her lips were trembling slightly and her eyes were half-closed and restless. He hastened to calm her, and to assure her that the whole matter had ended in a mere trifle.

'Did anyone call to see you today?' she asked.

'Yes, a certain person called on me, we had a discussion and we came to a most satisfactory conclusion.'

Gemma withdrew behind the counter.

She didn't believe me, he thought to himself . . . However, he went into the adjoining room and there found Frau Lenore. Her migraine had passed, but she was in a mood of melancholy. She welcomed him with a friendly smile, but at the same time warned him that he would be bored by her today, she was in no state to entertain him. He sat down beside her, and noticed that her eyelids were red and swollen.

'What is the matter, Frau Lenore? Surely you haven't been crying?'

'Sh . . . sh . . .' she whispered and motioned with her head towards the room where her daughter was. 'Don't say that so loudly.'

'But what have you been crying about?'

'Ah, Monsieur Sanin, I don't know myself.'

'Has someone caused you distress?'

'Oh, no. I suddenly grew very lonely. I also remembered Giovan' Battista . . . my youth . . . then I thought how quickly it had all passed. I am getting old, my friend, and I cannot reconcile myself to that. It seems to me as if I were the same as I was before . . . but old age . . . here it is, here it is!'

Traces of tears appeared in Frau Lenore's eyes.

'I can see that you are looking at me with astonishment –

but you too will grow old, my friend, and you will discover how bitter it is!'

Sanin began to comfort her, mentioned her children in whom her own youth was resurrected, even tried to tease her a little by assuring her that she was fishing for compliments. But she earnestly begged him to stop, and he realized for the first time that such despondency, the despondency that comes with the awareness of growing old, cannot ever be comforted or dispelled. One can but wait until it passes of its own accord. He suggested a game of *tresette*, and could have thought of nothing better. She immediately agreed, and seemed to grow more cheerful.

Sanin played cards with her before and after luncheon. Pantaleone also took part in the game. Never had his locks fallen so low upon his forehead, never had his chin sunk so deeply into his cravat. His every movement breathed such concentrated self-importance that merely to look at him gave rise to the involuntary thought: 'What is the secret that this man is guarding with such firm determination?'

But – *segredezza, segredezza!*

During that entire day, he tried in every way to show the deepest respect for Sanin. At table, he passed over the ladies and ceremoniously and firmly handed Sanin the dishes. During the game, he let Sanin take cards first and did not have the effrontery to claim any penalties. From time to time, without rhyme or reason, he would declare to all and sundry that the Russians are the most magnanimous, the bravest, and the most determined people in the world!

Oh, you old mummer! Sanin thought to himself.

But what amazed him more than the sudden change in Signora Roselli's mood was the way in which her daughter behaved towards him. It was not that she avoided him – rather the contrary: she kept on settling down a little away from him, listening to what he said, looking at him. But she decidedly did not wish to enter into conversation with him, and every time that he spoke to her, she would quietly rise from her seat and quietly disappear for a few moments. She would then reappear, and sit down again somewhere in a corner and there she remained motionless, as if meditating and wondering – wondering above all. Frau Lenore at last noticed her extraordinary behaviour and inquired once or twice what the matter was.

'Nothing,' replied Gemma. 'You know I am like this sometimes.'

'Yes, that is so,' her mother agreed.

And so passed the whole of that long day – neither gay nor dull – neither amusing nor boring. Who knows? Maybe if Gemma had behaved otherwise, Sanin would have been unable to resist the temptation to show off a little, or would simply have surrendered to the feeling of sadness at parting from her, possibly for ever . . .

But since he did not even have an opportunity of speaking to Gemma, he had perforce to content himself with sitting at the pianoforte picking out minor chords for a quarter of an hour, before evening coffee.

Emil returned late, and in order to avoid inquiries about Herr Klueber, withdrew to bed very shortly afterwards. The time came for Sanin, too, to take his leave.

He said goodbye to Gemma. For some reason, he remembered Lensky's parting from Olga in Pushkin's *Eugene Onegin*. He pressed her hand firmly, and attempted to look her in the eyes . . . but she turned aside slightly and released her fingers from his grasp.

XX

THE stars were out when he emerged on to the porch. And what an array of stars was scattered in the heavens. Large and small, yellow and red, and blue and white, they glowed in clusters, their rays dancing in the darkness. There was no moon in the sky, but even without moonlight each object was clearly visible in the shadowless, half-illuminated dusk. Sanin walked the length of the street . . . He did not want to return home at once; he felt the need to wander in the fresh air. He retraced his steps, and had hardly drawn level with the Rosellis' house, when one of the windows facing on to the street suddenly opened with a knock. On the black square surface of the opening (there was no light in the room), there appeared the figure of a woman and he heard his name called: 'Monsieur Dimitry!'

He rushed headlong to the window . . . Gemma!

She leaned forwards with her elbows on the sill.

'Monsieur Dimitry,' she began in a hesitant voice, 'all day long I have wanted to give you a certain thing . . . but could not summon up the courage. But now, suddenly seeing you again, I thought evidently this is something that is fated . . .' Gemma stopped involuntarily at this word. She could not go on: at that instant something quite extraordinary happened.

Suddenly, in the midst of the deep silence, in a completely cloudless sky, there arose such a rush of wind that the very earth seemed to quake beneath their feet. The thin light of the stars shuddered and scattered, and the very air was whirling around them. The onrush of wind, which was not cold but warm and even torrid, struck at the trees, at the roof of the house, at its walls, at the street. In an instant, it had whipped Sanin's hat from his head, and blown the black strands of Gemma's hair into disorder. Sanin's head was level with the windowsill. He leaned against it involuntarily, while Gemma gripped his shoulders with both hands and pressed her breast against his head. The noise, the ringing and the rattling lasted about a minute . . . The whirlwind sped away, as fast as it had risen, like a flock of enormous birds . . . Once again there was deep silence.

Sanin raised his head and saw above him such a wonderful, frightened, excited face, such enormous, such terrifying, such marvellous eyes, he saw a creature of such beauty, that his heart seemed to stop. He sank his lips in the thin spray of hair that had fallen across his chest. 'Oh, Gemma . . .'

'What was that? Was it lightning?' she asked, opening her eyes wide and keeping her bare arms on his shoulders.

'Gemma!' Sanin repeated.

She started, glanced behind her into the room, and then with a swift movement took from her bosom a rose that was already faded and threw it to Sanin.

'I wanted to give you this flower.'

He recognized the rose which he had won back the day before . . .

But the window was already slammed to, and there was nothing to be seen, no sign of any pale reflection behind the dark pane.

Sanin returned to his hotel without his hat : . . He had not even noticed that he had lost it.

XXI

IT was morning when he fell asleep, and no wonder! Under the impact of that sudden summer squall, he had realized almost as suddenly not that Gemma was a beautiful girl, not that she attracted him – he knew that before – but that he had . . . very nearly fallen in love with her. Love had swept down upon him as suddenly as the squall, and now there was this idiotic duel! He began to be tortured by gloomy forebodings. Well, he might not be killed. But what could come out of his love for this girl, who was engaged to be married to another man? No doubt this other man was not a very serious rival, and suppose even that Gemma would come to love him, Sanin, or loved him already – what then? How would it end? And such a beauty . . .

He walked about the room, sat down at the table, took a sheet of paper, scribbled a few lines on it, and straight away scratched them out . . . Then he recalled the wonderful image of Gemma, all blown about by the warm rush of wind, in the dark window under the rays of the stars . . . He remembered her arms which were like marble, like the arms of the goddesses on Olympus; he could feel their living weight on his shoulders . . . then he picked up the rose which she had thrown him . . . and it seemed to him that its faded petals gave off a scent which was even more fragrant than the usual scent of roses . . .

'But suppose I am killed or maimed?'

He did not go to bed, but fell asleep fully dressed on the divan.

Someone was shaking him by the shoulder. He opened his eyes and saw Pantaleone.

'Asleep, like Alexander of Macedon on the eve of the Babylonian battle,' exclaimed the old man.

'But what is the time?' Sanin enquired.

'A quarter to seven. It is two hours' drive to Hanau, and we must be first on the scene. The Russians always forestall their enemies. I have engaged the best carriage in Frankfurt.'

Sanin began to wash.

'And where are the pistols?'

'They will be brought by that *ferroflucto tedesco*. He will bring the doctor, as well.'

Pantaleone was evidently putting on a show of courage, as he had done the day before. But when he sat down beside Sanin in the carriage and the coachman had cracked his whip and the horses had set off at a brisk trot, the former singer and friend of the Padua Dragoons suffered a change. He became confused, and a bit frightened. It was as if something within him had crashed to the ground, like a badly aligned wall.

'What are we doing, dear God, *Santissima Madonna*?' he, exclaimed, in a voice which had suddenly become plaintive, and clutched at his hair. 'What am I doing, old fool that I am, old madman, *frenetico*?'

Sanin was surprised and laughed, and putting his arm lightly around Pantaleone's waist, reminded him of the French saying: '*Le vin est tiré – il faut le boire*' (or, as the Russians say, 'If you put your hand to the cart, you can't draw back').

'Yes, yes,' replied the old man, 'we will drain this cup together. But even so, I am off my head. Off my head! Everything was so quiet, so pleasant . . . and now suddenly: ta-ta-ta, tra-ta-ta.'

'Just like the passages for *tutti* in the orchestra,' Sanin remarked with a forced smile, 'but it is not your fault, after all.'

'I know it isn't – what next? Even so, this is such an impetuous action. *Diavolo, diavolo*,' Pantaleone kept repeating, shaking his mop of hair and sighing.

And the carriage rolled on and on.

It was a beautiful morning. The streets of Frankfurt, which had scarcely begun to stir, seemed so clean and comfortable. The window-panes on the houses sparkled like silver foil, as the sun played on them. And no sooner had the carriage left the town boundary than the shrill song of the larks came cascading down from the blue, but not as yet bright, sky. Suddenly, at a turning in the main road, a familiar figure appeared from behind a tall poplar tree, took a few steps forward and stopped. Sanin looked at it more closely. Dear God, it was Emil!

He turned to Pantaleone. 'Does he know anything?'

'Didn't I tell you that I am a madman?' the poor Italian almost shouted in his despair. 'This wretched boy gave me no peace all night, and at last, this morning, I told him everything.'

There's your *segredezza* for you, thought Sanin. The carriage drew level with Emil. Sanin told the coachman to stop and called the 'wretched boy' to him. Emil came towards him with uncertain, faltering steps, as pale as pale could be, as on the day of his fainting fit. He could hardly stand up.

'What are you doing here?' Sanin asked severely. 'Why are you not at home?'

'Please, please, allow me to drive with you,' Emil babbled in a trembling voice, his hands folded in entreaty. His teeth were chattering, as in a fever. 'I won't be in the way, only please take me with you.'

'If you feel the slightest affection or respect for me,' Sanin replied, 'you will return home or to Herr Klueber's shop immediately, will not say a single word to anyone and will wait for my return.'

Emil moaned, 'Your return . . .' and his voice rang out and then broke. 'And what if you . . .'

'Emil,' Sanin interrupted, motioning with his eyes at the coachman, 'remember yourself! Emil, please go home! Please listen to me, my friend. You assure me that you are fond of me. Please, do as I ask.'

He put out his hand to the boy, who lurched forward with a sob, pressed the hand to his lips, and then jumped off the road and ran back across a field in the direction of Frankfurt.

'There's another noble heart for you,' murmured Pantaleone, but Sanin glared at him. The old man sat huddled into his corner of the carriage. He knew he had done wrong. Besides, his amazement grew with every moment. Was it really possible that *he* had agreed to act as second in a duel, that *he* had procured the horses and made all the arrangements and had left his peaceful abode at six o'clock in the morning? On top of everything, his legs were aching painfully.

Sanin thought it necessary to put some heart into him, and found the right chord to strike, found the very word.

'Where is your former spirit, my worthy Signor Cippatola, where is *il antico valor?*'

Signor Cippatola sat up straight and frowned. '*Il antico valor?*' he repeated in a deep bass voice, '*Non è ancora spento il antico valor*' (The ancient valour is not yet all spent).

He preened himself, began to talk about his career, about the opera, and the great tenor Garcia, and arrived in Hanau full of vitality. When you come to think of it, there is nothing in the world more powerful – or more impotent – than a word.

XXII

THE little wood in which the battle was destined to take place was about a quarter of a mile from Hanau. As Pantaleone had foretold, he and Sanin were the first to arrive. They ordered the carriage to wait at the edge of the wood and walked deeper into the shade of the thickly grown and close-set trees. They had about an hour to wait.

The time spent waiting did not weigh too heavily on Sanin. He strolled up and down the little path, listened to the song of the birds, watched the dragonflies as they flew past and, like the majority of Russians in similar circumstances, tried not to think. He was only once plunged into melancholy reflections, and that was when he came upon a young lime tree, which had to all appearances been felled by yesterday's squall. The tree was actually dying, all its leaves were withering. What is this? An omen? flashed through his mind. But he immediately started to whistle, jumped over the very same lime tree and went striding along the path. As for Pantaleone, he grumbled away, abused the Germans, groaned and kept rubbing either his back or his knees. He even kept yawning from excitement, which gave his tiny, pinched and drawn face a most comical expression. Sanin nearly burst out laughing when he looked at him.

At last the sound of carriage wheels was heard on the soft

road. 'It is they,' muttered Pantaleone, alert now and straightening himself. He did shiver nervously for a moment, but proceeded to camouflage this with a 'brrr', and a remark that it was a fresh morning. The leaves and the grass were drenched with dew, but the heat of the day penetrated right into the wood.

The two officers soon appeared, framed at the edge of the forest. They were accompanied by a short, stoutish man with a phlegmatic, almost sleepy expression – the military doctor. He was carrying in one hand an earthenware jug of water, ready for any emergency. A satchel, containing surgical instruments and bandages, was dangling from his left shoulder. It was evident that he was more than used to expeditions of this nature. They formed one of the sources of his income: every duel was worth eight sovereigns to him, four from each combatant. Herr von Richter was carrying a box containing the pistols, Herr von Doenhof was twirling a small riding switch, probably in order to show off.

'Pantaleone,' Sanin whispered to the old man, 'if . . . if I am killed – after all anything can happen – get a paper from my side pocket – there is a flower wrapped in it, and give the paper to Signorina Gemma. Do you hear me? Do you promise?'

The old man looked at him dejectedly – and nodded his head . . . but goodness knows if he had understood Sanin's request.

The adversaries and their seconds exchanged bows, as is customary. The doctor alone did not move an eyebrow, but sat down on the grass with a yawn, as if to say, 'I have no time for these manifestations of knightly courtesies.' Herr von Richter proposed to Signor 'Cibbadola' that he should select the spot; Signor 'Cibbadola' replied, with his tongue hardly moving in his palate (the 'wall' in him had once again collapsed), 'You take the necessary action, my dear sir, and I will observe.'

And so Herr von Richter took the necessary action. He found there in the wood a very pretty clearing, all decked with flowers. He measured the paces and marked out the limits with two small twigs which he had hastily peeled, got the pistols out of the box, sat down on his heels and packed in the bullets. In a word, he made himself uncommonly busy, constantly mopping the sweat from off his face with a white handkerchief. Pantaleone, who accompanied him, looked more like a man shivering with cold. While all these preparations were going on, the two adversaries stood some distance apart, like two schoolboys who had been punished and who were showing resentment against their masters.

The moment of decision was come . . .

'Each took his pistol in his hand . . .'[1]

But at this point, Herr von Richter remarked to Pantaleone that as the senior second it was his duty, according to the rules of duelling, before pronouncing the fatal, 'One, two, three,' to address to the adversaries words of last-minute advice and to make a proposal for reconciliation; that while such proposals had never been known to lead to any results, and were in fact nothing more than an empty formality, nevertheless by going through with the formality, Signor Cippatola would divest himself of a certain degree of responsibility for the consequences; that while it was true that an allocution of this nature was the direct responsibility of the so-called impartial witness, *unparteiischer Zeuge*, nevertheless, since none such was present, he, Herr von Richter, would willingly yield this privilege to his respected confrère.

Meanwhile Pantaleone had had time to disappear so completely behind a bush as to be unable to see the officer who had been guilty of the insulting behaviour. At first, he understood nothing of Herr von Richter's oration, particularly since it had been delivered through the nose. But suddenly he sprang into action, stepped forward nimbly and, feverishly beating his chest, bellowed in his hoarse voice, in his comic mixture of

73

languages, '*A, la la la ... Che bestialità! Deux zeun' ommes come ça qué si battono – perchè? Che diavolo! Andate a casa!*'

'I am not willing to be reconciled,' Sanin said hurriedly.

'And I also am not willing,' his adversary repeated after him.

'Well then, call out, "One, two, three",' said von Richter, addressing himself to Pantaleone, who by now had completely lost his head.

Pantaleone instantly dived back into his bush, where he huddled, and with his eyes shut and his head averted yelled at the top of his voice:

'*Una ... due ... e tre!*'

Sanin fired first – and missed. The bullet struck a tree with a thud. Baron Doenhof fired immediately after him – deliberately to the side and into the air.

There followed a strained silence ... no one moved. Pantaleone uttered a weak 'Oh' –

'Do you wish to continue?' said Doenhof.

'Why did you fire into the air?' Sanin asked.

'That is not your business.'

'Does it mean that you will fire the second shot into the air as well?' Sanin asked him again.

'Perhaps. I don't know.'

'Please, gentlemen, please,' began von Richter. 'Adversaries in a duel have no right to converse with each other. That is quite out of order.'

'I renounce my right to fire,' said Sanin, and threw his pistol to the ground.

'And I, too, have no intention of going on with this duel,' exclaimed Doenhof and also threw down his pistol, 'and besides, I am now prepared to admit that I was in the wrong the day before yesterday.'

He took a few hesitant steps and stretched out his hand. Sanin quickly walked towards him and grasped the hand. Both young men looked at each other with a smile, and each of them blushed.

'*Bravi, bravi,*' Pantaleone suddenly bellowed like a madman, and, clapping his hands, ran out from the bush like a tumbler pigeon. The doctor, who had seated himself on a tree-stump a little way off, promptly rose to his feet, emptied the water from the jug and ambled lazily towards the edge of the wood.

'Honour is satisfied and the duel is concluded,' von Richter declared in a loud voice.

'*Fuori!*'[2] Pantaleone barked from force of habit.

Having exchanged bows with the officers and taken his seat in the carriage, Sanin was certainly conscious in his whole being of a sensation, if not of pleasure then of relief, like that which follows a successful operation. But another feeling stirred within him as well, something akin to shame . . . The duel in which he had just enacted his part now began to take on the appearance of something false, a pre-arranged regimental ceremonial, an ordinary piece of officer and student nonsense. He remembered the phlegmatic doctor and recalled how he had smiled – or rather wrinkled his nose – at the sight of his emerging from the wood practically arm-in-arm with Baron Doenhof. And then, while Pantaleone was paying over to that same doctor the four sovereigns which were his due . . . Oh dear . . . it was not very agreeable.

Yes, Sanin felt a little remorseful and ashamed . . . and yet, when he thought about it, what should he have done? Surely not have left the insolence of the young officer unpunished, and behaved like Herr Klueber? He had intervened on Gemma's behalf, he had defended her . . . That was so, but for all that, he was uneasy in his mind, and felt pangs of remorse and even of shame.

Pantaleone, on the other hand, was nothing less than triumphant. He was overwhelmed with pride. No general returning victorious from the field of battle could have looked around him with greater self-satisfaction. Sanin's behaviour during the duel had fired him with enthusiasm. He kept calling him a hero, and would not listen to protestations or to requests to desist. He compared him to a monument of marble, or of bronze, to the statue of the Commendatore in 'Don Giovanni'. As for himself, he admitted he had suffered a certain loss of nerve. 'But, after all, I am an artiste,' he remarked. 'I am highly-strung by nature, while you – you are a child of the snows and of the granite cliffs.'

Sanin simply did not know how to restrain the ardour of the old singer, who was now in full spate.

At about the same spot on the road where they had overtaken Emil a couple of hours before, the boy once again jumped out from behind a tree. With cries of joy, waving his cap above his head and jumping up and down with excitement, he rushed straight at the carriage, nearly falling under the wheels in the process. Then, without waiting for the horses to stop, he clambered over the closed carriage doors – and hurled himself on Sanin.

'You are alive, not wounded!' he kept exclaiming. 'Forgive me, I disobeyed you. I didn't return to Frankfurt . . . I couldn't do it . . . I waited for you here . . . Tell me about it. Did . . . did you kill him?'

Sanin had considerable difficulty in calming him and settling him down in his seat.

Pantaleone, with much rhetoric and evident pleasure, related all the details of the duel and of course did not omit to mention the bronze monument and the statue of the Commendatore. He even rose from his seat, stood legs apart to keep his balance, folded his arms across his chest, squinted haughtily over his shoulder, and gave a life-like impersonation of Commendatore Sanin! Emil listened reverently, occasionally interrupting the recital with an exclamation, or else rising swiftly to implant an equally swift kiss on his heroic friend.

The carriage wheels rattled on the paved roads of Frankfurt, and eventually stopped before Sanin's hotel.

Sanin was ascending the stairs to the second floor with his two companions, when suddenly a woman stepped briskly from a small, dark corridor. Her face was covered with a veil. She paused in front of Sanin, swayed slightly, heaved an agitated sigh, ran immediately down to the street, and disappeared – to the great surprise of the waiter who announced that, 'This lady has been waiting for the foreign gentleman to return for over an hour.' Although her appearance had been only momentary, Sanin had had time to recognize Gemma. He recognized her eyes under the thick silk of her brown veil.

'Was Fräulein Gemma then aware . . .?' he asked in German, slowly and with annoyance in his voice, turning to Emil and Pantaleone who were following closely on his heels.

Emil blushed and looked embarrassed.

'I was forced to tell her everything,' he mumbled. 'She guessed what was going on, and there was nothing I could . . . But it doesn't matter at all now,' he went on brightly, 'everything has ended so splendidly, and she has seen you well and unharmed!'

Sanin turned away.

'What a pair of gossips you are, the two of you,' he said crossly, as he went into his room and sat down on a chair.

'Oh, please don't be angry,' begged Emil.

'All right, I won't be angry.' (Sanin was not, in fact, angry – he could indeed have hardly wished that Gemma would discover nothing.) 'All right, that's enough embracing. You had better go now. I want to be alone. I am tired and will go to sleep.'

'An excellent thought,' exclaimed Pantaleone. 'You need repose, and you have fully earned it, most noble Signore. Come, Emilio. On tiptoes, on tiptoes . . . sh . . . sh . . .!'

Sanin had only said that he wanted to sleep in order to be rid of his companions. But, when he was alone, he did indeed feel a considerable weariness in all his limbs. He had scarcely closed his eyes during the whole of the previous night. He threw himself down on to the bed and immediately fell into a deep sleep.

XXIII

HE slept for several hours without waking. Then he began to dream that he was once again fighting a duel, that the adversary before him was Herr Klueber, while on a pine tree sat a parrot, which was, in fact, Pantaleone, and which kept snapping its beak and saying, 'One, one, one! One, one, one!'

'One, one, one.' He was now awake. He opened his eyes and raised his head . . . Someone was knocking at the door.

'Come in!' Sanin called out.

A waiter appeared and announced that a lady was very anxious to see him.

Gemma flashed through his mind . . . but the lady turned out to be her mother, Frau Lenore.

As soon as she had entered the room, she sank down on a chair and began to weep.

'What is the matter, dear, good Signora Roselli?' Sanin began, sitting down beside her and touching her hand with a gentle caress. 'What has happened? Please calm yourself, I beg of you . . .'

'Oh, Herr Dimitry, I am very, very unhappy.'

'Unhappy? You?'

'Oh, desperately. How was I to expect this? Suddenly like a clap of thunder from a clear sky . . .' She was drawing breath with difficulty.

'But what is happening? Won't you explain? Would you like a glass of water?'

'No, thank you.' Frau Lenore wiped her eyes with her handkerchief, then burst out weeping with renewed abandon. 'You see, I know everything, everything . . .'

'What do you mean by everything?'

'Everything that happened today, and the reason . . . I know about that, too . . . You behaved like an honourable man. But what a miserable chain of circumstances! I never liked the idea of the trip to Soden, and I was right – quite right.' (Frau Lenore had implied nothing of the kind on the day of the trip, but had now convinced herself that she had had a 'premonition'.) 'It is because you are an honourable man and a friend that I have come to you, though I only first set eyes on you some five days ago . . . But I am a widow, a lonely widow . . . my daughter . . .!' Tears drowned Frau Lenore's words. Sanin did not know what to think.

'Your daughter?' he repeated.

'My daughter, Gemma,' Frau Lenore's words burst out with something like a groan, from under the tear-soaked handkerchief, 'declared to me today that she does not wish to marry Herr Klueber, and that I must break off the engagement.'

Sanin actually backed away from her slightly. He had not expected this.

'I say nothing of the disgrace,' Frau Lenore went on. 'This is something that has never happened before in the history of the world, for a girl to break off an engagement. This means ruin for us, Herr Dimitry!' She carefully and methodically rolled up her handkerchief into a tight little ball, exactly as if she wished to roll up her grief in it. 'It is no longer possible for us to live on the income from the shop, Herr Dimitry, and Herr Klueber is very rich and will in time be even richer. And why should the engagement be broken, just because he did not stand up for his fiancée? Well, perhaps that wasn't quite right of him, but after all he is a civilian, he hasn't been to a university and it was only right for a solid businessman like him to treat a light-hearted prank of an unknown little officer with contempt. And in any case, what *was* there insulting about it, Herr Dimitry?'

'Forgive me, Frau Lenore, you seem to be condemning my own behaviour.'

'No, indeed not, indeed I don't condemn you for what you did. It is quite a different matter for you. You are a military man, like all Russians . . .'

'But forgive me, I am not . . .'

'You are a foreigner, passing through the town. I am grateful to you.' Frau Lenore went on, not listening to Sanin. She was quite breathless, gesticulating, and then once again unrolling the handkerchief and blowing her nose. It was evident, if only from the way in which she gave expression to her grief, that she had not been born under northern skies.

'And how is Herr Klueber to do business in his shop if he spends his time fighting with his customers? It makes no sense at all. And now I am to break off the engagement! And what are we going to live on? Formerly, we were the only shop to make maiden-skin and nougat with pistachio nuts, and we had special customers for these things, but now everyone makes maiden-skin. Just think: even as it is, everyone in town will be talking about your duel . . . How can these things be kept secret? And suddenly, the wedding is off! But it will mean a scandal, a real scandal! Gemma is an excellent girl and she is very fond of me, but she is a stubborn republican and quite defiant about what others think. You alone can persuade her to change her mind.'

Sanin was even more amazed now.

'I, Frau Lenore?'

'Yes, you and only you. Only you. That is why I have come to you – I was at my wits' end! You are such a learned, such a good, man and you stood up for her, she will listen to you. She *must* listen to you – after all, you risked your own life! You will prove to her – I can't do anything more with her. You will prove to her that if she persists she will ruin both herself and all of us. You saved my son – now save my daughter! You were sent to us by God Himself . . . I am ready to go down on my knees to beg you to do it!'

And Frau Lenore half rose from the chair, as if with the intention of throwing herself at Sanin's feet. He restrained her.

'Frau Lenore! For Heaven's sake! What are you doing?'

She seized his hands. She was trembling all over.

'Do you promise?'

'But think, Frau Lenore, why should I . . .?'

'Do you promise? Or do you wish me to die, here in front of you, this very moment?'

Sanin lost his head. This was the first time in his life that he had had to deal with a case of hot Italian blood.

'I will do everything you wish!' he cried. 'I will speak to Fräulein Gemma.'

Frau Lenore gave a cry of joy.

'Only I really do not know what the outcome will be.'

'Oh please, don't refuse again, don't refuse!' Frau Lenore entreated. 'You have already agreed. And I am sure the outcome will be excellent. In any case, there is nothing more that I can do. She will certainly not listen to *me*.'

'And she was very definite about her refusal to marry Herr Klueber?' Sanin asked after a short silence.

'Like a cut from a knife. She is the image of her father, Giovann' Battista. A real madcap!'

'A madcap? She?' Sanin sounded incredulous.

'Yes . . . yes . . . but she is an angel, too. She will listen to you. You will come, and come soon? Oh, my dear Russian friend!' Frau Lenore rose impulsively from her chair, and just as impulsively seized the head of Sanin who was sitting before her. 'Receive a mother's blessing – and give me some water.'

Sanin brought Signora Roselli a glass of water, promised faithfully that he would come without delay and escorted her downstairs into the street. When he got back to his room, he was in such a state of confusion that he wrung his hands and his eyes were staring.

There, he thought, now life really is spinning round and spinning so fast that it makes me giddy. He did not even attempt to try to fathom what was happening inside him –

bedlam, and there's an end on it! 'What a day, what a day,' he whispered involuntarily ... 'A madcap, according to her mother. And I am supposed to advise her – her! And what advice am I to give?'

Sanin's head was spinning now and above all this whirligig of sensations, impressions and unuttered thoughts he could see the image of Gemma – the image which had been so indelibly stamped on his mind on that warm, electrically charged night, framed in that dark window, beneath the light of the clustering stars.

XXIV

As Sanin approached Signora Roselli's house his steps were hesitant. His heart was beating wildly: he could distinctly feel and even hear it thumping against his ribs. What was he going to say to Gemma? How would he start the conversation? He did not enter the house through the shop, but by the back porch. In the small front room he met Frau Lenore. She was pleased to see him and at the same time alarmed.

'I was waiting for you, waiting for you,' she whispered, shaking his hand with each of her own in turn. 'Go into the garden, she's there. And remember: all my hopes are on you!'

Sanin set off into the garden. Gemma was sitting on a bench near the path, engaged in selecting the ripest fruit from a large basket filled with cherries, and putting them on to a plate. The sun was low in the sky – it was already after six – and there was more red than gold in the broad, slanting beams with which it was warming the whole of Signora Roselli's little garden. From time to time the leaves exchanged a scarcely audible, leisurely whisper. Some belated bees occasionally uttered a sharp buzz as they navigated from one flower to the next. Somewhere a dove was cooing monotonously and interminably.

Gemma was wearing the same big hat which she had worn

for the expedition to Soden. She glanced at Sanin from under its down-turned brim, and once more bent over her basket.

Sanin approached Gemma, involuntarily taking shorter and shorter steps as he did so and . . . and . . . and he could think of nothing better to say than to ask her why she was picking over the cherries.

Gemma did not reply immediately.

'These riper ones,' she said softly at last, 'are for jam; the others are for the filling of tarts. You know those round tarts that we sell, with sugar on them?'

Having said these words, she bent her head even deeper. Her right hand, which held two cherries, paused in the air between the basket and the plate.

'May I sit beside you?' Sanin asked.

'You may.' Gemma moved slightly along the bench. Sanin sat down beside her, thinking, 'How am I to begin?' But she helped him out of his difficulty.

'You fought a duel today,' she began in a spirited manner, turning her face full towards him, her lovely features aflame with a modest blush. And oh, the profound gratitude that shone in her eyes! 'And you are so calm! Does that mean that danger simply does not exist for you?'

'For Heaven's sake! I was in no danger of any kind. Everything went off very successfully and quite harmlessly.'

Gemma moved a finger to the right and to the left in front of her eyes. Another Italian gesture.

'No, no, you must not say that. You can't deceive me. Pantaleone told me everything.'

'That's a fine source of information! I expect he compared me with the statue of the Commendatore?'

'His way of putting things may be comic, but there is nothing comic either about his feelings or about what you did today. And it was all because of me . . . for me . . . I will never forget this.'

'But Fräulein Gemma, I assure you . . .'

'I will never forget this,' she repeated, stressing each word, then looked at him intently and turned away.

He could now see her slender, clear profile. It seemed to him that he had never seen the like before, and had never in his life experienced what he felt at that moment. He was all aflame.

'And what about my promise?' flashed through his thoughts.

'Fräulein Gemma . . .' he began, after a moment's hesitation.

'Yes?'

She did not turn towards him, she went on picking over the cherries, carefully holding the tips of the little stalks in her fingers, attentively lifting the leaves . . . but what trust and warmth were to be heard in that one word, 'Yes'.

'Has your mother not told you anything . . . concerning . . .?'

'Concerning what?'

'Concerning me?'

Gemma quite suddenly let the cherries in her hand fall back into the basket.

'Did she have a talk with you?' she asked in turn.

'Yes.'

'And what did she tell you?'

'She told me that you . . . that you suddenly decided to change . . . your former intentions.'

Gemma's head dropped again. She disappeared entirely under her hat: all that was visible was her neck, supple and delicate like the stem of a large flower.

'What intentions?'

'Your intentions – concerning . . . the future arrangement of your life.'

'Do you mean . . .? Are you referring to Herr Klueber?'

'Yes.'

'And Mother has told you that I do not wish to become the wife of Herr Klueber?'

'Yes.'

Gemma moved. The basket tipped over and fell . . . several cherries went rolling along the path . . . A minute passed – then another. At last her voice could be heard saying:

'Why did she tell you this?'

Sanin could still only see Gemma's neck. Her breast rose and fell more rapidly than before.

'Why? Your mother thought that since you and I have, as it were, become friends in this short time, and you have acquired some slight confidence in my judgement, that I might be in a position to give you some helpful advice . . . and that you would follow it.'

Gemma's hands quietly slipped to her knees. She began fingering the folds of her dress.

'And what advice will you give me, Monsieur Dimitry?' she asked, after a short pause.

Sanin could see that Gemma's fingers were trembling on her knees. In fact, she was only playing with the folds of her dress to conceal the trembling. Very quietly, he laid his hand on those pale, quivering fingers.

'Gemma,' he murmured, 'why are you not looking at me?'

Instantly, she threw her hat back over her shoulder and fixed her eyes on him – they were full of trust and gratitude as before. She waited for him to speak . . . but the sight of her face confused him and seemed to blind him. The warm rays of the evening sun lighted up her youthful head – and the radiance of this head was lighter and brighter than the sunlight.

'I will do what you tell me, Monsieur Dimitry . . .' she began, with a very faint smile and a very slight lift of the eyebrows. 'What is your advice to me going to be?'

'My advice?' Sanin repeated. 'Well now, you know that your mother thinks that to break off your engagement to Herr Klueber just because he did not show particular bravery the day before yesterday . . .'

'Just because?' Gemma echoed, bending down to pick up the basket which she placed beside her on the bench.

'That . . . generally speaking . . . it is imprudent for you to break off the engagement; that this is a step of such gravity that it is necessary to weigh all the consequences carefully; and finally, that the very state of your business affairs imposes a certain obligation on each and every member of your family . . .'

Gemma interrupted him.

'These are all my mother's opinions; these are her words. I know them. But what is your opinion?'

'My opinion?' Sanin was silent. He felt as if a lump had come up into his throat and stopped him breathing. 'I also am of the opinion . . .' he began with some effort.

Gemma stiffened.

'Also? You also?'

'Yes – at least . . . that is to say . . .' Sanin could not, definitely could not, add a single word.

'Very well,' said Gemma, 'if you, as a friend, advise me to change my decision . . . I mean, not to change my former decision, I will think the matter over.' Without noticing what she was doing, she began putting the cherries back from the plate into the basket. 'Mother hopes that I will listen to your advice. Well, perhaps I really will listen to your advice.'

'But, Fräulein Gemma, I should first like to know what the reasons were which compelled you . . .'

'I will take your advice,' Gemma repeated, but as she spoke, she kept frowning, her cheeks went pale, and she bit at her lower lip. 'You have done so much for me that it is my duty to do what you wish me to do. I am under an obligation to fulfil your wishes. I will tell Mother . . . I will think it over. Here she comes, as it happens.'

So it was indeed: Frau Lenore appeared on the threshold of the door leading from the house into the garden. She was consumed with impatience: she could not keep still. By her reckoning, Sanin ought to have completed his discussion with Gemma ages ago, although his conversation with her had not lasted so long as a quarter of an hour.

'No, no no! For God's sake, don't say anything to her yet!' Sanin exclaimed quickly, in alarm. 'Wait a little. I will tell you. I will write to you, and meanwhile take no decision of any kind . . . Wait!'

He squeezed Gemma's hand tightly, jumped up from the bench, and, to the great amazement of Frau Lenore, rushed past her, raised his hat, muttered something quite incomprehensible, and vanished. She went up to her daughter.

'Gemma, please tell me . . .'

The girl rose abruptly and embraced her.

'Mother dear, can you wait just a little while, just a tiny little while . . . till tomorrow? Can you? And not a word about it all until tomorrow? Oh!'

She suddenly burst into a flood of radiant, and for her quite unexpected, tears. This astonished Frau Lenore all the more because the expression on Gemma's face far from being sad in fact looked joyful.

'What's the matter with you? You, who never weep, and now suddenly . . .'

'It's nothing, Mother, nothing. Just you wait. We must both wait. Don't ask me about anything until tomorrow – and let us sort out the cherries before the sun goes down.'

'But you are going to be sensible?'

'Oh, I am always sensible.' Gemma nodded her head wisely. She began tying the cherries into little bunches, holding them up high in front of her face which was blushing faintly. She did not wipe away the tears; they dried of their own accord.

XXV

SANIN almost ran back to his lodgings. He felt, he knew, that only here, alone with himself, would illumination come and he would discover what was happening to him. And so it was. He had hardly entered the room, had barely had time to sit down at the writing desk before he exclaimed, in a dull and mournful voice, his elbows on the desk and with both palms pressed to his face: 'I love her, I love her madly.' At that moment, everything within him burst into a glow, like coal from which the layer of dead ashes has suddenly been blown away. Only one instant . . . and he was no longer capable of understanding how it had been possible that he had been sitting next to her – to her! and talking to her, without feeling that he worshipped the hem of her dress, that he was ready, as the young men put it, 'to die at her feet'.

That last meeting in the garden had decided everything. When he thought of it now, he no longer pictured her with her hair all blown about under the light of the stars. He saw her seated on the bench. He saw her throw back her hat with a sudden movement and look at him so trustingly – and the fever and the longing of love coursed through all his veins. He remembered the rose which he had been carrying in his pocket since the day before. He pulled it out and pressed it to his lips with such feverish strength that he involuntarily flinched with pain. He was no longer debating anything inwardly, no longer reflecting, calculating, looking ahead. He had left the past entirely behind him, he had taken a leap forward: he had plunged headlong off the dreary shores of his solitary bachelor life into a gay, bubbling and mighty flood. Never mind what grief it might bring, never a thought for where the flood would carry him or indeed for the possibility that it would dash him to pieces against a cliff! Here were no longer the quiet streams of the Uhland Romanze which had lulled him not so long ago. Here were mighty waves which could not be restrained; they were flying, racing forward, and he along with them.

He took a sheet of paper and, without making a single blot, scarcely lifting the pen from the paper, he wrote the following:

Dear Gemma,

You know what advice I undertook to urge upon you, you know what your mother wants, and what she asked me to do. What you do not know, and what I am now in duty bound to tell you, is that I love you, love you with all the passion of a heart that has felt love for the first time. This fire has flared up within me suddenly, but with such force, that I cannot find words! When your mother came to me and made her request, the fire was only just smouldering within me – otherwise, as an honest man, I would certainly have refused to carry out her wishes . . . the admission which I am now making to you is the admission of an honest man. It is essential for you to know with whom you are dealing – there must be no misunderstanding between us. You see now that I can give you no advice of any kind . . . I love you, I love you, I love you – and there is nothing else in me, in my mind or in my heart.

D. Sanin

Having folded and sealed this note, Sanin at first thought of ringing for the waiter and sending it by him . . . but no, that seemed a little embarrassing. Send it with Emil? But to go to the store and search for him among the other shop assistants was also embarrassing. Besides, it was already dark and Emil would probably have left. For all these reflections, Sanin nevertheless put on his hat and went out into the street. He turned one corner and then another and – to his boundless delight – saw Emil in front of him. A satchel under his arm and a roll of paper in his hand, the young enthusiast was hurrying homewards.

'It is not for nothing that they say that every lover has his lucky star,' thought Sanin and called out to Emil.

The boy turned, and immediately rushed at Sanin.

Sanin cut short his raptures, gave him the note, and explained to whom and in what manner it was to be delivered. Emil listened attentively.

'You want no one to see me deliver it?' he asked, assuming a purposeful and mysterious expression, as if to say, We understand all about this affair!

'Yes, my dear boy,' said Sanin, who was beginning to feel slightly awkward, but nonetheless patted Emil's cheek ... 'and if there should be an answer ... you will bring me the answer, won't you? I will stay in.'

'Oh, you need not worry about that,' Emil whispered gaily and ran off, nodding to him once again as he ran.

Sanin returned to his room, threw himself on the divan without lighting the candles, put his arms above his head, and abandoned himself to those sensations of newly apprehended love which it is pointless to describe. He who has experienced them knows their languor and sweetness; there is no way of explaining them to one who has not.

The door opened and Emil's head appeared.

'I've brought it,' he said in a whisper. 'Here it is, the answer.' He raised a folded paper above his head and showed it to Sanin.

Sanin leapt from the divan, and snatched the note from Emil's hand. His ardour was by now deeply aroused and he had no time for concealment or keeping up the politenesses, even in front of this boy, her brother. Had he but been in a state to observe such proprieties, his conscience would have pricked him, and he would have forced himself to be more restrained. He went to the window, and by the light of the street lamp, which stood immediately in front of the building, he read the following lines:

I ask you, I beg of you – *not to come to us the whole of tomorrow*, *not to make an appearance.* This is necessary to me, absolutely necessary, everything will be decided then. I know you will not refuse me this request, because ...

Gemma

Sanin read the note through twice – how touching, sweet and beautiful her handwriting seemed to him. Then he thought for a moment, turned to Emil (who, in order to convey what a tactful young man he was, was standing with his face to the wall and excavating it with his fingernail) and called his name loudly.

Emil immediately ran up to him.

'Sir?'

'Listen, my friend ...'

'Monsieur Dimitry,' Emil interrupted in a piteous voice, 'why do you not say *tu* to me?'

Sanin laughed.

'Oh, very well. Listen, my friend.' (Emil gave a little jump of joy at the sound of the word *écoute.*) 'Listen to me. Over *there*, you understand, you are to say that everything will be carried out to the letter.' (Emil pursed his lips and nodded importantly.) 'As for yourself – what are you doing tomorrow?'

'I? What am I doing? What do you wish me to do?'

'If you are allowed to, come here in the morning early, and we shall go for a walk in the neighbourhood of Frankfurt until evening. Would you like that?'

Emil gave another jump.

'Good gracious, as if there could be anything better in the world! To go walking with you – but that will be simply marvellous! I will certainly come.'

'And what if they don't let you?'

'They'll let me all right!'

'Listen. Don't say anything *there* about the fact that I have asked you to go for a whole day's walk.'

'Why should I say anything? I'll simply slip away. I don't care!'

Emil imprinted a great kiss on Sanin and ran off.

As for Sanin, he walked about the room for a long time and went to bed late. He abandoned himself to the same sensations as before, in which apprehension was mingled with sweetness, and to the same joyful trepidation in the face of a new life. Sanin was very pleased that he had thought of asking Emil to spend the following day with him: the boy was like his sister to look at. He will remind me of her, he thought.

But what surprised him more than anything was to think that he could have felt differently yesterday from the way he felt today. It seemed to him that he had loved Gemma since the beginning of time – and had loved her exactly in the way in which he loved her now.

XXVI

THE following morning, at eight o'clock, Emil reported to Sanin with Tartaglia on a lead. He could not have carried out his instructions more meticulously had he been a born German. He had lied at home. He had said that he was going for a walk with Sanin before breakfast and would then go on to the shop. While Sanin was dressing, Emil touched on the subject of Gemma and of the broken engagement to Herr Klueber – though he did so rather hesitantly. Sanin met this with grim silence and Emil, having indicated by his expression that he understood the reason why so important a topic should not be broached in so light a fashion, returned to it no more. But from time to time he assumed a look of concentration, even of severity.

Having finished their coffee, the two friends set off – on foot, of course – for Hausen, a little village surrounded by woods not very far from Frankfurt. The whole Taunus mountain range is visible from there, as if spread out on the palm of one's hand. The weather was superb: the sun was bright and warming, but not oppressive. A fresh breeze rustled vigorously among the green leaves. The shadows of little round clouds high up in the sky glided swiftly and gracefully across the ground, forming small dark patches. The young men soon left the town behind them and stepped out gaily and energetically along the well-swept road.

They went into a wood and spent a long time wandering around in it. Then they ate a very solid breakfast in a village inn; then they climbed up hills, admired the views, rolled stones and clapped their hands at the amusing and strange way in which the stones bobbed about like rabbits – until a passer-by down below, whom they had not seen, abused them roundly in a ringing voice. Then they lay outstretched on some dry, short moss of a yellowish-violet colour; then they drank beer at another inn, then they raced and made bets on who could jump farthest. They discovered an echo, and had a conversation with it, they sang, they yodelled, they wrestled; they broke off branches, they decorated their hats with ferns, and they even danced. Tartaglia participated in all these activities to the best of his ability. It is true that he did not throw any stones, but he dashed down headlong after them, howled when the young men sang, and even drank beer, though with evident disgust. (He had been taught this art by a student to whom he had once belonged.) He was not, incidentally, very obedient to Emil – it was very different when his master Pantaleone gave the orders. When Emil ordered him to 'talk' or to 'sneeze' all he did was wag his tail and stick his tongue out in a little roll.

The young people also talked. At the beginning of the walk, Sanin, as the older of the two and the better informed, started a conversation on such subjects as Fate and predetermined Destiny and the meaning of a man's Calling and in what it consisted. But the discussion soon took a less serious turn. Emil began questioning his friend and protector about Russia, about the way they fought duels there, and whether the women were beautiful, and whether the Russian language could be learned quickly, and what Sanin felt when the officer was aiming his pistol at him.

Sanin in turn questioned Emil about his father, his mother and their family affairs, trying in every way not to mention Gemma's name, and thinking of nothing but her. Strictly speaking, he was not really thinking about her, but about the following day, that mysterious morrow that was to bring him undreamed-of happiness, such as had never been known before. It was as if a curtain, a thin, light, slightly swaying curtain, was suspended before his mind's eye – and beyond the curtain he sensed . . . he sensed the presence of a young, quite motionless, divine image with a gentle smile on its lips, the lashes lowered severely, but with mocking severity. And this image was not Gemma's face – it was the face of happiness itself – and now at last *his* hour has struck, the curtain sweeps upwards, the lips open, the eyelashes are raised – and his divinity has seen him and there is light like the light of the sun, and delight and ecstasy without end! He thinks of this morrow – and once again his soul is still with joy and elation – waiting and longing, waiting and longing!

And this waiting and longing is in no wise disturbing. It is with him all the time – and makes no difference of any kind. It does not stop him from enjoying an excellent lunch with Emil in yet a third inn. Just occasionally, like a brief flash of lightning, the thought would strike him: just suppose that anyone in the whole world knew about it all? His longing does not stop him from playing leap-frog with Emil after luncheon. The game takes place in a small, open green field . . . Imagine Sanin's astonishment and confusion when, to the accompaniment of Tartaglia's shrill bark, he has just taken a flying leap with his legs apart, over the crouching Emil, and suddenly sees in front of him, at the very edge of the green field, two officers whom he immediately recognizes as yesterday's adversary and his second – Herr von Doenhof and Herr von Richter! Each officer fixes a piece of glass in his eye and grins ... Sanin falls on his feet, turns away, quickly puts on his top-coat which he had cast aside, and utters a curt word to Emil. Emil also puts on his jacket, and the two of them immediately make themselves scarce.

They returned to Frankfurt very late.

'They will scold me,' Emil told Sanin as they parted, 'but what does it matter? I have spent such a wonderful, wonderful day!'

When he returned to his hotel, Satin found a note from Gemma. In it she appointed a meeting for the following day, at seven o'clock in the morning, in one of the many public parks with which Frankfurt is surrounded.

Oh, how his heart jumped! How glad he was that he had obeyed her so implicitly. And, dear God, what was in store for him ...? What was in store for him on this morrow, this unprecedented, unique and impossible – and never-to-be doubted morrow?

His eyes devoured Gemma's note. The long and eloquent tail of the letter G, the initial of her name, which was at the bottom of the sheet of paper, reminded him of her lovely fingers, of her hand. The thought crossed his mind that he had not once touched this hand with his lips ...

Italian women, he thought, in spite of their reputation, are modest and strictly behaved ... And Gemma above all! An Empress – a Goddess – marble, pure and virginal – but the day will come – and it is not far off ...

There was one happy man that night in Frankfurt. He slept, but he could have said of himself in the words of the poet:

'I sleep ... but ever wakes my sentient heart!'[1]

And his heart beat as gently as the wings of a moth which is clinging to a flower and is drenched with the rays of the summer sun.

XXVII

SANIN woke at five and was dressed by six. At half past six, he was already walking in the public garden within sight of the small summerhouse which Gemma had mentioned in her note.

It was a quiet, warm, grey morning. Sometimes it seemed as if it was going to rain any moment, but if one stretched out a hand one could feel nothing, and it was only when one looked at one's sleeve that one noticed traces of tiny drops like the smallest of beads; but that stopped very soon. As for wind – it was as if there had never been any wind in the whole world. Sounds did not so much fly through the air as flow in enveloping waves. In the distance, white mist was forming, and there was the scent of mignonette and white acacia flowers all around.

The shops in the street were still closed, but a few people had already appeared. Occasionally the sounds of a solitary carriage could be heard . . . There were no visitors in the park. A gardener was scraping the path in a desultory manner with a spade, and a decrepit old woman in a black cloak hobbled across an alley. Not for a moment could Sanin have mistaken this poor creature for Gemma, but for all that his heart jumped, and his eyes followed with close attention the black shape disappearing into the distance.

Seven o'clock. The hours boomed from a near-by tower.

Sanin stopped in his tracks. Was she not coming then? A cold shiver suddenly ran through him. A few moments later he felt the same cold shiver, but for another reason. He heard a light footstep behind him, and the soft rustle of a woman's clothes . . . He turned – it was she!

Gemma was walking along the path behind him. She was wearing a light grey mantle and a small dark hat. She glanced at Sanin and averted her head – and, as she drew level with him, walked briskly past him.

'Gemma,' he murmured, almost inaudibly. She gave him a slight nod, and continued walking. He followed her.

He was breathing in gasps. His legs did not obey him very well.

Gemma passed the summerhouse, turned right, walked past a small shallow pond where a sparrow was busily preening itself, stepped behind a clump of tall lilacs, and sat down on a bench. It was a comfortable and well-sheltered spot. Sanin sat down beside her.

A minute went by – and neither spoke a word. She did not even look at him, and he did not look at her face, but at her folded hands in which she held a small umbrella. What was there to say? What words could be uttered which were not totally meaningless compared to the fact that they were here, alone, so early in the morning, so close together?

'You . . . are not angry with me?' Sanin murmured at last.

It would have been difficult for Sanin to have said anything more stupid – he realized that himself – but at least the silence had been broken.

'I?' she replied. 'Why should I be? No.'

'And you believe me?' he continued.

'You mean what you wrote to me?'

'Yes.'

Gemma dropped her head and said nothing. The umbrella slipped from her hands. She hurriedly retrieved it before it fell.

'Oh, believe me, believe what I wrote to you!' Sanin exclaimed. His timidity had suddenly vanished and he spoke with passion. 'If there is any truth on this earth, any sacred truth which cannot be doubted, it is that I love you, love you passionately, Gemma!'

She threw him a brief sidelong glance, and once again nearly dropped her umbrella.

'Believe me, believe me,' he urged – he was imploring her, stretching out his hands towards her, not daring to touch her. 'What do you want me to do to convince you?'

She glanced at him again.

'Tell me, Monsieur Dimitry,' she began, 'the day before yesterday, when you came in order to persuade me, you did not know then ... did not feel ...?'

'Yes, I did feel it,' Sanin interrupted, 'but I did not know it. I loved you from the very first moment, but did not at once realize what you had come to mean to me. And besides, I learned that you were engaged to be married. As for carrying out your mother's request – well, in the first place, how could I refuse? And secondly, I think I passed on her message in such a manner that you could guess ...'

There came the sound of heavy footsteps, and a stout man, evidently a foreigner, with a travelling bag slung on his shoulder, appeared from behind the lilac bushes. With the lack of ceremony which revealed the visiting stranger, he eyed the couple on the bench, coughed loudly and went on his way.

'Your mother,' said Sanin, as soon as the sound of heavy feet was gone, 'told me that your breaking your engagement would cause a scandal' (Gemma frowned slightly), 'that it was I who had in some measure given cause for the unseemly gossip and that ... consequently ... to some extent ... it was my duty to persuade you not to break your engagement to marry ... Herr Klueber.'

'Monsieur Dimitry,' said Gemma, passing her hand over her hair on the side closest to Sanin, 'please do not refer to my engagement to marry Herr Klueber. I will never be his wife. I have refused him.'

'You have refused him? When?'

'Yesterday.'

'You told him this to his face?'

'Yes. At our house. He called.'

'Gemma! That means you love me?'

She turned towards him.

'Otherwise ... would I have come here?' she whispered, and let both her hands fall on the bench.

Sanin seized those listless hands as they lay, palms upwards, and pressed them to his eyes, to his lips . . . This was the moment when the curtain, which he had kept seeing the day before, swept up. Here it is, here is happiness with its radiant countenance!

He raised his head and looked at Gemma boldly, straight in the eyes. She was looking at him, too – with a slightly downward glance. There was scarcely any lustre in her half-closed eyes: they were flooded with shining tears of joy. But her face was not smiling . . . No! It was laughing, with soundless laughter that was also the laughter of bliss.

He wanted to draw her to his breast, but she resisted him, and, still laughing silently, shook her head. 'Wait,' her happy eyes seemed to be saying.

'Gemma!' Sanin exclaimed. 'Could I have ever imagined that you' (his heart vibrated like a string when his lips first formed the word *tu*), 'that you would love me!'

'I did not expect it myself,' Gemma said quietly.

'How could I ever have thought,' Sanin went on, 'how could I ever have thought, as I drove into Frankfurt, where I only intended to stay for a few hours, that I should find happiness here for the whole of my life!'

'For the whole of your life? Is that really true?'

'Yes, for the whole of my life, for ever and for all time!' cried Sanin with a new burst of emotion.

The gardener's spade could suddenly be heard scraping a few paces away from the bench where they sat.

'Let us go home,' Gemma whispered, 'let us go together. *Veux tu?*'

If at that moment she had said to him, 'Throw yourself into the sea – *veux tu?*' she would hardly have had time to complete the second syllable before he would have been flying headlong into the depths of the ocean.

They left the garden together and set off for the house, not by the town streets but through the outskirts.

XXVIII

SANIN sometimes walked by Gemma's side, sometimes a little behind her. He never once took his eyes off her, and never stopped smiling. As for her – at times she seemed to be hurrying, at times about to stop. Truth to tell, both of them – he all pale, she all pink with excitement – moved forward as in a trance. What they had done together a few moments before, this mutual surrender of one soul to another, was so shattering, so novel, so disturbing. Everything in their lives had changed and had been re-ordered so suddenly that neither had yet regained composure. They were only conscious of the sudden rush of wind which had swept them away, like the powerful gust which a few nights ago had all but hurled them into each other's arms. As Sanin walked, he felt that he was even looking at Gemma in a different manner: he instantly noted certain characteristics of her gait, her way of moving, and oh, dear God, how infinitely precious and delectable they seemed to him! And she in turn sensed that he was looking at her 'like that'.

Sanin and Gemma were in love for the first time, and all the miracles of first love were happening for them. First love is exactly like a revolution: the regular and established order of life is in an instant smashed to fragments; youth stands at the barricade, its bright banner raised high in the air, and sends its ecstatic greetings to the future, whatever it may hold – death or a new life, no matter.

'Look – surely that is our old man?' said Sanin, pointing at a muffled-up figure which was quickly edging its way along, as if trying to remain unnoticed. In his state of overflowing bliss, Sanin felt the need to talk to Gemma about something other than love – love was a settled and holy matter.

'Yes, that is Pantaleone,' Gemma replied gaily and happily. 'I expect he left the house with the intention of following me. He was already watching every step I took yesterday. He has guessed!'

'He has guessed!' repeated the enraptured Sanin. Was there anything that Gemma could have said that would not have sent him into raptures?

Then he asked her to tell him in detail everything that had occurred the day before.

She immediately began her account, hurriedly and in some confusion, smiling, periodically uttering brief little sighs, and exchanging quick, radiant glances with Sanin. She told him that after their conversation of the day before yesterday, her mother had persistently tried to elicit something definite from her, Gemma, and she had avoided the importunities of Frau Lenore by promising to reveal her decision within twenty-four hours; how she had begged for this delay and how difficult it had been to get her mother to agree to it; how Herr Klueber had appeared quite unexpectedly, looking more pompous and starched than ever; how he had declared his indignation over the puerile, and unforgivable and for him, Klueber, deeply insulting (this was his actual expression) escapade of the Russian stranger ('he meant *ton duel*') and how he demanded that the door of the house should be *te défendu*. 'Because,' added Herr Klueber – and at this moment Gemma gave a slight imitation of his voice and manner – 'this casts a reflection on my honour. As if I could not have intervened to protect my fiancée had I considered this course necessary or desirable! The whole of Frankfurt will know tomorrow that some stranger fought a duel with an officer over my fiancée – what a state of affairs! It is a stain on my honour!'

'Mother was agreeing with him – just imagine! But at this point I suddenly declared that he was wasting his efforts in worrying about his honour and his position in the matter, that he had no reason to be affronted by any gossip about his fiancée, since I was no longer engaged to be married to him and would never be his wife! I confess that I had wanted to have a talk *avec vous . . . avec toi* – before finally breaking off the engagement; but he came . . . and I just could not restrain myself . . . Mother was so frightened that she even began to shout, and I went into the other room and fetched his ring – you did not notice that I stopped wearing this ring two days ago – and gave it to him. He was terribly offended. But he is so vain and so self-opinionated that he did not want to discuss the matter any further and left. As you can imagine, I had a very difficult time with Mother, and it distressed me greatly to see her so upset. I even thought that I had been somewhat hasty, but I already had your note – and in any case, I knew without it . . .'

'That I love you,' Sanin interrupted.

'Yes – that you had fallen in love with me.'

Such was Gemma's account, told with a good deal of confusion. She smiled as she talked, and lowered her voice or became completely silent every time anyone came towards her or passed her on the way. And Sanin listened in a state of euphoria, delighting in the sound of her voice, much as he had doted on her handwriting the day before.

'Mother is extraordinarily upset,' Gemma began again, her words tumbling out one after another with great rapidity. 'She simply will not even consider that Herr Klueber could have become repugnant to me, that in any case I was not marrying him for love, but because of her persistent pleas . . . She suspects . . . *vous* . . . *toi* . . . to put it plainly, she is certain that I have fallen in love with you. This is all the more painful to her because the day before yesterday this possibility had not even occurred to her, and she had even commissioned you to persuade me. It was rather a strange commission, was it not? Now she has honoured *toi* . . . *vous* . . . with the title of a man of cunning, of a deceiver, and says that you betrayed her trust and warns me that you will deceive me . . .'

'But Gemma,' Sanin exclaimed, 'surely you told her . . .?'

'I told her nothing. What right had I to tell her anything before I had discussed it *avec vous*?'

Sanin actually wrung his hands with agitation.

'Gemma, I hope that now at any rate you will admit

everything to her, that you will take me to her. I want to prove to your mother that I am not a deceiver.'

Sanin's breast was literally heaving from the onrush of noble, fiery emotions.

Gemma looked him full in the face.

'You (*vous*) really want to go and see Mother with me now? Mother, who keeps saying that all that kind of thing is impossible between us ... and can never take place?'

There was one word which Gemma could not bring herself to utter ... it scorched her lips; but Sanin pronounced the word all the more readily.

'To marry you, Gemma, to become your husband – I can imagine no greater happiness.'

He could now no longer conceive of any limits to his love, to his magnanimity, or to his resolution!

When she heard these words, Gemma who had almost stopped for a moment, now walked on faster ... it was as if she wished to run away from this too great and too unexpected happiness.

Suddenly her legs swayed beneath her. From round the corner of a side street, a few steps in front of her, attired in a new hat and short overcoat, straight as a ramrod and curled like a poodle, there appeared the figure of Herr Klueber. He saw Gemma and he saw Sanin – and then gave a kind of inward smirk. With a backward bend of his elegant trunk, he walked towards them with an air of bravura. Sanin was momentarily disconcerted. But then he glanced at the Klueber face to which its owner was trying, within the limits of his ability, to give an expression of contemptuous surprise and even condolence, and the sight of this pink, common face suddenly threw him into a rage. Sanin stepped forward.

Gemma seized his arm, put her arm through it with quiet determination, and looked her former betrothed straight in the face. Klueber narrowed his eyes, hunched his shoulders, stepped quickly aside, muttered through his teeth, 'That's the way the song usually ends' (*Das alte Ende vom Liede*), and went on his way with the same air of bravura and with a slight spring in his gait.

'What did the scoundrel say?' asked Sanin and was about to rush after him. But Gemma stopped him and they walked on. She did not remove her arm from his.

The Roselli establishment appeared in front of them. Gemma stopped once again.

'Dimitry, Monsieur Dimitry,' she said, 'we have not yet entered the house, we have not yet seen Mother ... If you (*vous*) want to think it over, if ... you are still free, Dimitry.'

Instead of replying, Sanin pressed her hand very tightly to his breast and drew her onwards.

'Mother,' said Gemma as they entered the room where Frau Lenore was sitting, 'I have brought the real one!'

XXIX

HAD Gemma announced that she had brought along the cholera or even death itself, Frau Lenore could not conceivably have received the news with greater despair. She immediately sat down in a corner with her face to the wall, burst into a flood of tears and almost began to keen, for all the world like a Russian peasant woman at the side of her husband's or son's coffin. To begin with Gemma was so much put out that she did not even go up to her mother, but stood as still as a statue in the centre of the room. Sanin was completely at a loss and very nearly ready to burst into tears himself. This disconsolate weeping went on for a whole hour, for a whole, entire hour!

Pantaleone thought it wise to lock the outer door of the patisserie in case some stranger should come in, although happily it was still early morning. The old man was himself a bit put out. He did not approve of the haste with which Gemma and Sanin had acted, but he was reluctant to condemn them and was ready, in case of need, to give them his support – his dislike for Klueber was so strong. Emil saw himself as the intermediary between his sister and Sanin, and was really rather proud of the fact that everything had succeeded so magnificently. He simply could not understand Frau Lenore's desolation, and decided there and then that women, even the best of them, suffer from the lack of capacity for rational judgement. Sanin was the worst off of all. As soon as he approached Frau Lenore, she raised a great outcry and waved him away with her arms. His efforts on several occasions to pronounce in a loud voice, stationed at a distance, 'I ask for the hand of your daughter,' were completely in vain. Frau Lenore particularly could not forgive herself for the fact that she 'had been so blind', that she 'had seen nothing'. 'If only my Giovan' Battista had been alive,' she kept repeating through her tears, 'nothing of the kind could have happened!' Heavens! What is all this about? Sanin thought to himself. This is absolutely preposterous! He dared not look at Gemma, nor did she have the courage to raise her eyes to glance at him. She contented herself with patiently looking after her mother, who at first pushed even her aside.

At long last, the storm began to abate. Frau Lenore stopped weeping, allowed Gemma to ease her out of the corner in which she had immured herself, to settle her in an armchair near the window, and to give her a drink of water flavoured with orange blossom. She suffered Sanin – not to approach her, oh no – but at least to remain in the room (up till then, she had kept on demanding that he should leave) and did not interrupt him.

Sanin immediately made the most of the calm which had descended, and displayed amazing eloquence: he would hardly have been capable of expounding his intentions and his feelings to Gemma herself with such fervour and with such conviction. These feelings were of the most sincere quality and the intentions of the very purest – like those of Almaviva in

the 'Barber of Seville'. He did not conceal either from Frau
Lenore or from himself the disadvantageous aspects of these
intentions; but these disadvantages were more apparent than
real! True, he was a foreigner, one with whom they had only
recently become acquainted, and of whose person and property
they had no certain information. But he was prepared to
adduce all the necessary proof that he was of respectable
character, and not without means: he would call in aid the
most incontrovertible evidence of his compatriots. He hoped
that Gemma would be happy with him, and that he would find
a way of making the separation from her family less painful.
The mention of separation – the very word 'separation' –
nearly spoiled the whole business. Frau Lenore was thrown
into a tremble of agitation. Sanin hastened to point out that
the separation would only be a temporary one – and indeed
that perhaps, in the end, there would be no need for any
separation at all!

His eloquence was not in vain. Frau Lenore began to cast
glances at him which, although still full of grief and reproach,
were no longer charged with rage and repugnance. Then she
allowed him to approach her, and even to sit down at her side.
(Gemma was sitting on the other side.) Then she began to reproach him – not with looks alone, but in words, which
clearly indicated a certain softening in her attitude. She began
to complain, and her complaints became quieter and gentler.
They were interspersed with questions addressed now to
Sanin, now to her daughter. Then she allowed him to take her
hand, and did not immediately snatch it away ... Then she
burst into tears again, but they were tears of quite a different
kind ... Then she smiled sadly and expressed regret at the
absence of Giovan' Battista, but already in quite a different
sense from before ... Another instant passed – and both
criminals, Sanin and Gemma, were kneeling at her feet, and
she was placing her hands on the head of each in turn. Then,
after another moment, they were embracing and kissing her,

and Emil, his face radiant with delight, came running into the room and threw himself at this closely united family group.

Pantaleone glanced into the room, gave a combined smirk and frown, then went into the patisserie and unlocked the street door.

XXX

FRAU LENORE's transition from despair to sadness, and from sadness to quiet resignation, took place fairly rapidly. But before long the quiet resignation was swiftly transformed into secret satisfaction. However, for the sake of decency, this was concealed and restrained in every way. Frau Lenore had very much taken to Sanin from the first day of their acquaintance. Having once got used to the idea that he was to be her son-in-law, she no longer found the prospect altogether unpleasing, though she considered it her duty to preserve an expression of affront – or perhaps rather of concern – on her face. Besides, everything that had happened in the last few days had been so extraordinary . . . One thing led to another!

As a practical woman and as a mother, Frau Lenore also considered it her duty to submit Sanin to all kinds of questions. Sanin, who had had no thought of marriage in his mind when he had set out that morning to meet Gemma – truth to tell, he had thought of nothing at all at the time, and simply surrendered himself to the driving force of passion – very readily, and indeed enthusiastically, entered into the part of the future husband. He willingly answered the interrogation to which he was submitted, with full and circumstantial details. Frau Lenore first satisfied herself that he was a genuine member of the nobility by right of birth, and even expressed some slight surprise that he was not a prince. She then put on a serious mien and gave him 'fair warning' that she would speak frankly and without ceremony, since she was bound to do so by her sacred duty as a mother. To this, Sanin replied that he had indeed expected nothing else from her, and most earnestly requested her not to spare him.

Thereupon Frau Lenore remarked that Herr Klueber (at the mention of the name she gave a slight sigh, pursed her lips and hesitated for a moment), that Herr Klueber, Gemma's *former* fiancé, was already in possession of an income of eight thousand guldens, and that this income would increase rapidly year by year. And what might Monsieur Sanin's income be?

'Eight thousand guldens,' Sanin repeated the words meditatively, 'in our money that is around fifteen thousand paper roubles . . . My income is considerably less. I have a small estate in Tula province . . . if properly run, it can yield . . . indeed, it certainly must yield, five or six thousand . . . And then if I take an appointment in the public service, I can easily earn a salary of about two thousand.'

'Service in Russia?' exclaimed Frau Lenore. 'That means I shall be parted from Gemma!'

'It will be possible for me to arrange to enter the diplomatic service,' Sanin interjected quickly. 'I have certain connections . . . It will then be possible for me to serve abroad. And here is another idea – and that is far and away the best plan: sell my estate and invest the capital in some lucrative undertaking. For instance, we could use it to make a going concern of your patisserie.'

Sanin knew that he was talking nonsense, but he was possessed by an incomprehensible foolhardiness. One glance at Gemma (who, as soon as the 'practical' discussion began, kept on rising from her chair, walking about the room and sitting down again) – one glance at Gemma, and all difficulties vanished. He was ready to arrange everything straight away in the best possible manner, to do anything to stop her worrying.

'Herr Klueber also wished to give me a small sum for the improvement of the patisserie,' said Frau Lenore after a moment's hesitation.

'Mother! For God's sake! Mother!' Gemma cried in Italian.

'It is necessary that these things should be discussed in good time, my daughter,' replied Frau Lenore in the same language. She turned once again to Sanin, and began questioning him about the law relating to marriage in Russia, and in particular whether there were any difficulties in the way of a Russian marrying a Catholic, as there were in Prussia. (At that date, in 1840, the whole of Germany still remembered the quarrel between the Prussian Government and the Archbishop of Cologne on the subject of mixed marriages.) But when Frau Lenore learned that, by marrying a Russian nobleman, her daughter would herself become a member of the nobility, she showed some signs of pleasure.

'But surely it will be necessary for you first to return to Russia?'

'Why?'

'Surely, to obtain permission from your Emperor?'

Sanin explained that this was quite unnecessary. He went on to say that he might indeed have to pay a very brief visit to Russia before the wedding. (Even as he spoke the words, his heart was wrenched with grief, and Gemma, who was watching him, guessed what he felt, blushed and became pensive.) He would try to use his time in Russia to sell his estate . . . but in any case he would obtain the money that was necessary.

'I should be grateful if you would bring me back some good Astrakhan lambskins for a cape,' said Frau Lenore. 'According to what I hear, they are remarkably good there, and remarkably cheap.'

'Certainly, with the greatest of pleasure, I will bring some for you and for Gemma,' exclaimed Sanin.

'And I would like a Morocco leather cap, embroidered with silver,' Emil interrupted, putting his head through the door from the next room.

'All right, you shall have one – and Pantaleone shall have some slippers.'

'Now, now what *is* all this about?' Frau Lenore remarked. 'We are discussing serious things now. But there is another matter,' added this practical lady, 'you say: sell your estate. But how will you do this? Do you mean that you will sell your peasants as well?'

Sanin felt as if he had been struck. He remembered that in the course of conversation with Signora Roselli and her daughter on the subject of serfdom in Russia, which, as he had told them, aroused in him feelings of the deepest indignation, he had assured them more than once that he would never contemplate selling his peasants for any consideration whatever, because he regarded such sales as immoral. He now spoke with some hesitation.

'I will try to sell my estate to someone whom I know to be a decent person, or perhaps the peasants will wish to redeem themselves.'

'That would be best of all,' Frau Lenore agreed, 'because really, the sale of live human beings . . .'

'*Barbari!*' growled Pantaleone, who had made an appearance at the door after Emil, then shook his mane and disappeared.

This is a nasty business, Sanin thought to himself, and stole a glance at Gemma. She did not appear to have heard his last words. Well, that's all right! he thought again.

The practical conversation continued in this manner until it was almost lunchtime. In the end, Frau Lenore was quite softened. She was already calling Sanin 'Dimitry', shaking her finger at him affectionately, and promising to revenge herself on him for his treacheries. She asked him many detailed questions about his family, because 'this is also a very important matter'. She also made him describe to her the marriage ceremony according to the rites of the Russian Orthodox Church, and was delighted at the thought of Gemma in a white dress with a golden crown on her head.

'You know, she is as beautiful as a queen,' Signora Roselli

spoke with a mother's pride, 'and indeed there is no queen in the world like her.'

'There is no other Gemma in the whole world!' Sanin cried out.

'Yes, that is the reason why she is Gemma.' (In Italian, of course, 'Gemma' means a precious stone.)

Gemma rushed to kiss her mother . . . it was only now that she felt herself again, as if a crushing weight had been lifted from her heart.

As for Sanin, he suddenly felt overwhelmed with happiness. His heart was filled with childlike joy. To think that the dream in which he had indulged so short a while ago in these very rooms had come true, had actually come true! He was in such transports of rapture that he went straight to the shop: he was determined, whatever happened, to do some selling behind the counter, as he had done a few days before . . . 'After all, I now have every right to do so! I am now one of the family!'

He actually took his place behind the counter, and actually did some selling – that is to say, he sold a pound of sweets to two girls who came in, giving them fully two pounds in weight and charging them only half the price.

At lunch, he sat next to Gemma by right of his status as her betrothed. Frau Lenore continued with her practical reflections. Emil kept on laughing, and pestered Sanin to take him with him to Russia. It was decided that Sanin would leave for Russia in two weeks' time. Only Pantaleone looked gloomy, so much so that even Frau Lenore said to him reproachfully, 'And to think that he even acted as second!' Pantaleone glared at her from under his thick eyebrows.

Gemma was silent most of the time, but her face had never been more radiant or beautiful. After lunch she called Sanin into the garden for a moment and, stopping at the same bench where she had sat picking over the cherries two days before, said:

'Dimitry, do not be angry with me, but I want to remind you again that you must not regard yourself as bound . . .'

He would not let her finish.

Gemma turned her face aside.

'And about what Mother mentioned, the difference in our faith, do you remember? Well, look' – she seized a small garnet cross which hung on a thin cord about her neck, and pulled at it sharply. The cord broke, and she handed him the little cross.

'If I am yours, then your faith is my faith.'

Sanin's eyes were still moist when he returned with Gemma to the house.

By the evening everything was normal again. They even played a few hands of *tresette*.

XXXI

SANIN awoke very early next day. He was at the very pinnacle of human well-being, but it was not for this reason that he had been unable to sleep longer. One question had disturbed his rest – a question of life and destiny: how was he to sell his estate for the best possible price, and at the earliest possible moment? All kinds of plans kept forming in his mind, but so far he could not see his way clearly. He went out of the hotel into the street to clear his brain and for a breath of air. He wanted to appear before Gemma with a cut-and-dried plan – nothing else would do.

Now whose is this thick-legged solid figure walking in front of him, actually quite well dressed, rolling from side to side as it hobbles along? Where had he seen the back of that head, thickly thatched with flaxen-coloured hair? Where had he seen that head which looked as if it had been set straight on to the shoulders, and that soft, fat back, and those puffy hands, dangling limply? Could it be – could it be Polozov, his school-mate of long ago, whom he had completely lost sight of for five years? Sanin overtook the figure in front of him and turned to look back . . . He saw a broad, yellowish face with small pig's eyes and white eyebrows and lashes, a short, flat nose, thick lips which looked as if they had been stuck together, a round, hairless chin, and that expression on the face, a bit sour, lazy and suspicious – there was no doubt, it was he, Ippolit Polozov. 'Perhaps my lucky star is at work again!' flashed through Sanin's mind.

'Polozov! Ippolit Sidorych! Is that really you?'

The figure stopped in its tracks, raised its tiny eyes, waited a little – and then, at last, having unstuck its lips, spoke in a hoarse falsetto.

'Dimitry Sanin?'

'None other,' exclaimed Sanin, and wrung one of Polozov's hands. Encased in ash-coloured smooth-fitting kid gloves, they hung as before, lifelessly against his rotund thighs. 'Have you been here long? Where have you come from? Where are you staying?'

'I arrived yesterday from Wiesbaden,' Polozov replied un-hurriedly, 'to do some shopping for my wife, and I am returning to Wiesbaden this very day.'

'Oh, of course, you are married – and they say to a great beauty.'

Polozov made a sideward movement with his eyes.

'Yes, so they say.'

Sanin laughed.

'I see you are still the same – as phlegmatic as you were at school.'

'Why should I change?'

'And they say,' Sanin added, placing a special emphasis on the word 'say', 'that your wife is very rich.'

'Yes, they say that too.'

'But surely you know all about this yourself, Ippolit Sidorych?'

'My friend Dimitry . . . Pavlovich – yes, it is Pavlovich – I don't meddle in my wife's affairs.'

'You don't meddle? Not in any of her affairs?'

Polozov made the same movement with his eyes.

'None at all, my friend. She goes her way, and – well – I go mine.'

'And where are you going now?' Sanin asked.

'I am going nowhere at the moment: I am standing in the street talking to you. But when we have finished our conversation, I shall go to my hotel and have luncheon.'

'Would you like to have me as a companion?'

'Do you mean as a companion for luncheon?'

'Yes.'

'By all means, it is much more convivial to eat *à deux*. You are not a chatterbox, I take it?'

'I don't think so.'

'Well, all right then.'

Polozov moved forward. Sanin followed at his side. Polozov's lips were stuck together again; he kept silent and rolled along, wheezing. Meanwhile Sanin was thinking to himself: How on earth had this oaf succeeded in landing a beautiful and rich wife? He was neither rich nor famous nor clever. At school he had been considered a dull and dreary boy, sleepy and gluttonous. His nickname had been 'Dribbler'. Wonders would never cease!

'But if his wife is really very rich – they say her father owned state concessions – maybe she will buy my estate? Although he says that he does not interfere in any of his wife's affairs, one can scarcely believe that. Besides, I will ask an attractive price which will give her some profit. Why shouldn't I try? Perhaps this is my lucky star again . . . So be it! I will try.'

Polozov led Sanin towards one of the best hotels in Frankfurt, in which, of course, he had taken the best room. On the

tables and chairs there were heaped boxes, parcels and cartons
... 'These are all purchases for Maria Nikolaevna, my friend.'
(That was the name of Polozov's wife.) Polozov sank into an
easy chair, groaned, 'Oh, this heat,' and unknotted his
necktie. Then he rang for the head waiter and ordered an
elaborate luncheon with many detailed instructions. 'And my
carriage is to be ready at one o'clock. Do you hear, at one
o'clock sharp!'

The head waiter bowed obsequiously, and vanished like the
perfect slave. Polozov unbuttoned his waistcoat. From the
very way in which he raised his eyebrows, puffed and wrinkled
his nose, it was evident that all conversation was going to be a
great effort to him, and that he was somewhat anxious to
discover whether Sanin would force him to set his tongue in
motion, or would take upon himself the whole burden of
conducting the conversation.

Sanin sensed his companion's mood, and therefore did not
tax him with too many questions. He restricted himself to
discovering the necessary minimum: that Polozov had been
in military service for two years (in the Light Cavalry, of all
things – he must have been a pretty sight in a short tunic!),
that he had married three years ago, and that he was already
spending a second year abroad with his wife, 'who is now
taking a cure for something or other in Wiesbaden', and was
then going on to Paris. Sanin, for his part, was also not very
communicative, either about his past life or his plans. He
went straight to the point – that is to say he broached the
question of his intention to sell his estate. Polozov listened
silently, only now and again casting a glance at the door
through which luncheon was due to appear. It arrived at last.
The head waiter, accompanied by two other servants, brought
in a few dishes, surmounted by silver covers.

'Is that your estate in Tula province?' Polozov asked, sitting
down at the table and tucking a napkin into the collar of his
shirt.

'Yes.'

'In the Efremov district ... I know it.'

'You mean you know my Alekseevka?' asked Sanin, also sitting down at the table.

'Yes, of course I know it.' Polozov stuffed a piece of truffle omelette into his mouth. 'Maria Nikolaevna, my wife, has an estate next to it. Waiter, open this bottle! It is quite a decent piece of land – only the peasants have cut down your forest. Why are you selling?'

'I need money, my friend, I am prepared to sell quite cheaply. Why don't you buy it, it is an opportunity ...'

Polozov swallowed a glass of wine, wiped his mouth with his napkin and once again resumed chewing – slowly and noisily.

'Hm – yes,' he said at last. 'I don't buy estates: I haven't any capital. Pass the butter, will you? My wife might buy it. You talk to her about it. If you don't ask too much, she likes that kind of thing ... But what asses these Germans are. They don't know how to boil fish. You would think it was the simplest thing in the world. And these are the people, if you please, who talk about the need to unite the *Vaterland*. Waiter, take this revolting stuff away.'

'But do you mean that your wife deals with these business matters herself?'

'Oh, yes. Now these cutlets are good. I recommend them ... I have told you, Sanin, that I don't meddle in any of my wife's affairs and I am telling you so again.'

Polozov continued to chew noisily.

'Hm ... But how can I discuss the matter with her?'

'Very simply. Go to Wiesbaden. It isn't far. Waiter, have you any English mustard? No? Animals! Only don't delay. We are leaving there the day after tomorrow. Let me pour you a glass of wine: it has bouquet, it isn't the usual vinegar.'

Polozov's face became animated and flushed: it only came to life when he was eating or drinking.

'Well, but ... I really don't know if I can do that ...' muttered Sanin.

'Anyway, what has suddenly happened to make you so desperate for money?'

'That's the whole point, I am desperate, my friend.'

'Do you need a large sum?'

'Yes – I – how should I say? I have it in mind to get married.'

Polozov put down the wine glass which he had been about to raise to his lips.

'Married!' he said in a hoarse voice, a voice which had turned hoarse from surprise, and folded his puffy hands on his stomach. 'And so precipitately?'

'Yes, quite soon.'

'The girl is in Russia, of course?'

'No, not in Russia.'

'Where then?'

'Here, in Frankfurt . . .'

'And who is she?'

'A German – that is to say not a German, an Italian, she lives here.'

'With capital?'

'No, without capital.'

'So it must be a case of being very seriously in love?'

'How odd you are! Yes, very seriously.'

'And that's what you need the money for?'

'Well, yes . . . yes . . .'

Polozov swallowed some wine, rinsed out his mouth, washed his hands and dried them carefully on his napkin, selected a cigar and lit it. Sanin watched him in silence.

'There is only one remedy,' Polozov boomed at last, throwing back his head and blowing out the smoke in a thin stream. 'Go and see my wife. If she is so inclined, she can resolve all your troubles with a wave of her hand.'

'But where am I to see your wife? You say that you are leaving the day after tomorrow?'

Polozov closed his eyes.

'Listen, do you know what I am going to suggest?' he said at last, turning his cigar around with his lips and sighing. 'You run off home, get yourself ready as quickly as you can, and then come back here. I leave at one o'clock, there is plenty of room in my carriage, and I will take you with me. That will be the best way. And now I am going to sleep. That is how it is, my friend: as soon as I have eaten, I must sleep without fail. Nature demands it, and indeed I don't resist her. And don't you disturb me.'

Sanin considered the matter for a while. Suddenly, he raised his head: he had made up his mind.

'All right, I agree. And thank you. I shall be back here at half past twelve, and we shall set off for Wiesbaden together. I hope that your wife will not be annoyed . . .'

But Polozov was already wheezing. He murmured, 'Don't disturb me', made a few movements with his legs and fell asleep like a baby.

Sanin threw another glance at the heavy figure, the head and neck, and the chin, raised high in the air and round as an apple. He then left the hotel and walked briskly towards the Roselli patisserie. Gemma had to be warned.

XXXII

HE found her with her mother in the front shop. Frau Lenore was bending down measuring the distance between the two windows with a small folding footrule. When she saw Sanin, she straightened up and greeted him gaily, but not without some slight hesitation.

'After what you said yesterday,' she began, 'I keep on turning over in my mind ideas for improving our shop. Here, for example, I think we should have two small cupboards with mirror shelves. You know, they are very fashionable now. And then . . .'

'Splendid splendid . . .' Sanin interrupted. 'We must think

about all that . . . but come in here now, I have something to tell you.'

He took Frau Lenore and Gemma by the arm and led them into the next room. Frau Lenore was alarmed, and dropped the footrule. Gemma was also alarmed at first, but a closer look at Sanin reassured her. His face appeared worried it was true, but at the same time it showed animation, confidence and resolution. He asked both ladies to be seated, and took up a position in front of them. Waving his arms in the air and ruffling his hair, he told them everything: his meeting with Polozov, his imminent visit to Wiesbaden, and the possibility of selling his estate.

'Just imagine my good fortune!' he exclaimed at last. 'Things have so turned out that it may well prove unnecessary for me to go to Russia. And we shall be able to arrange the wedding much sooner than I expected!'

'When do you have to leave?' asked Gemma.

'This very day, in an hour's time. My friend has hired a carriage, and will take me with him.'

'Will you write to us?'

'Immediately. As soon as I have had a talk with this lady, I will write at once.'

'This lady, you say, is very rich?' asked the practical Frau Lenore.

'Exceedingly rich. Her father was a millionaire, and left her everything.'

'Everything? To her? Well, that is your good luck. Only be careful that you do not ask too little for your estate. Be sensible and firm. Do not let yourself be carried away! I can understand your desire to become Gemma's husband as soon as possible, but . . . caution before all else! Don't forget: the higher the price you get for the sale of the estate, the more there will be left for the two of you – and for your children.'

Gemma turned away, and Sanin began waving his arms again.

'You can have absolute confidence in my prudence, Frau Lenore! I am not even going to bargain! I will name the proper price. If she accepts, well and good; if not, then let her be!'

'Do you know her . . . this lady?' Gemma asked.

'I have never set eyes on her.'

'And when will you be back?'

'If nothing comes of the business, the day after tomorrow. But if things appear to be going well, it may be necessary to stay a day, or even two days, longer. In any event I will not delay a moment longer than is necessary. You know that I am leaving my soul behind! But I must not go on talking – I still have to rush back to my lodgings before leaving . . . Give me your hand for luck, Frau Lenore – that is our custom in Russia.'

'The right hand or the left?'

'The left, nearest the heart. I will be back the day after tomorrow – bearing my shield, or borne upon my shield! Something tells me I shall return victorious! Goodbye, my dear, good friends!'

He embraced and kissed Frau Lenore, and asked Gemma to go into her room with him for a moment, since he had something very important to tell her. He only wanted to say goodbye to her alone. Frau Lenore realized this, and therefore showed no curiosity about the very important matter . . . Sanin had never before been in Gemma's room. No sooner had he crossed the hallowed threshold than all the love which possessed him, its fire, its rapture and its sweet terrors, overwhelmed his whole being and burned within him . . . He glanced around him with tender adoration, fell at the feet of his beloved, and pressed his face to her body . . .

'*Tu es mien?*' she whispered. 'You will come back soon?'

'I am yours . . . I will come back.' His breath came in gasps as he murmured his assurance.

'I shall be waiting for you, my darling.'

A few moments later, Sanin was running down the street

towards his lodgings. He never noticed that a bedraggled Pantaleone had leapt out after him from the door of the patisserie and shouted something at him, holding his arm high in the air and shaking it wildly in what looked like a menacing gesture.

At exactly a quarter to one, Sanin reported to Polozov. A four-horse carriage stood ready at the gates of the hotel. When he saw Sanin, Polozov only muttered, 'Ah, so you've made up your mind,' and then, having put on his hat, great-coat and galoshes, and stuffed his ears with cotton wool, although it was summertime, came out on to the porch. Under his directions, the waiters disposed his numerous articles of shopping in the interior of the carriage, lined a place for him to sit on with little silk-covered cushions, bags and bundles, placed a basket of provisions at his feet, and lashed his trunk to the coachman's box. Polozov distributed generous largesse and climbed into the carriage, grunting and supported, from behind it is true, but respectfully, by the obsequious porter. It was only after thoroughly pressing down everything around him to make himself comfortable, and after selecting and lighting a cigar, that he signed to Sanin, as if to say, all right you can get in too. Sanin sat down beside him. Polozov, through the porter, ordered the postillion to drive carefully if he wished to be tipped. There was a rattle of steps and a banging of doors, and the carriage rolled off.

XXXIII

NOWADAYS it takes less than an hour by railway from Frankfurt to Wiesbaden. In those days, the journey by express post horses took about three hours. The horses were changed some five times. Polozov either dozed or else just sat swaying, holding his cigar in his teeth and talking very little. He did not once look out of the window. He was not interested in picturesque views, and even declared that 'Nature was death to him'. Sanin also kept silent, and did not admire the scenery: he had other things to think about. He was completely sunk in his thoughts and memories. At every stage, Polozov paid what was due, checked the time on his watch, and rewarded the postillions – generously or less generously, according to their efforts. When they were about halfway to their destination, Polozov extracted two oranges from the provisions basket, selected the better of the two, and offered the other to Sanin. Sanin looked closely at his companion – and suddenly burst out laughing.

'What's all this about?' asked the other, carefully peeling the orange with his short white nails.

'What's it about?' Sanin repeated. 'Why, about this journey of ours.'

'What of it?' asked Polozov again, inserting into his mouth one of the long segments into which an orange divides.

'It is a very strange business. Yesterday, truth to tell, I had as little thought of you as of the Emperor of China, and here I am today, driving with you in order to sell my estate to your wife, about whom I know absolutely nothing.'

'All kinds of things happen,' Polozov replied. 'If you live long enough, you will see everything in your time. For example, can you imagine me, mounted as an orderly officer? But I was. And the Grand Duke Michael shouted: "At the canter! That fat subaltern there, at the canter! Faster, at the full canter!"'

Sanin scratched his ear.

'Now tell me please, Polozov, what is your wife like? What kind of a woman is she? After all, I must know.'

'It's all very well for him to give the order, at the canter,' Polozov went on, with sudden heat, 'but what about me, I ask you, what about me? And I thought to myself: "Take all your ranks and your epaulettes, you can keep them." Oh yes . . .

you were asking about my wife. Well – what is she like? Human like everyone else. Don't trust her too far – she doesn't like it. The main thing is, talk as much as possible so as to give her something to laugh about. Tell her about your love affair, perhaps, but you know, make it amusing.'

'How do you mean, amusing?'

'Just that. You tell me that you are in love and want to get married. Well, just describe all that to her.'

Sanin was offended.

'And what do you find so funny about that?'

Polozov merely made a movement with his eyes. The juice from the orange was running down his chin.

'Was it your wife who sent you into Frankfurt to do the shopping?' Sanin inquired after a while.

'It was.'

'And what have you been buying?'

'Toys, obviously.'

'Toys? Have you got children?'

Polozov actually moved away from Sanin.

'What next! Why on earth should I have children? I mean women's playthings . . . Trimmings. For their dressing-up.'

'But do you know anything about such things?'

'Certainly.'

'Then how is it that you told me that you don't meddle in any of your wife's affairs?'

'This is the only affair of hers in which I do interfere. This . . . is not so bad. It relieves boredom a bit. Besides, my wife trusts my taste. And I am extremely good at beating down the tradesmen.'

Polozov had begun to speak in jerks. He was already exhausted.

'And is your wife very, very rich?'

'Oh yes, she's rich enough. Only mostly for herself.'

'Still, it looks as if you don't have much to complain about!'

'Well, after all, I am her husband. It would be a fine thing if

I did not benefit from it. And I am pretty useful to her. She's got quite a good bargain in me. I am a convenient husband!'

Polozov wiped his face with a silk handkerchief and puffed heavily, as if to say, 'Have mercy on me, don't force me to utter another word. You can see what a strain I find it.'

Sanin left him in peace, and once again sank into his own reflections.

The hotel in Wiesbaden, in front of which the carriage stopped, looked like a real palace. A ringing of bells resounded immediately from its depths, and a flurrying and scurrying began. Distinguished-looking persons in black frock-coats sprang about at the main entrance. A doorman, covered with gold, flung open the carriage door with a flourish.

Polozov dismounted like an emperor in triumph, and began to ascend the well-carpeted and sweet-smelling staircase. A man, also very well-dressed, but with a Russian face, hurried up to him – it was his valet. Polozov remarked to the servant that in future he must take him with him, since the evening before, in Frankfurt, he, Polozov, had been abandoned for the whole night without any warm water. The valet's face expressed due horror, and he bent down briskly to remove his master's goloshes.

'Is Maria Nikolaevna at home?' asked Polozov.

'Yes, sir, she is dressing, sir. She is going to dine with Countess Lasunskaia.'

'Ah, with that ... Wait, there are some things in the carriage, get them all out and bring them in. And you, Sanin – get yourself a room and come along in three-quarters of an hour. We will have dinner.'

Polozov swam on his way, and Sanin asked for a modest room. He changed and had a short rest, and then set off for the enormous suite occupied by His Serene Highness (*Durchlaucht*) Prince von Polosoff.

He found the 'Prince' enthroned on a luxurious, velvet-covered armchair in the middle of a most magnificent drawing-room. Sanin's phlegmatic school-fellow had already had time to take a bath and to envelop himself in a dressing-gown of the richest satin. He wore a crimson fez on his head. Sanin approached him and stood for some time examining him. Polozov sat motionless like an idol: he did not even turn his face towards Sanin, nor move an eyebrow, nor emit any sound. It was, in truth, a majestic spectacle! Having admired the scene for almost two minutes, Sanin was about to speak and to shatter the hieratic silence, when suddenly the door from a neighbouring room opened: there appeared on the threshold a young and beautiful woman in a white silk dress trimmed with black lace, her hands and neck decked with diamonds. It was herself – Maria Nikolaevna Polozova. Her thick fair hair, which had not yet been dressed, hung in two heavy plaits.

XXXIV

'OH, do forgive me,' she said with a smile, in which confusion and mockery were equally blended, immediately seizing the end of one of her plaits with her hand, and fixing her large, bright grey eyes on Sanin, 'I had no idea that you had already arrived.'

'Dimitry Pavlovich Sanin, a childhood friend,' murmured Polozov, still without turning round or rising from his chair, but pointing a finger at him.

'Yes . . . I know. You told me already. Very glad to make his acquaintance. But I wanted to ask you to do something for me, Ippolit Sidorych . . . my maid seems unable to do anything right today . . .'

'You want me to do your hair?'

'Yes, yes, please. Forgive me,' Madame Polozov repeated with her former smile. She gave Sanin a quick nod and, turning swiftly, disappeared through the door, leaving behind her a fleeting but elegant impression of a beautiful neck, wonderful shoulders, and a wonderful figure.

Polozov rose, and lumbered heavily after her. Sanin never had a moment's doubt that his presence in 'Prince Polozov's' drawing-room was perfectly well known to the lady of the house: the whole object of the incident had been to display her hair, which was indeed very fine. In his heart Sanin was even rather pleased by Madame Polozov's performance: if, he thought, her ladyship wanted to impress me, to cut a fine figure in front of me, then perhaps – who can tell? – she will show less resistance when it comes to the price of my estate. He was so wholly absorbed by Gemma that other women no longer had any significance for him. Indeed, he scarcely noticed them, and on this occasion only went so far as to think, 'Yes, what they say is true, this fine lady is not bad looking.'

However, had he not been in this exceptional state of mind, he would probably have expressed himself differently: Maria Nikolaevna Polozova, born Kolyshkina, was a very remarkable personality. Not that her beauty was beyond challenge: in fact the traces of her plebeian origins were evident enough. Her forehead was low, her nose somewhat fleshy and upturned. She could boast neither a delicate skin nor elegant hands and feet – but what did this matter? It was not the 'hallowed shrine of beauty', to use Pushkin's phrase, that would have made any man who met her stand and stare. It was the overwhelming presence of a Russian, or perhaps gipsy, woman's powerful body in full flower. Yes, any man would have been willing enough to stop and admire her.

But Gemma's image protected Sanin, like that triple armour of which the poets sing.

Some ten minutes later Madame Polozov reappeared with her husband. She came up to Sanin . . . and how she walked! In fact, some extraordinary fellows in those, alas! far distant days, would go out of their minds just from seeing her walk. 'When this woman walks towards you, it is as if she is bringing you all your life's happiness' – as one of them used to put it. She came up to Sanin, offered him her hand and said, in Russian, in her gentle and strangely withdrawn voice: 'You will wait up for me, won't you? I will be back soon.'

Sanin bowed respectfully while Maria Nikolaevna was already disappearing behind the heavy curtain which hung, before the outer door. As she vanished, she once more turned, looked over her shoulder and smiled, and once again left behind her the former impression of elegance. When she smiled, not one, not two, but three dimples appeared in each cheek and her eyes smiled more than her lips – her long, scarlet, tempting lips with two tiny birthmarks on the left.

Polozov lumbered into the room, and once again ensconced himself in the armchair. He was as silent as before. But from time to time a slight smile puffed out his colourless and prematurely wrinkled cheeks.

He looked old, although only three years senior to Sanin. The dinner with which he entertained his guest would certainly have satisfied the most exacting gourmet, but to Sanin it seemed endless and insufferable. Polozov ate slowly, 'with feeling, sense and measure',[1] bending attentively over his plate, and sniffing at almost every morsel. He would first swill the wine round his mouth and only then swallow it, and smack his lips. But when the roast was served, he suddenly burst into conversation – and on what a subject! He spoke of pedigree Merino sheep, of which he intended to import a whole flock, describing everything in the greatest detail, with tender affection, using diminutives throughout.

Having drunk a cup of coffee which was almost at boiling point (he had several times reminded the waiter in lachrymose tones of irritation that the other day he had been served coffee which was quite cold, cold as ice) and having inserted a Havana cigar between his crooked yellow teeth, he dozed off in his customary manner. This delighted Sanin, who began to walk slowly and noiselessly up and down the deep-piled carpet, and abandoned himself to daydreams of life with Gemma, and of the news which he would bring back to her. However, Polozov woke up earlier than usual, as he himself remarked, since he had only slept an hour and a half. He drank a glass of iced soda water and swallowed about eight spoonfuls of jam, Russian jam, which his valet brought him in a genuine dark green Kiev jar. He could not live without it – to quote his own words. He then fixed his puffed eyes on Sanin, and inquired if he would like a game of Old Maid. Sanin readily agreed. He was afraid that Polozov might once again begin to talk about Merino rams, ewe lambs and fat-tail sheep.

Host and guest went into the drawing-room, a waiter brought cards and the game began – not for money, of course.

They were engaged in this innocent pastime when Maria Nikolaevna returned from her visit to Countess Lasunskaia. She burst out laughing as soon as she entered the room and saw the cards and the open card table. Sanin jumped up from his seat, but she exclaimed: 'Please go on with your game. I will go and change and return at once' – and again she vanished with a rustle of skirts, pulling off her gloves as she went.

She did indeed return very soon. She had changed her fine dress for a voluminous lilac-coloured silk robe with loose, wide sleeves. A thick plaited cord was knotted about her waist. She sat down by her husband, waited until he had lost the hand, and then said to him: 'Well, Fatty, that's enough' (at the word 'Fatty' Sanin looked at her with amazement, and she smiled gaily in answer to his look, displaying all the dimples in her cheeks). 'That's enough. I can see that you are sleepy. Kiss my hand and take yourself off, while Monsieur Sanin and I have a talk on our own.'

'I am not sleepy,' Polozov murmured, rising heavily from the chair, 'but I will take myself off, and I will kiss your hand.'

She extended the palm of her hand, but continued to smile and kept her eyes on Sanin.

Polozov also glanced at him, and left without saying goodnight.

'Well, come on now, tell me everything,' Maria Nikolaevna said eagerly, placing her bare elbows on the table and impatiently tapping her nails together. 'Is it true that you are getting married?'

Having said these words, Madame Polozov even inclined her head a little so as to look Sanin in the eyes the more attentively and the more searchingly.

XXXV

MADAME POLOZOV's easy manner would probably have put Sanin off from the start – although he was no novice in society, and had rubbed along a good deal in the world – had he not once again interpreted this ease and familiarity of manner as a good omen for his enterprise. Let us indulge the caprices of this rich lady, he decided inwardly, and answered her with the same informality of manner as she employed for her questions.

'Yes, I am getting married.'

'To whom? To a foreigner?'

'Yes.'

'Did you meet her recently? In Frankfurt?'

'Just so.'

'And who is she? May one inquire?'

'Certainly. She is the daughter of a pastry-cook.'

Maria Nikolaevna opened her eyes wide and raised her eyebrows.

'But how perfectly delightful!' she said, drawing out the words. 'This is wonderful! And I thought that there were no longer any young men like you left in the world. The daughter of a pastry-cook!'

'I can see that this surprises you,' Sanin observed, not without some show of dignity. 'But in the first place, I am entirely free of those prejudices . . .'

'In the *first place* I am not in the least surprised,' interrupted Madame Polozov, 'and I have no prejudices either. I am a peasant's daughter myself. So we're quits. What surprises and delights me is the fact that here is a man who is not afraid of loving. You do love her, don't you?'

'Yes.'

'And is she very good-looking?'

Sanin was slightly put out by the last question. However, it was too late to retreat.

'As you know, Maria Nikolaevna,' he began, 'every man thinks that his beloved is better looking than anyone else. But my future wife is indeed a very beautiful girl.'

'Really? And in what style? The Italian? The antique?'

'Yes. She has very regular features.'

'Have you her portrait with you?'

'No.' (In those days no one had thought of photographs. Even daguerreotypes were hardly known.)

'What is her name?'

'She is called Gemma.'

'And what are you called?'

'Dimitry.'

'And your patronymic?'

'Pavlovich.'

'Do you know what?' said Madame Polozov, still in the same deliberate drawl. 'I like you very much, Dimitry Pavlovich. I am sure you are a very good man. Give me your hand. Let us be good friends.'

She gripped his hand firmly with her beautiful, white, strong fingers. Her hand was slightly smaller than his, but much warmer and smoother, softer and more vital.

'But do you know what has occurred to me?'

'What?'

'Are you sure you won't be angry? Sure? You say you are engaged to be married to this girl. But was it . . . was it really absolutely necessary?'

Sanin frowned.

'I don't understand you, Maria Nikolaevna.'

She laughed quietly and shook her head so as to throw back the hair that was falling on her cheeks.

'There is no doubt about it – he is a delight!' she said in a half-meditative, half-absent way, 'a knight in armour – and now, after this, just try to believe those who insist that there are no more idealists left!'

Maria Nikolaevna spoke all the time in Russian, in a remarkably pure Moscow form of speech, but as spoken by the lower classes, not the gentry.

'You were presumably educated at home in a patriarchal, god-fearing family?' she inquired. 'In what province?'

'In Tula province.'

'Well, then we were fed at the same trough. My father . . . But you must know who my father was?'

'Yes, I know.'

'He was born in Tula . . . a Tula man . . . Well, all right.' (Maria Nikolaevna pronounced the Russian word *khorosho'* deliberately now in a plebeian manner – *khersho . . oo*.) 'Well, let us get down to business.'

'What do you mean – get down to business? What do you mean by that?'

Madame Polozov narrowed her eyes.

'What then have you come here for?'

(When she narrowed her eyes, their expression became very gentle and a little mocking: but when she opened them to their full extent something cruel, something threatening showed through their clear and chilly brilliance. Her thick and slightly close-set eyebrows, which were in truth like sable, lent a special beauty to her eyes.)

'You want me to buy your estate, don't you? You need

money for the celebration of your marriage? Is that not so?'

'Yes, that is so.'

'And do you need a great deal of money?'

'I should be content with a few thousand francs to start with. Your husband knows my estate. You can ask his advice. I am prepared to accept a low price.'

Madame Polozov shook her head.

'In the *first place*,' she began, stressing each word, tapping the tips of her fingers on the cuff of Sanin's coat, 'I am not in the habit of asking my husband's advice – except, perhaps, in the matter of dress, on which he is a great expert. And *secondly*, why are you telling me that you are asking a low price? I do not wish to take advantage of the fact that you are now in love and ready for all sacrifices . . . I am not going to accept any sacrifice from you. Are you suggesting that, instead of encouraging . . . how can I best put it? – encouraging your noble feelings – is that right? I am to skin you like a rabbit? I am not in the habit of doing that. I can sometimes be quite ruthless with people – but certainly not in this way.'

Sanin was at a complete loss to make out whether she was laughing at him or speaking seriously, but he kept thinking to himself, 'You have to keep your wits about you with this one.'

A servant came in with a Russian samovar, a tea-set, cream, rusks and the like on a large tray, distributed all this bounty on the table between Sanin and Madame Polozov, and withdrew.

She poured a cup of tea.

'Do you mind?' she asked, putting sugar in his cup with her fingers – and the sugar tongs were lying in front of her.

'For Heaven's sake! From such a fair hand . . .'

He did not finish the phrase, and nearly choked over his mouthful of tea, while she observed him attentively and serenely.

'The reason I mentioned a low price for my estate,' he continued, 'is because I could not assume, since you are now abroad, that you would have much free capital at your disposal, and, in a word, I myself feel that the sale ... or the purchase of an estate in such circumstances is something unusual and that I must take all this into account.'

Sanin talked confusedly and with hesitation, while Madame Polozov leaned quietly against the back of the chair with her arms crossed, and kept looking at him in the same attentive and serene manner. At last he stopped.

'That's all right, go on, go on,' she said, as if coming to his rescue. 'I am listening to you, I like listening to you. Go on talking.'

Sanin started to describe his estate, its acreage, its position, its assets and the profit that it could be made to yield ... He also mentioned the picturesque situation of the house; meanwhile, Maria Nikolaevna kept on looking at him, even more fixedly and openly. Her lips were moving slightly, but without a smile, and she kept biting at them a little. At last he began to feel awkward, and fell silent once again.

'Dimitry Pavlovich,' began Madame Polozov, and then paused to think. 'Dimitry Pavlovich,' she repeated, 'do you know what? I am certain that the purchase of your estate is a very profitable business for me, and that we shall agree on a price. But you must give me two days, yes, two days' time. You are surely capable of parting for two days from your beloved? I will not keep you here any longer against your will – I give you my word of honour. But if you are now in need of five or six thousand francs it would give me great pleasure to offer to lend you the money – we can settle up later.'

Sanin rose.

'I have to thank you, Maria Nikolaevna, for your open-hearted and courteous readiness to help a man who is almost a complete stranger to you ... But if it is your wish, I should prefer to await your decision about the estate, and I will stay for two days.'

'Yes, it is my wish, Dimitry Pavlovich. And will it be very difficult for you? Very? Tell me.'

'I love Gemma, Maria Nikolaevna, and it is not easy for me to be parted from her.'

'Oh, you are a man with a heart of gold,' Maria Nikolaevna said with a sigh. 'I promise not to torment you too much. Are you going?'

'It is late,' observed Sanin.

'And you must rest after your journey, and after your game of Old Maid with my husband. Tell me, are you a great friend of my husband?'

'We went to the same boarding school.'

'Was he already like that – in those days?'

'How do you mean, "Like that"?'

Madame Polozov suddenly burst out laughing, and laughed until her whole face was scarlet. She put a handkerchief to her lips, rose from her chair, and, swaying as if from fatigue, went up to Sanin and held out her hand.

He took his leave and walked towards the door.

'Be here as early as possible tomorrow, will you? Do you hear?' she called after him.

As he left the room, he glanced back and saw that she had once again sunk into her armchair and had thrown her arms above her head. The wide sleeves of her robe had dropped almost to her shoulders. No one could deny that the pose of those arms, and the whole of that figure were of fascinating beauty.

XXXVI

THE lamp in Sanin's room burned far into the night. He sat at the desk and wrote to 'his Gemma'. He told her everything. He described the Polozovs, husband and wife – though incidentally, he enlarged mainly on the subject of his own feelings – and ended with making an appointment in three days' time!!! (with three exclamation marks). Early next morning, he took the letter to the post, and went for a walk in the gardens of the Kurhaus, where the music was already playing. There were as yet few people about. He paused in front of the bandstand, listening to a pot-pourri from 'Roberto Diavolo' and, after drinking some coffee, went down a secluded side alley, sat down on a small bench, and plunged into thought.

A parasol handle tapped him briskly and quite sharply on the shoulder. He came to with a start . . . before him, attired in a light grey-green dress of Barège silk, a white tulle hat and suède gloves, stood Maria Nikolaevna, rosy and fresh as a summer morning. Her glance and her movements were still soft with the glow of untroubled sleep.

'Good morning,' she said. 'I sent for you this morning, but you had already gone out. I have just finished my second tumbler – you know they make me drink the waters here, God knows why. If I am not perfectly well, then who is? And now I have to walk for a whole hour. Would you like to come with me? And after that we will drink coffee.'

'I have already had my coffee,' said Sanin, rising to his feet, 'but I should be delighted to walk with you.'

'Then give me your arm . . . don't be afraid, your intended is not here – she will not see you.'

Sanin gave a forced smile. He had a disagreeable feeling every time Madame Polozov referred to Gemma. However, he quickly and obediently offered his arm – Maria Nikolaevna's arm sank slowly and softly on to his, glided along, and clung as if welded to it.

'Come along, this way,' she said, tossing her open parasol over her shoulder. 'I am at home in this park and will take you to the prettiest spots. And, do you know' (she often used these three words) 'we shan't talk any business now – we will have a good discussion about that after breakfast. But you must now tell me about yourself so that I know what kind of man I am dealing with. And after that, if you like, I will tell you something about myself. Agreed?'

'But, Maria Nikolaevna, what possible interest can you have . . .?'

'Stop, stop! You have misunderstood me, I have no wish to flirt with you.' Maria Nikolaevna shrugged her shoulders. 'The man is engaged to a girl who looks like a classical statue, and I should flirt with him! But you have something to sell, and I am a business woman. So I want to know all about your goods. Well, show me – what are they like? I want to know not only what I am buying, but from whom I am buying. That was my father's rule. So begin . . . Well, not from childhood, perhaps – but, have you been abroad long, for instance? And where have you been up till now? Only don't walk so fast – we are in no hurry.'

'I came here from Italy, where I spent a few months.'

'It seems as if you are drawn towards everything Italian. How strange that you did not find your particular object *there*. Do you like art? Paintings? Or do you prefer music?'

'I love art . . . I love everything that is beautiful.'

'Music, too?'

'Yes, music as well.'

'And I don't like it at all. All I like is Russian songs, and then only in the country and in spring – songs and dances, you know . . . the red cotton of the peasants' clothes, the girls' bead head-dresses, young grass on the common pasture land, the smell of smoke in the air – marvellous! But we are not talking about me. Go on with your story. Go on, go on with your story.'

Madame Polozov walked on, and kept glancing at Sanin as she walked. She was tall – her face was very nearly level with his.

He began his account, reluctantly at first and not very skilfully, but then he got into his stride and even became talkative. Madame Polozov was a very good listener. Besides, she seemed so frank herself that she had the effect of inducing frankness in others, however unwilling. She possessed the great gift of putting a man at his ease, *le terrible don de la familiarité*, which is mentioned by Cardinal de Retz. Sanin spoke of his travels, of his life in St Petersburg, of his youth ... Had Maria Nikolaevna been a society woman, with refined manners, he would never have let himself go in this way. But she referred to herself as a 'good fellow' who could not bear any ceremony: it was in these very terms that she had described herself for Sanin's benefit. And at the same time, here was the 'good fellow' walking beside him softly like a cat and leaning slightly against him, looking up at him. What is more, the 'good fellow' was cast in the image of a young female creature who simply radiated that destructive, tormenting, quietly inflammatory temptation with which Slav natures alone – and then only some of them, and sometimes not pure Slav at that, but with a dash of something else – know how to drive us poor men, us sinful, weak men, out of our minds.

So Sanin walked in the company of Madame Polozov, and his conversation with her lasted for over an hour. And they did not stop once, but kept on walking along the interminable avenues, now going uphill, admiring the view on the way, now down into the valley, into the cover of dense shadows – and all the time arm in arm. There were moments when Sanin felt a certain irritation: never had he walked so long with Gemma, his darling Gemma – and here this grand lady had taken possession of him, and that was that!

'Are you not tired?' he inquired on several occasions.

'I am never tired,' she replied.

Occasionally, other walkers would cross their path. Nearly all of them bowed to her – some respectfully, some even obsequiously. To one of them, an extremely good-looking and very well-dressed man with dark hair, she called out from some distance in the best Paris accent: '*Conte, vous savez il ne faut pas venir me voir – ni aujourd'hui, ni demain.*' The man raised his hat without saying a word, and gave a deep bow.

'Who was that?' asked Sanin, betraying the bad habit of idle curiosity with which all Russians are afflicted.

'That? That's a little Frenchman – there are many of them running around here. He's one of those dancing attendance on me. But it's time for coffee. Let's go home: I imagine you must be hungry. I expect my old man has got his eyes unstuck by now.'

' "Old man". "Got his eyes unstuck," ' repeated Sanin to himself. And she speaks such excellent French . . . what a curious character . . .

Maria Nikolaevna was not mistaken. When she and Sanin returned to the hotel, the 'old man', or 'Fatty', was sitting, with the inevitable fez on his head, at a table laid for breakfast.

'I got tired of waiting for you,' he exclaimed, screwing up his face in a sour grimace. 'I was about to have coffee without you.'

'That's all right, that's all right,' replied his wife gaily. 'Were you angry? That's good for you, otherwise you will become completely ossified. Here, I have brought a guest. Go on, ring! Let us drink coffee, the very best coffee, in Dresden china cups on a snow-white tablecloth!'

She threw off her hat and her gloves, and clapped her hands. Polozov peered at her from under his eyebrows.

'What has made you go off at the gallop today, Maria Nikolaevna?' he asked in a low voice.

'That's not your business, Ippolit Sidorych. You ring the bell. Dimitry Pavlovich, sit down and drink coffee for the second time. Oh, what fun it is to give orders! There is no greater pleasure in the world!'

'When people obey them,' grunted her husband.

'Just so, when people obey me. That is why I enjoy myself. Especially with you. Isn't that so, Fatty? And here is the coffee.'

Lying on the enormous tray brought in by the waiter there was also a theatre playbill. Madame Polozov immediately seized it.

'Tragedy!' she cried indignantly. 'German tragedy! Never mind, that's better than German comedy. Will you tell them to reserve a box for me in the pit tier – no, better take the *Fremden Loge*,' she said, turning to the waiter. 'Do you hear, the *Fremden Loge* without fail!'

'But what if the *Fremden Loge* is already taken by His Excellency, the Town Director (*Seine Excellenz der Herr Stadt-Direktor*)?' the waiter ventured to object.

'Then you give His Excellency ten talers – and see that I get the box. Do you hear?'

The waiter inclined his head, submissively and sadly.

'Dimitry Pavlovich, you will come to the theatre with me, will you not? German actors are terrible, but you will come, won't you? Yes? Yes? Oh, how polite you are. And you, Fatty, will you come?'

'Just as you say,' Polozov said into his cup, which he had lifted to his mouth.

'Do you know what, stay at home. You always sleep at the theatre, and in any case you know practically no German. I will tell you what you can do. You can write an answer to the estate manager about our mill – do you remember? About the peasants' milling. Tell him that I won't do it, that I won't do it, and again that I won't do it. That will provide you with an occupation for the whole evening.'

'Very well,' Polozov agreed.

'That's excellent. You're my clever boy. And now, gentlemen, this talk of the estate manager reminds me that we must discuss our principal business. And so, as soon as the waiter has cleared the table, you, Dimitry Pavlovich, will tell us all about your estate – how, and why, and how much you want, and what deposit you require – everything.'

At last, thought Sanin, thank goodness!

'You did tell me a little about it, and I think I remember that you gave a wonderful description of the garden, but Fatty wasn't there at the time . . . Let him hear it all. I expect he may even contribute a relevant grunt. It is very agreeable for me to think that I can help you to get married, and besides I promised that after breakfast I would devote myself to your affairs. I always keep my promises – is that not so, Ippolit Sidorych?'

Polozov rubbed his face with the palm of his hand.

'Yes, that is true, and it is only right to say so. You never deceive anyone.'

'Never. And I never *will* deceive anyone. Now Dimitry Pavlovich, please state your case, as we say in the Senate.'

XXXVII

SANIN began to state his case, that is, for the second time, to describe his estate, but omitting from this recital references to natural beauty, and occasionally seeking confirmation from Polozov of some fact or figure. But Polozov only muttered 'Hm . . . m', and shook his head – and whether this was a sign of assent or of dissent, the devil himself would probably have been unable to determine. In any case, Maria Nikolaevna was in no need of his assistance. She revealed such extraordinary commercial and administrative talents as to leave one amazed. She had complete mastery of every minute detail of the estate. She questioned Sanin closely and exactly about everything and explored every aspect. Each time she used a word she hit the mark, and dotted the I's. Sanin did not expect such an examination and was unprepared for it. It lasted for all of an hour and a half. He experienced all the sensations of a prisoner on trial, seated on a very narrow bench, before a severe and searching judge. 'Why, this is a cross-examination,' he whispered to himself unhappily. Madame Polozov was laughing a little all the time, as if she were making a joke of the whole affair, but this did not improve matters for Sanin. He even broke out in a cold sweat in the course of the 'cross-examination' when it became evident that he was not certain of the exact meaning of the words used in peasant households for land re-allocation, or for plough lands.

'All right,' Maria Nikolaevna decided at last. 'Now I know your estate ... as well as you do. What price are you asking for a soul?' (In those days, it will be recalled, the price of estates was determined by the number of souls, that is to say peasants.)

'Yes ... Well ... I think ... that it would hardly be possible to take less than five hundred roubles,' Sanin managed to say with difficulty. (Oh, Pantaleone, Pantaleone, where are you? This would have made you say once more: *Barbari!*)

Madame Polozov raised her eyes to the heavens as if making her calculations.

'Well,' she said at last, 'this price seems inoffensive to me. But I obtained two days' grace for myself – and you must wait until tomorrow. I expect that we shall agree, and you will then tell me what deposit you require. And now, *basta cosi!*' she added, having noticed that Sanin was about to make some objection, 'we have spent enough time on filthy lucre – *à demain les affaires!* Do you know what, I am now releasing you' (she glanced at the small enamelled watch which she kept tucked into her waist-band), 'until three o'clock ... I must, after all, let you have a rest. Go and have a game of roulette.'

'I never gamble,' remarked Sanin.

'Really? Why, you are perfection itself! As a matter of fact, I don't gamble either. It is stupid to throw one's money to the winds – and that is what it certainly means. But go to the gaming room, and have a look at the characters. There can be some very amusing ones. There is an old woman with a moustache and a lapdog – wonderful! There is also one of our Princes, he is pretty good too. A majestic figure, an aquiline nose, and every time he stakes a taler, he crosses himself secretly under his waistcoat. Read the journals, go for a walk – in short, do what you like. But I expect you at three o'clock . . . *de pied ferme*. We must dine early. These comic Germans start their theatre performances at half past six.' She stretched out her hand. '*Sans rancune, n'est-ce pas?*'

'Good gracious, Maria Nikolaevna, and why should I have any ill feelings towards you?'

'Because I have been tormenting you. You wait, I have something else in store for you,' she added, half-closing her eyes, so that all her dimples appeared at once in her cheeks, which were flushed. '*Au revoir!*'

Sanin bowed and turned to leave the room. There was a burst of merry laughter behind him – and the following scene was reflected in a looking-glass as he passed it: Madame Polozov had pushed her husband's fez down over his eyes, and he was struggling helplessly, with his arms waving about in the air.

XXXVIII

OH, what a deep sigh of relief and joy Sanin breathed as soon as he found himself alone in his room! Maria Nikolaevna had spoken truly – he needed a rest, a rest from these new acquaintances, impacts and conversations. He needed time to dispel the fumes which this unexpected and unasked-for intimacy with a woman so alien to him had generated in his heart and head. And think when it was happening – almost the day after he had discovered that Gemma loved him and he had become engaged to her! Why, it was blasphemy! In his thoughts he sought forgiveness a thousand times from his innocent dove, although truth to tell there was nothing for which he could blame himself; he pressed a thousand kisses on the little cross which she had given him. Had he not had every hope of concluding quickly and successfully the business which had brought him to Wiesbaden, he would have rushed back headlong to dear Frankfurt, to that house which he loved, and which had now become a part of his life, to the feet of his beloved . . . But there was nothing to be done. The cup had to be drained, he must dress, go to dinner . . . then on to the theatre. If only she would let him go as early as possible tomorrow!

There was another matter which dismayed and angered him. He kept thinking of Gemma, with love akin to worship, with rapture, with gratitude, thinking of the life which the two of them would share, of the happiness which lay before him – and all the time this strange woman, this Madame Polozov, incessantly appeared – no, hung around, as Sanin expressed it, with a feeling of especially malicious pleasure – hung around in front of his eyes, and he could not get rid of her image, could not shut out the sound of her voice or put the things she had said out of his mind. He could not even free himself of the memory of that particular delicate, fresh and penetrating scent, like the scent of yellow lilies, which came from her clothing. This woman was obviously making a fool of him, and making every kind of overture. Why? Why did she do it? Was it really just the whim of a spoiled, rich, almost immoral woman? And that husband? What sort of a creature was he? What was his relationship with her? And why did these questions bedevil him, Sanin, who in truth had no concern with either Polozov or his wife? Why could he not dismiss this persistent image, even at a time when his soul was wholly turned towards the vision of another, clear and serene as God's daylight? How dare *those* features even show themselves against the vision of *hers*, which were almost divine? Show themselves – why, they leered at him provocatively. Those grey eyes, like those of a bird of prey, those dimples, those plaits which looked like snakes – was it really possible that they had so possessed him that he could not shake himself free? Did he lack the will to do it?

Nonsense, nonsense! Tomorrow all this would vanish without trace. Ah, but would she let him go tomorrow? Yes . . . he asked himself all these questions, and meanwhile three o'clock was drawing near. So he put on a black evening coat and, after a short walk in the park, set off for the Polozovs.

In their drawing-room he found an Embassy secretary of German origin, a long, thin individual with a horse's profile, fair hair, and a parting at the back of his head (this was just coming into fashion in those days). But, wonder of wonders, whom else? None other than von Doenhof, the officer with whom he had fought a duel a few days before. Sanin had never expected to meet him here and could not help being put out, although he exchanged bows with him.

'You know each other?' asked Maria Nikolaevna. Sanin's confusion had not escaped her.

'Yes . . . I have had the honour,' murmured Doenhof, with a slight bow towards Madame Polozov, and added softly with a smile, 'It is the same one . . . your compatriot . . . a Russian.'

'Impossible!' she exclaimed, also in an undertone. She shook her finger at him and immediately began to make her farewells both to him and to the long secretary, who was obviously head over heels in love with her, since he stood gaping every time she looked at him. Doenhof left at once, politely submissive, like a friend of the house who only needs a hint to know what is expected. The secretary tried to stall, but Madame Polozov saw him off without ceremony.

'You go along to your high-powered personage,' she told him. (A certain Principessa di Monaco was then living in Wiesbaden, who looked remarkably like a somewhat low-grade cocotte.) 'Why should you waste your time on a plebeian like me?'

'For heaven's sake, Madame,' the unhappy secretary began to assure her, 'all the princesses in the world . . .'

But Madame Polozov was quite merciless – and the secretary took himself off, parting and all.

Maria Nikolaevna had dressed herself up very much to her '*avantage*', as our grandmothers used to say. She was wearing a rose-coloured dress of watered silk, with sleeves in the fashion of the Comtesse de Fontanges, and a large diamond in each ear. Her eyes shone no less brilliantly than the diamonds, and she seemed to be in a good mood and on top of her form.

She placed Sanin beside her and began to talk about Paris, where she intended going in a few days' time. She told him how bored she was with the Germans, who were stupid whenever they tried to be clever, and suddenly inappropriately clever when they were being stupid; then, quite suddenly, out of the blue – as they say, *à brule pourpoint* – she asked him if it was true that he had fought a duel on account of some lady a few days ago with the very same officer who had been sitting there a short while back?

'But how do you know about this?' muttered the startled Sanin.

'The world is full of rumours, Dimitry Pavlovich. But I know, by the way, that you were in the right, a thousand times in the right, and behaved like a man of honour. Tell me, was this lady your betrothed?'

Sanin frowned slightly.

'All right, all right, I won't ask,' Madame Polozov said hurriedly, 'since you find it unpleasant to talk about it. Forgive me, I won't say any more; don't be angry!' Polozov appeared from the room next door with a newspaper in his hand. 'What are you up to? Or is dinner ready?'

'Dinner will be served in a minute; you have a look at what I have read in "The Northern Bee" – Prince Gromoboy has died.'

Maria Nikolaevna raised her head.

'Oh well, God rest his soul! Do you know,' turning to Sanin, 'every year in February, for my birthday, he used to fill all my rooms with camellias, but this still does not make it worth spending the winter in St Petersburg. I suppose he was over seventy?' she asked her husband.

'Yes. There is a description of his funeral in the paper. The whole court was there. And there is a poem by Prince Kovrizhkin[1] for the occasion.'

'Splendid!'

'Would you like me to read it to you? The Prince calls him a man of counsel.'

'No, thank you. Some man of counsel! He was simply his wife's, Tatiana Yurievna's, man. Let us go to dinner. Life is for the living. Dimitry Pavlovich, your arm.'

The dinner was superb – like that of the day before, and passed with much animation. Maria Nikolaevna knew how to tell a story – a rare gift among women, and Russian women at that! She had no reticence in choosing her words: her female compatriots were particular targets for her wit. Sanin was more than once forced to burst out laughing at the aptness and vividness of her characterizations. Above all, Maria Nikolaevna could not bear hypocrisy, the empty phrase or the lie ... She found all these about her everywhere. She seemed actually to parade and to boast of the humble surroundings in which her life had begun, told a number of rather odd stories about her relations from the time of her childhood, and described herself as a peasant girl, not a whit worse than Natalia Kirillovna Naryshkina.[2] It became evident to Sanin that she had, in her time, lived through far more than the great majority of women of her own age.

Meanwhile, Polozov ate with concentration, drank attentively, and only occasionally threw, now at Sanin, now at his wife, a glance from his colourless eyes, which looked blind, but were, in fact, extremely keen.

'What a clever boy you are!' exclaimed his wife, turning to

him. 'How well you carried out all those errands for me in Frankfurt! I would give you a little kiss on your forehead, only you don't care for that sort of thing very much.'

'No, I don't,' replied Polozov, and cut open a pineapple with a silver knife.

Maria Nikolaevna looked at him, and drummed on the table with her fingers.

'So our bet is on,' she said in a meaningful manner.

'Yes.'

'Very well. You will lose.'

Polozov stuck out his chin.

'This time, you had better not be too confident, Maria Nikolaevna: my opinion is that you are going to lose.'

'What is the bet about? May I know?' asked Sanin.

'No . . . not now,' replied Maria Nikolaevna, and laughed.

Seven o'clock struck. A waiter announced that the carriage was ready. Polozov accompanied his wife to the door, and then immediately waddled back to his armchair.

'Now, remember! Don't forget the letter to the manager!' she called to him from the hall.

'Don't worry, I will write. I am a methodical man.'

XXXIX

IN 1840 the Wiesbaden Theatre was not only ugly to look at, but bad. Its pathetic company was distinguished for its ranting mediocrity, and its productions for their plodding vulgarity. In fact it did not rise one whit above the standard which can be considered normal to this day for all German theatres. (The most perfect example of German theatre has in latter days been offered us by the company at Karlsruhe, under the 'celebrated' direction of Herr Devrient.)[1]

Behind the box which had been reserved for 'Her Serene Highness, Frau von Polosoff' (Goodness only knows how the waiter had contrived to secure it – could he really have bribed the *Stadt Direktor*?) there was a small room furnished with little settees. Before entering, Maria Nikolaevna asked Sanin to close the shutters which screened the box from the auditorium.

'I don't want to be seen,' she said, 'otherwise they'll start coming in here.'

She also made him sit beside her, with his back to the auditorium, so that the box should look empty.

The orchestra played the overture to the 'Marriage of Figaro', the curtain rose and the play began.

It was one of those innumerable home-grown products in which well-read but talentless authors, using stilted, lifeless language, bring before the audience some 'profound' or 'palpitating' thought. They portray a so-called tragic conflict, diligently but clumsily, and induce boredom – Asiatic boredom, much the same as there is Asiatic cholera.

Maria Nikolaevna patiently listened through the first half of the first act. But when the First Lover, having learned that his beloved had been false to him, stuck both his fists on his chest, pushed his elbows out at acute angles and howled for all the world like a dog, she could stand it no more. (The First Lover, incidentally, was dressed in a long white coat, with puffed sleeves and a plush collar, a striped waistcoat and mother-of-pearl buttons, green pantaloons braided with patent leather, and white chamois leather gloves.)

'The very last French actor in the very last provincial town acts better and more naturally than the greatest German celebrity,' she declared indignantly, and moved into the back room.

'Come here,' she said to Sanin, tapping the space beside her on the settee. 'Let us talk.'

Sanin obeyed.

Maria Nikolaevna threw him a glance.

'Ah, I can see you are as soft as silk. Your wife will have an easy time with you. This clown,' she continued, pointing with the end of her fan at the actor who had started howling (he was playing the part of a domestic tutor), 'has reminded me of my youth. I was also in love with a tutor. That was my first . . . no, my second passion. I fell in love for the first time with a young lay brother in the Don monastery in Moscow. I was twelve. I only saw him on Sundays, he wore a velvet cassock, sprayed himself with lavender water, and, as he made his way through the crowd with the censer, would say to the ladies in French "*Pardon, excusez*". He never raised his eyes, but his lashes were that length' – she marked off a whole half of her little finger with her thumbnail and showed Sanin. 'My tutor was called Monsieur Gaston. I must tell you that he was terribly learned and extremely strict, a Swiss – and what a dynamic face he had! He had side whiskers as black as tar, a Greek profile, and his lips looked as if they had been cast in iron. I was terrified of him! He was in fact the only man I have ever been afraid of in my life. He was also my brother's tutor – that was my brother who died later . . . He was drowned . . . A gipsy once foretold that I too would die a violent death, but that's nonsense. I don't believe it. Just imagine my husband with a dagger in his hand!'

'There are other ways of dying than by a dagger,' remarked Sanin.

'All that kind of thing is nonsense. Are you superstitious? I am not a bit. But what is to be, will be. Monsieur Gaston lived in our house, and his room was over mine. I used to wake up sometimes at night and hear his footsteps – he went to bed very late – and my heart would miss a beat from sheer veneration . . . or some other feeling. My father could scarcely read or write, but he gave us a good education. Do you know that I can understand Latin?'

'You? Latin?'

'Yes – I. Monsieur Gaston taught me. We read the *Aeneid* together. It's a dull thing, but there are some good parts in it. Do you remember when Dido and Aeneas are in the forest . . .?'

'Yes, I remember,' Sanin said hurriedly. He had forgotten all his Latin long ago, and had only the faintest notion about the *Aeneid*.

Maria Nikolaevna glanced at him in her characteristic manner – with a sidelong look from under lowered lids.

'But you mustn't imagine that I am very well-educated. Oh, good gracious me, no, I am not educated at all, and I have no accomplishments. I can scarcely write – truly, and I can't read aloud. I can't play the piano or draw or sew – nothing. That's what I'm like – all here!'

She flung her arms wide.

'I am telling you all this,' she went on, 'first, in order not to have to listen to those dolts' (she pointed to the stage: at that moment instead of an actor, an actress was setting up a howl, and she too had thrust her elbows forward); 'and secondly, because I am in your debt: you told me about yourself yesterday.'

'It was your pleasure to ask me to tell you about myself,' remarked Sanin.

Maria Nikolaevna suddenly spun round at him.

'And is it not "your pleasure" to know what kind of a woman I really am? However, I am not surprised,' she added, eaning back once again on the cushions of the settee. 'Here is a man, about to get married, and moreover for love, and on top of that after a duel . . . how would you expect him to think of anything else?'

She became pensive, and began to bite the handle of her fan with her large, regular teeth, which were as white as milk.

But to Sanin it seemed that the fumes which he had been unable to drive away for two days, were once again beginning to rise to his head.

He and Maria Nikolaevna were talking in low voices, almost in whispers – and this only increased his irritation and his excitement . . .

When, oh when, would all this come to an end? Weak

people never make an end themselves – but keep waiting for the end.

Someone was sneezing on the stage. The sneeze had been introduced by the author as a comic 'moment' or 'element'. Certainly, the play had no other element of comedy, and the spectators had to be satisfied with this tiny crumb of light relief, and were laughing.

This laughter also irritated Sanin. There were moments when he simply did not know – was he angry or pleased? Bored or entertained? Oh, if only Gemma could see him!

'You know, it really is strange,' Maria Nikolaevna suddenly spoke again, 'a man announces in the calmest manner, "I intend to get married, don't you know?" And yet no one will ever say calmly, "I intend to jump into the water." But, when you come to think of it, what is the difference? It really is strange.'

Sanin was now really annoyed.

'There's a very big difference, Maria Nikolaevna. For some people, there is nothing very frightening about jumping into water – there are those who can swim. Besides . . . so far as strange marriages are concerned . . . if that is what we . . .'

He stopped suddenly, and bit his tongue. Maria Nikolaevna struck her fan against the palm of her hand.

'Finish what you were saying, Dimitry Pavlovich, finish what you were saying! I know what you meant to say: "If that is what we are discussing, my most respected Maria Nikolaevna Polozova" – you wanted to say – "It would be difficult to imagine a stranger marriage than yours. After all, I have known your husband since childhood." That is what you wanted to say – you expert swimmer!'

'But, really . . .' Sanin tried to interpose.

'Isn't that right? Am I not right?' she persisted. 'Now, look me in the eyes and tell me that what I have said is untrue.'

Sanin did not know where to look.

'All right, as you please, it is true, if you insist on knowing,' he said at last.

Maria Nikolaevna nodded her head.

'That's right, that's right ... Well – but have you, who know how to swim, ever asked yourself what the reason might be for such strange conduct by a woman who is not poor ... and not stupid ... and not plain? Perhaps you are not interested – but never mind. I will tell you the reason, but not now – as soon as the interval is over. I keep on worrying in case someone should come in ...'

She had indeed hardly had time to finish her sentence before the outer door was half opened. A head was thrust into the box: it was red, oily and sweating, young but already toothless, with flat, long hair, a long pendant nose, enormous ears like a bat's, with golden spectacles in front of its inquisitive and dull little eyes, and a pince-nez on top of the spectacles. The head took in the scene, noticed Madame Polozov, broke into a mean grin, started to nod ... a scraggy outstretched neck was visible behind the head ...

Maria Nikolaevna waved her handkerchief at the apparition.

'I am not at home! *Ich bin nicht zu Hause, Herr P.! Ich bin nicht zu Hause* ... Shoo ... Shoo ...'

The head showed signs of astonishment, emitted a forced laugh and said, with something like a sob, in imitation of Liszt at whose feet he had once grovelled, '*Sehr gut, sehr gut*,' and disappeared.

'Who is that character?' asked Sanin.

'That? The Wiesbaden critic. "*Litterat* – or *Lohn Lakai*",[2] as you prefer. He is in the pay of the local concessionaire, and is therefore obliged to praise everything and to enthuse about everything, while at the same time he is overflowing with spiteful bile, which he does not even dare to discharge. But I am afraid: he is a terrible gossip, and will immediately run off and tell everyone that I am in the theatre. Well, never mind.'

The orchestra played a waltz, the curtain soared again ... the grimacing and the simpering began once more upon the stage.

'Well, now,' began Maria Nikolaevna, sinking back on to the settee, 'since you are trapped and have to sit with me, instead of enjoying the bliss of being near your beloved – now, don't roll your eyes and don't get angry, I understand your predicament and I have already promised to let you go free as the wind – now listen to my confession. Do you want to know what I love more than anything else in the world?'

'Freedom,' Sanin prompted.

She placed her hand on his.

'Yes, Dimitry Pavlovich,' she said, and there was a special note in her voice, a note which suggested solemnity and absolute sincerity. 'Freedom more than anything else, and before everything else. And don't imagine that I am boasting about this – there is nothing very praiseworthy about it, but *that's* how it is, and that's how it will be for me to the end of my days. I suppose I saw a great deal of slavery in my childhood, and suffered from it.[3] And of course, Monsieur Gaston, my tutor, opened my eyes. Perhaps you understand now why I married Polozov: with him I am free, completely free, as free as the air, as the wind ... and I knew all that before the wedding, I knew I should be as free as a bird with him.'

Maria Nikolaevna fell silent and threw aside her fan.

'I will tell you something else. I am quite a reflective woman, it's amusing, and that's what our minds are for. But I never reflect about the consequences of anything I do myself, and when something goes wrong I don't indulge in self-pity – not *that much*: it's not worth it. I have a favourite saying – *Cela ne tire pas à conséquence* – I don't know how to put it in Russian. And just so – what does *tire à conséquence*? No one is going to demand an account from me *here* on this earth; as for there' (she lifted a finger in the air), 'well, they can do what they think best up there. When the time comes for them to judge

153

me *there*, I shall no longer be *I*. Are you listening to me? Are you bored?'

Sanin was sitting with his head bowed. He raised his head.

'I am not at all bored, Maria Nikolaevna, and I am listening to you with great interest. But I . . . I confess, I am asking myself why you are telling me all this.'

Maria Nikolaevna made a slight movement on the settee.

'You are asking yourself? . . . Are you so bad at guessing? Or so modest?'

Sanin raised his head even higher.

'I am telling you all this,' she continued in a calm voice, which did not, however, match the expression on her face, 'because I like you very much; yes, don't be surprised, I am not joking; because, having met you, it would be unpleasant for me to think that you might remember me in a bad light . . . or perhaps not so much in a bad light – I don't care about that – but simply a wrong light. That is why I have inveigled you in here, and am remaining alone with you, and that is why I am talking so frankly. Yes, yes, frankly – I don't lie. And, please note this, Dimitry Pavlovich, I know that you are in love with someone else, that you plan to marry her . . . at least give me credit for my disinterestedness . . . but, by the way, here is the chance for you to say in your turn "*Cela ne tire pas à conséquence*".'

She laughed, but the laughter stopped abruptly, and she sat motionless, as if amazed by her own words; her eyes, usually so gay and so bold, showed for a moment a hint of shyness, even grief.

Oh, she's a snake, Sanin thought meanwhile, but what a beautiful snake!

'Give me my lorgnette,' Maria Nikolaevna said suddenly. 'I want to see if the leading lady is in fact as plain as she seems. Really, one might think that the authorities had selected her with a moral purpose – to prevent young men from being too much carried away!'

Sanin handed her the lorgnette: as she took it from him she quickly, but almost imperceptibly, placed both her hands on his.

'None of this solemnity, if you please,' she whispered with a smile. 'Do you know what? No one can put chains on me, but then I don't put chains on others. I love freedom and recognize no ties – and that goes not only for me. And now move up a little, and let us listen to the play.'

Maria Nikolaevna directed her lorgnette at the stage. Sanin began to look at the stage too, sitting by her side in the half-darkened box, and breathing in, however unwillingly, the warmth and the fragrance of her magnificent body, and equally unwillingly turning over in his mind everything she had said to him in the course of the evening – and especially during the last few minutes.

XL

THE play continued for another hour or more, but Maria Nikolaevna and Sanin soon stopped looking at the stage. Before long they started to talk again, and their conversation followed the same course as before: only this time Sanin was less silent. In his heart he was angry both with himself and with Maria Nikolaevna: he tried to prove to her how much her 'theory' lacked foundation – as if she was interested in theories! He began arguing with her, at which she was secretly very pleased: once he has started arguing, she thought, it means that he is giving in, or will give in. He is beginning to eat out of my hand, he is coming on, he no longer shies away! She argued back, laughed, agreed with him, reflected, attacked him ... and meanwhile their faces came closer, his eyes no longer evaded her gaze ... her eyes, as it were, wandered over, circled around his features, and he smiled back – politely, but still, he smiled. It suited her book very well that he should be indulging in abstractions: discussing honesty in mutual relationships, duty, the sanctity of love and marriage . . . It is a well-known fact, after all, that these abstractions are exceedingly useful as a start, as a point of departure . . .

Those who knew Madame Polozov well used to insist that whenever her powerful and vital personality suddenly showed signs of something like tenderness or modesty, something almost like virginal pudicity – though, when one thinks of it, where *did* these qualities come from? – then, why then, things were taking a dangerous turn!

It seems that things were taking just such a dangerous turn for Sanin . . . Had he been able to concentrate even for a moment, he would have despised himself. But he had no time for either concentration or for self-contempt.

She certainly lost no time – and all this was happening because he was not bad looking! One is indeed forced to say: 'Take heed you find not that you did not seek!'

The play came to an end. Maria Nikolaevna asked Sanin to throw her shawl about her, and stood motionless while he wrapped the soft fabric around her truly regal shoulders. Then she took his arm, went out into the corridor – and nearly screamed: right by the door of the box, like some kind of ghost, Doenhof was hovering. Behind his back was visible the odious figure of the Wiesbaden critic. The oily face of this '*Littérateur*' was positively radiant with malicious pleasure.

'Will you allow me, Madame, to find your carriage for you?' the young officer asked Maria Nikolaevna, his voice trembling with ill-concealed rage.

'No, thank you most kindly,' she replied, 'my servant will find it. Stay here,' she added in a whispered tone of command, and quickly made off, taking Sanin with her.

'Go to the devil! Why are you pestering me?' Doenhof suddenly barked at the '*Littérateur*'. He had to vent his rage on someone.

'*Sehr gut, sehr gut,*' murmured the literary gentleman, and made himself scarce.

Madame Polozov's servant was waiting in the foyer, and

immediately found her carriage. She jumped lightly into it; Sanin followed. The doors were briskly shut – and Maria Nikolaevna burst out laughing.

'Why are you laughing?' Sanin was curious to know.

'Oh, forgive me, please, but it has just occurred to me, suppose Doenhof should fight another duel with you . . . about me, this time . . .? Wouldn't that be fun?'

'Do you know him very well?' asked Sanin.

'Him? That boy? He's just my errand boy. You needn't worry.'

'Oh, I'm not at all worried.'

Maria Nikolaevna sighed.

'Ah, I know that you are not worried. But listen, you are such a dear boy, you must not refuse me a last request. Don't forget, in three days' time I am leaving for Paris, and you are returning to Frankfurt . . . When shall we ever meet again?'

'What is the request?'

'You ride, of course?'

'Yes.'

'Well, then. Tomorrow morning I will take you with me and we will ride out of town. We shall have excellent horses. Then we shall come back, finish our business, and amen! Don't be surprised, don't tell me that I am capricious or mad – all of which is quite possible – just say: "I agree." '

She turned her face towards him. It was dark in the carriage, but her eyes shone even in the darkness.

'As you please, I agree,' murmured Sanin with a sigh.

'Ah, you sighed!' Maria Nikolaevna mocked him. 'That means – "I have put my hand to the plough, I can't draw back." But no . . . no, no. You're delightful, you're a good man – and I will keep my promise. Here is my hand, my right hand, my business hand, with no glove on it. Take it and trust this handshake. I don't know what kind of a woman I am, but I am an honest human being . . . and you can trust me in business matters.'

Only half aware of what he was doing, Sanin put her hand

to his lips. She quietly withdrew it, and suddenly fell silent, and remained silent until the carriage stopped.

She began to dismount ... What was that? Did Sanin imagine it, or did he really feel a swift and burning touch on his cheek?

'Until tomorrow,' Maria Nikolaevna whispered to him, as they stood on the stairs which were all illuminated by the four candles of a candelabra which a gold-bedecked porter had grasped as soon as she appeared. She kept her eyes lowered. 'Until tomorrow.'

When he returned to his room, Sanin found a letter from Gemma on the table. For a moment he took fright ... and then immediately was overjoyed, the more quickly to hide his alarm from himself. The letter consisted of a few lines. She was pleased about the successful start of the 'business', counselled him to be patient, and added that all were well at home, and were looking forward to his return. Sanin found the tone of the letter a little dry. However, he picked up pen and paper – and then threw them aside. 'What's the point of writing? I shall be back tomorrow ... It's high time, high time.'

He went to bed immediately, and tried to get to sleep as soon as possible. Had he stayed up and awake he would certainly have started thinking about Gemma – and for some reason he felt too ashamed to think of her. His conscience was troubling him. But he comforted himself with the thought that tomorrow everything would be over for all time, and then he would say goodbye for ever to this crazy woman, and forget all this nonsense! When weak people talk to themselves, they are fond of using forceful turns of speech. *Et puis ... Cela ne tire pas à conséquence!*

XLI

THAT is what Sanin thought as he went to bed. But history does not relate what he thought on the following day when Maria Nikolaevna knocked impatiently at his door with the coral handle of her riding switch; when he saw her on the threshold of his room, holding the train of her dark blue riding habit over her arm, a small, masculine hat on her thick, plaited hair, a veil thrown over her shoulder, and with a provocative smile on her lips, in her eyes, on her whole face – this history does not relate.

'Well, are you ready?' her voice rang out gaily.

Sanin quickly buttoned his coat, and picked up his hat, without saying a word. Maria Nikolaevna threw him a radiant glance, nodded and ran quickly down the stairs. And he ran after her. The horses were already standing in front of the porch. There were three of them. For Madame Polozov, a pure-bred golden chestnut mare, somewhat lean, but beautiful, and as spirited as fire. She had delicate legs like those of a deer, a spare, fine-boned muzzle, showing the teeth a little, and black, slightly prominent eyes. For Sanin a powerful, broad, rather heavy black steed without markings; the third horse was intended for the groom.

Maria Nikolaevna sprang lightly on to her mare ... the animal pawed the ground and began to circle, raising its tail and pressing up its haunches, but Maria Nikolaevna (who was an excellent horsewoman) kept her collected.

It was necessary to take leave of Polozov, who, with his fez, from which he was never parted, and with his dressing-gown thrown open, appeared on the balcony, waving a lawn handkerchief. He was not smiling, however, but almost frowning. Sanin also mounted. Maria Nikolaevna waved to her husband with her switch, and then struck the flat, arched neck of her mare. The mare reared, leapt forward and then began to step out in tiny, short, collected paces, trembling all over and mouthing at the bit, snatching at the air and snorting violently. Sanin rode behind, observing Maria Nikolaevna: her elegant, supple figure, closely corseted but unconstrained, swayed gracefully, effortlessly and confidently as she rode. She turned her head and signed to him with a look. He drew level with her.

'Well, there you are, you see how wonderful it is,' she said. 'Let me tell you this, now that the party is coming to an end, and before we finally separate: you are delightful – and you won't regret this.'

As she spoke, she nodded her head several times, as if in confirmation of her words and to make him feel their significance.

She seemed so utterly happy that Sanin was amazed. Her face even showed that placid expression that can sometimes be seen on the faces of children, when they are very, very pleased. They walked their horses to the town limit, which was not far away, and then broke into a brisk canter along the highway. The weather was superb, a real summer's day: the wind rushed at them as they rode, and roared and whistled agreeably in their ears. Life was good. Both were possessed by a sense of young and healthy vitality and of the bounding freedom of the ride. Their sense of well-being increased with every instant.

Maria Nikolaevna reined in her horse, and once again set off at a walk. Sanin followed her example.

'There,' she began with a deep and blissful sigh, 'this is the only thing that makes life worth living. If you have succeeded in doing something you wanted to do, something that seemed impossible – well, then, make the most of it, with all your heart, to the very brim.' She drew her hand across her throat. 'And how kind one feels when it happens! Now take me – how kind I am at this moment. I feel I could embrace the whole world! Well, no, not the whole world ... I don't think I could embrace him' – she pointed with her whip at an old beggar, who was making his way along the side of the road. 'But I am ready to make him happy. Here, take this!'

she called out loudly in German, and threw a purse at his feet. The heavy little bag (in those days, no one had even thought of the modern form of purse) fell on the road with a thud. The passer-by was astonished and stopped, while Maria Nikolaevna burst into a roar of laughter, and set her horse off at a gallop.

'Do you find riding so amusing?' asked Sanin, when he had overtaken her.

Maria Nikolaevna once again reined in her mare with a sharp movement, as she always did when she wished to stop her.

'All I wanted to do was to get away from gratitude. As soon as someone starts thanking me all the pleasure is gone. After all, I didn't do it for him, but for myself. So how dare he thank me? I didn't catch what you said, what were you asking me?'

'I was asking . . . I wanted to know why you are so gay today.'

'Do you know what?' said Maria Nikolaevna, who had either not heard what Sanin had asked her, or else did not think it necessary to answer his question. 'I am very bored with the groom hanging around; I expect that all he's thinking of is when the gentry will decide to go home. How can we get rid of him?' She swiftly produced a note-book from her pocket. 'Shall we send him back to town with a letter? No . . . that will not do. Ah? I've got it. What is that over there? An inn?'

Sanin glanced in the direction she had indicated.

'Yes, it looks like an inn.'

'Splendid! I shall tell him to stay at this inn and drink beer until we return.'

'But what will he think?'

'What's that to do with us? In any case, he won't even think: he will just drink beer.'

'Well, Sanin' (it was the first time that she had addressed him by his surname alone), 'forward, at the canter!'

When they had drawn up at the inn, Maria Nikolaevna called the groom over and gave him his orders. The groom, a man of English origin and English temperament, said nothing, raised his hand to his cap, jumped off his horse and took hold of the reins.

'Well, now we are as free as the birds!' Maria Nikolaevna exclaimed. 'Where shall we make for? The north, the south, the east or the west? Look – I am like the King of Hungary at his coronation ceremony' (she pointed with the end of her whip at the four corners of the earth). 'It's all ours! No, do you know what? Do you see these wonderful hills, and what wonderful hills they are, and what woods! Let us ride up there to the hills, to the hills! *In die Berge, wo die Freiheit thront!*'[1]

She turned off the road and galloped along the narrow, uneven path, which seemed indeed to lead up to the mountains. Sanin galloped after her.

XLII

THE path soon turned into a track and eventually disappeared completely, barred by a ditch. Sanin advised turning back, but Maria Nikolaevna said 'No! I want to go to the mountains. Let's go straight on, as the birds do!' and put her horse over the ditch. Sanin also jumped. Beyond the ditch was a meadow, which was dry at first, then became rather wet, and finally completely marshy. Water was welling up everywhere, forming big puddles. Maria Nikolaevna purposely put her horse at the puddles, laughing heartily and saying repeatedly: 'Let's go mad!'

'Do you know,' she asked Sanin, 'what splash-hunting means?'[1]

'Yes,' Sanin replied.

'My uncle used to splash-hunt with dogs,' she continued. 'I used to go out with him, on horseback, in the spring. Wonderful! Now you and I will go splash-hunting – the only thing is that here are you, a Russian, but you want to marry an Italian. Well, what of it – that's your funeral! What's this, another ditch? Up!'

The horse jumped the ditch, but Maria Nikolaevna's hat fell off and her hair tumbled all over her shoulders. Sanin was about to dismount to retrieve the hat, but she called out to him: 'Don't move, I'll get it myself', bent low from the saddle, caught the veil with the handle of her whip, and did indeed seize the hat. She put it on, but did not gather up her hair, and was off again at the gallop, even uttering a shout as she went.

Sanin sped along beside her, jumped at her side over ditches, fences and streams, tumbled through them and scrambled up again, flying around the hills, into the hills, and looking at her face all the time.

And what a face it is! It is all, as it were, open, the eyes are open, predatory, bright and wild; the lips and nostrils are open too, breathing avidly. She keeps her eyes steadily fixed in front of her, and it seems as if this creature wishes to be mistress of everything she sees before her – the earth, the sky, the sun and the very air – and regrets one thing only, that there are not enough dangers – she would surmount them all. 'Sanin!' she shouts. 'Why, this is just like Buerger's *Lenore*,[2] only you're not dead, or are you? Not dead? Not dead . . .? *I* am alive!'

Wild forces are now in play. Here is no Amazon putting her steed to the gallop – a young female Centaur gallops along, half-beast and half-goddess. The placid and well-bred German countryside lies amazed at the trample of her wild Russian Bacchanalia.

At last Maria Nikolaevna drew in her horse: it was covered with foam and sweat, and swayed under her. Sanin's powerful but heavy mount was also breathing hard.

'Well, is it good?'[3] whispered Maria Nikolaevna with some kind of magic in her voice.

'It is good,' the elated Sanin rejoined. His blood was also aflame.

'You wait, you don't know what's coming.' She stretched out her hand. The glove was torn.

'I said I would bring you to the forest, to the mountains.

There they are, the mountains!' She was right. Some two hundred paces beyond the point where these bold riders had emerged rose the mountains. They were covered with tall trees. 'Look, there is the path, let us collect ourselves, and go on. But at a walk, we must let the horses recover their breath.'

They set off. Maria Nikolaevna threw back her hair with one strong sweep of her hand. Then she looked at her gloves and drew them off.

'My hands will smell of leather. But you don't mind, do you?'

She was smiling and Sanin was smiling too. This mad gallop seemed finally to have brought them together and made them friends.

'How old are you?' she asked suddenly.

'Twenty-two.'

'No! I am also twenty-two. A good age! Add our years together and it's still a long way from old age. But it's hot! I suppose my face is all red?'

'As red as a poppy.'

She wiped her face with a handkerchief.

'Once we get into the forest we shall be cool. What an old forest it is – like an old friend. Have you any friends?'

Sanin thought for a moment.

'Yes ... But not very many. No real friends.'

'Well, I have some real friends – but not very old ones. This mare – she's a friend, too. How carefully she carries me. Oh, how wonderful it is here. Am I really going to Paris the day after tomorrow?'

'Yes, is it possible?'

'And you will be going to Frankfurt?'

'Yes, I am certainly going to Frankfurt.'

'Well, good luck to you! But this day is ours ... ours ...'

*

The horses reached a glade and entered. The shadow of the forest closed in on them from every side, soft and expansive.

'Oh, but this is paradise!' Maria Nikolaevna exclaimed. 'Come on, Sanin, deeper, farther into the shade!'

The horses moved quietly 'deeper into the shade', swaying and blowing a little. The path along which they were moving suddenly turned, and led into a narrow gully. A powerful, soporific scent of heather, ferns, pine resin and of last year's decaying leaves pervaded the place. From the crevasses between the brown rocks, a strong sense of dampness assailed them. On each side of the little path rose round mounds covered with green moss.

'Stop!' exclaimed Maria Nikolaevna. 'I want to sit down and rest on this velvet. Help me down!'

Sanin jumped off his horse and ran towards her. She leaned on his shoulders, jumped swiftly to the ground and sat down on one of the mossy clumps. He stood in front of her, holding the reins of both horses.

She looked up at him.

'Sanin, do you know how to forget?'

Sanin remembered what had happened the night before in the carriage.

'What is this – a question or a reproach?'

'I have never reproached anyone in all my life. Do you believe in love charms?'

'What do you mean?'

'Love charms. You know, the kind that they talk about in our folk-songs, in the Russian peasant songs.'

'Oh, that's what you mean,' Sanin said slowly.

'Yes, that. I believe in them, and so will you.'

'Love charms? That's a kind of folk magic,' repeated Sanin. 'Everything in life is possible. I never believed in them, but now I do. I don't recognize myself.'

Maria Nikolaevna was thoughtful for a while, and then looked about her.

'Do you know, I have the impression that I know this spot. Have a look, Sanin, is there a red wooden cross behind that broad oak tree – or am I wrong?'

Sanin took a few paces to the side.

'Yes, yes, there is.'

Maria Nikolaevna grinned.

'Ah, good, very good. I know where we are, we are not lost so far. What is that knocking? A wood-cutter?'

Sanin looked into the woods.

'Yes, there's a man chopping down the dry branches.'

'I must put my hair in order,' said Maria Nikolaevna. 'He might see me and think the worst of me.' She removed her hat and began to plait her long hair, silently, solemnly. Sanin stood in front of her . . . the contours of her handsome limbs were clearly apparent to him under the dark folds of the cloth to which some strands of moss were clinging.

Suddenly one of the horses gave a shudder behind Sanin's back, Sanin too trembled involuntarily from head to foot. Everything was confounded inside him – his senses were as tense as strings. He had been right when he said he could not recognize himself. He was, in fact, bewitched. His whole being was filled with . . . one thought and one desire. Maria Niko-laevna glanced at him searchingly.

'Well, everything is now as it should be,' she said, putting on her hat. 'Won't you sit down? Here. No, wait . . . don't sit down. What is that?'

A dull, quaking sound rolled over the tops of the trees and through the forest air.

'Can that be thunder?'

'It sounds like thunder,' said Sanin.

'Well, well, what could be better, this is a real holiday! That's the only thing that was missing.'

The dull boom sounded again. It rose through the air, then fell, scattering itself in full force.

'Bravo! *Bis!* Do you remember I was telling you yesterday

about the *Aeneid*? They were also overtaken by a storm in the woods. However, we must get away.' She jumped to her feet. 'Bring my horse up, will you . . . Give me a leg-up – that's right . . . I'm not heavy . . .' She swung into the saddle like a bird. Sanin also mounted his horse.

'Are you going home?' he asked in a faltering voice.

'Home!!' she replied, dwelling on the word, and then gathered up the reins. 'Follow me!' she ordered, almost brutally. She moved out on to the path, avoiding the red cross, rode down a hollow, reached an intersection, turned right, and then uphill once again . . . Evidently she knew where she was going . . . and the way she took led farther and farther into the depths of the forest. She did not say a word, and did not look round; she moved forward imperiously, and he followed, obedient and submissive, drained of every spark of will and with his heart in his mouth. A few drops of rain began to fall. She quickened the pace of her horse, he kept close behind her. At last, through the dark greenery of the pine brush, he caught a glimpse of a woodman's humble shelter, with a low door in its wattle wall, set under an overhanging grey rock. Maria Nikolaevna forced her horse through the brush, jumped to the ground and found herself by the entrance to the hut. Turning to Sanin she whispered: 'Aeneas!'

Four hours later Maria Nikolaevna and Sanin, accompanied by the groom, who was nodding in the saddle, returned to Wiesbaden to the the hotel.

Polozov came forward to greet his wife, holding in his hand the letter to the estate manager. However, having taken a closer look at her, he showed a certain displeasure in his expression – and even muttered:

'Surely I haven't lost my bet?'

Maria Nikolaevna merely shrugged her shoulders.

*

And on the same day, two hours later, Sanin stood before her in his room, like a lost man, a man destroyed.

'So where are you going?' she was asking him. 'To Paris, or to Frankfurt?'

'I am going wherever you are, and I will be with you until you drive me away,' he replied in despair, and pressed himself against the hands of his sovereign mistress. She released her hands, placed them on his head and seized his hair with all ten fingers. Slowly she handled and twisted his unresponsive hair ... She drew herself up, quite straight. Her lips curled in triumph. Her eyes, so wide and shining that they looked almost white, showed only the pitiless torpor of one sated with victory. A hawk clawing at a bird caught in its talons sometimes has this look in its eyes.

XLIII

THIS is what Dimitry Sanin remembered when, on going through his old papers in the quiet of his study, he found the little garnet cross among them. The events which I have related appeared clearly and in their proper order before his mind's eye. But, when he came to the moment when he had turned imploringly to Madame Polozov, when he had so far abased himself, when he had thrown himself at her feet, when his enslavement had begun – then he turned aside from the images which he had conjured up; he did not wish to remember more. Not that his recollection was unclear – oh no! He knew, he knew all too well everything that had happened after that moment, but shame stifled him, even then, so many years later. He was afraid of the feeling of self-contempt which he knew he could not conquer, and which he knew beyond doubt would wash over him, and, like a tidal wave, drown all other sensations, as soon as he allowed his memory to speak. But try as he might to turn away from the mental images which welled up inside him, he was powerless to obliterate them all.

He remembered the wretched, lachrymose, lying, miserable letter which he had sent to Gemma and which remained unanswered ... To appear before her, to return to her, after such deceit, after so great a betrayal – no, no, no! He had had enough conscience and honour left not to do that. Besides, he had lost all confidence in himself and all self-respect, he would no longer have been responsible for anything that might have happened. Sanin also recalled how later – oh, shame, shame! – he had dispatched the Polozovs' servant to Frankfurt to fetch his things, how afraid he had been, with only one thought in his mind: to Paris, to Paris, to get to Paris as soon as possible! Then, how on Madame Polozov's orders, he had made himself agreeable to her husband and tried to adapt to his ways – and had exchanged politenesses with Doenhof, on whose finger he observed an iron ring, identical with the one that Maria Nikolaevna had presented to him! There followed recollections which were even worse, even more shaming ...

A waiter hands him a visiting card – and on it is engraved the name of Pantaleone Cippatola, Court Singer to His Royal Highness, the Duke of Modena. He tries to hide from the old man, but cannot escape a meeting in the passage. And now there rises before him an indignant face beneath a mane of upstanding grey hair: the old eyes burn like coals of fire, and the air resounds with terrible admonitions and maledictions – *maledizione!* There are some frightening words, too: *Cobardo! Infame traditore!* Sanin closes his eyes and shakes his head, trying again and again to shut out the memories. And yet, now he sees himself seated in a travelling *dormeuse*, on the narrow front seat. On the rear and comfortable seat recline Polozov and his wife. Four well-matched horses are bearing them at the canter along the Wiesbaden road – to Paris! To Paris! Ippolit Sidorych Polozov is eating a pear which he, Sanin, has just peeled for him, while Maria Nikolaevna gazes at him and mocks him with a smile which, as a bondsman or serf, he already knows so well – the smile of the serf owner, of the sovereign lord and master ...

And, oh God! Is that not Pantaleone again, standing at the corner of the street, not far from the limits of the town? And who is that with him? Can it be Emilio? Yes, it is he, that boy who was so full of enthusiasm and devotion. Why, only the other day his young heart was ready to worship his hero, his ideal – and now? His pale and beautiful face – so beautiful a face that Maria Nikolaevna notices it and leans out of the carriage window – this noble face is now ablaze with anger and contempt; his eyes – so like *those* eyes – are riveted on Sanin and his lips are tight – and then open suddenly to utter an insult . . .

And Pantaleone extends his arm and points out Sanin – to whom? – why, to Tartaglia, who is standing at his side, and Tartaglia barks at Sanin: the very bark of this honest dog sounds like the hardest insult of all to bear . . . Oh terrible, terrible!

And then, life in Paris, all the degradations and vile sufferings of a slave, who is not permitted either to be jealous or to complain, and who is discarded in the end like a worn-out garment . . . Then, the return to Russia, the poisoned life, emptied of all meaning, the petty flurries and the petty worries, the bitter and fruitless contrition, and the equally fruitless and bitter oblivion – the punishment, although it was not evident, was constant, every minute of the day, like some insignificant but incurable pain, a repayment in farthings of a debt which cannot even be calculated . . .

The cup is overflowing – enough!

What strange chance had preserved the little cross which Gemma gave to Sanin? Why had he not returned it? How had it happened that he had not discovered it until today? He sat for a long, long, time, plunged in thought and, for all that experience had taught him over so many years, was still quite unable to understand how he had been capable of abandoning

Gemma, whom he had loved so tenderly and passionately, for a woman whom he had never loved at all. The next day he surprised all his friends and acquaintances: he announced that he was leaving for abroad.

Society was at a complete loss. Sanin was leaving Petersburg, right in the middle of winter, having only just rented and furnished excellent chambers, and having even taken a season ticket for the performances of Italian opera, in which Madame Patti herself – her very self – Madame Patti in person, was going to appear. His friends and acquaintances were at a loss – but people are not generally given to concerning themselves for long with the affairs of others. And so, when Sanin departed for abroad, there was no one to see him off at the railway station except for a French tailor – and he had only come in the hope of being paid for a little unsettled account '*pour un saut-en-barque en velours noir, tout à fait chic*'.

XLIV

SANIN told his friends that he was going abroad, but did not tell them precisely where he was going. My readers will easily guess that he made his way straight to Frankfurt. Thanks to the widespread expansion of the railway system, he was already there on the fourth day after leaving St Petersburg. He had not visited the town since that very year of 1840. The White Swan Hotel was still in the same spot, and flourishing, but was no longer considered first-class. Frankfurt's main street, the Zeile, had changed very little. But there was no trace left of Signora Roselli's house, nor indeed of the street where her patisserie had once stood. Sanin wandered in a daze through places that had once been so familiar, and could recognize nothing. The buildings that had been there had disappeared, and their place had been taken by new streets, flanked by enormous houses, one adjacent to the other, and by elegant villas. Even the public park, the scene of the avowals of mutual love between him and Gemma, had grown so large and was so changed, that Sanin had to ask himself whether it really was the same place. What was he to do? How, and where was he to make inquiries? After all, thirty years had passed since those days . . . it was no easy matter. No one of whom he inquired had ever heard the name Roselli. The owner of his hotel advised him to ask at the public library where they would have the old newspapers. But what use they might be the hotel owner was unable to explain.

In despair, Sanin inquired after Herr Klueber. This name was well known to his host – but once again, the search was no further advanced. The elegant shop-walker, after resounding success in commerce which raised him to the status of a capitalist, had over-reached himself, gone bankrupt, and died in prison . . . This information, incidentally, did not cause Sanin the least distress. He was beginning to think that his journey might have been somewhat precipitate . . . and then one day, while he was idly turning over the pages of a Frankfurt street directory, he happened upon the name von Doenhof, Major, retired (*Major a.D.*). He immediately took a carriage, and drove to the address – though why should *this* Doenhof necessarily be *that* Doenhof? And in any case, why should *that* Doenhof be able to give him any information about the Roselli family? But, no matter, A drowning man clutches at a straw.

Sanin found Major von Doenhof (retired) at home, and immediately recognized his former duelling opponent in the grey-haired man who received him. Doenhof likewise recognized Sanin, and was even pleased to see him: he brought back memories of his youth and of its follies. Sanin learned from him that the Roselli family had long, long ago moved to America, to New York; that Gemma had married a business-man; that, incidentally, he, Doenhof, had an acquaintance, also a businessman, who would probably know the address of Gemma's husband, since he had many commercial dealings with America. Sanin persuaded Doenhof to go round to see his acquaintance and – oh joy! – Doenhof brought him the address of Gemma's husband, Mr Jeremiah Slocum: Mr J. Slocum, New York, Broadway, No. 501. Unfortunately, the address dated from 1863.

'Let us hope,' exclaimed Doenhof, 'that our one-time Frankfurt beauty is still alive and has not left New York! Incidentally,' he added, dropping his voice, 'what about that Russian lady? The one who was then, you remember, on a visit to Wiesbaden – Frau von Bo . . . von Bozoloff – is she still alive?'

'No,' replied Sanin, 'she died years ago.'

Doenhof looked up but, noticing that Sanin had turned away with a frown, did not say another word and withdrew.

That same day, Sanin sent a letter to Mrs Gemma Slocum in New York. He told her that he was writing from Frankfurt, having come there for the sole purpose of discovering some trace of her; that he was only too conscious of the degree to which he had lost the slightest right to expect any answer from her, that he had done nothing to deserve her forgiveness; and that his only hope was that in the midst of the happiness with which she was surrounded, she had long forgotten his very existence. He added that he had plucked up the courage to remind her of himself as a result of a chance circumstance which had only too vividly brought back to him the image of past events; he told her about his life, his solitary life, without family and without joy; implored her to understand the reasons which had moved him to write, and not to let him carry with him to his grave the bitter sense of his guilt – long paid for in suffering, yet not forgiven; and asked her to bring him some happiness by sending him even the briefest account of her life in the new distant world to which she had removed. 'If you write me even one word,' so Sanin concluded his letter, 'you will be doing a good deed, worthy of your fine and generous spirit, and I will thank you for it until I draw my last breath. I am staying here, in the *White Swan Hotel* (he underlined the name) and I will wait – I will wait until the spring for your answer.'

He dispatched the letter and began his vigil. He lived for six whole weeks in the hotel, hardly leaving his room, and seeing absolutely no one. No one could possibly write to him, from Russia or from anywhere else. This was just what he wanted: if a letter should arrive addressed to him, he would know at once that it was *the* letter, the one he was waiting for. He read from morning till night – not the journals, but serious books, works of history. This long period of reading, the silence, the hermit life of the snail in its shell, were all exactly what best suited his state of mind – for that alone he was grateful to Gemma. But was she alive? Would she answer his letter?

It arrived at last: a letter with an American postage stamp, addressed to him from New York. The handwriting on the envelope was English in style. He did not recognize it, and his heart sank . . . It was some time before he could summon up courage to open the letter. He glanced at the signature: Gemma! Tears started from his eyes: the very fact that she had signed her Christian name alone without surname meant for him an earnest of forgiveness and reconciliation. He unfolded the thin blue sheet of writing paper, and as he did so a photograph slipped out. He quickly picked it up – and was rooted to the spot with amazement. It was Gemma, Gemma to the life, and young as he had known her thirty years before. The eyes, the lips were the same, it was the same face. The back of the photograph was inscribed with the words, 'My daughter Marianna'.

The whole letter was friendly and simple. Gemma thanked Sanin for not hesitating to turn to her, for showing trust in her; she did not conceal from him that, after his flight, she had lived through some painful moments, but added at once that, for all that, she regarded and had always regarded her meeting with him as a source of happiness, since it had prevented her from becoming the wife of Herr Klueber, and thus, if only indirectly, had been the cause of her marriage; that she had lived for over twenty-seven years with her husband in complete happiness, contentment and prosperity: their house was known all over New York. Gemma informed Sanin that she had five children, four sons and an eighteen-year-old daughter, engaged to be married: she enclosed her photograph because, by general consent, they were very much alike. Sad news was reserved for the end. Frau Lenore had died in New York, where she had moved to join her daughter and son-in-law, but she had lived long enough to derive pleasure from the happiness of her children and to enjoy her grandchildren. Pantaleone had also made plans to move to New York, but had died just before he was due to leave Frankfurt. 'And Emilio, our darling, incomparable Emilio, died a hero's death for the freedom of his country in Sicily, where he had been numbered among that thousand who were led by the great Garibaldi. We shed many tears at the death of our brother, who was very dear to us; but even as we wept, we felt proud of him, and we will be eternally proud of him, and we keep his memory sacred. His noble, selfless spirit was worthy of a martyr's crown.' Then Gemma expressed her regret that Sanin's life seemed to have unfolded so unhappily, wished him, above all, consolation and peace of spirit, and said that she would be glad to meet him again, although she realized that such a meeting was most unlikely to prove possible . . .

I cannot attempt to describe what Sanin felt when he read this letter. There are no phrases adequate for such feelings: they are deeper and stronger than any words, and cannot be defined. Music alone could convey them.

Sanin replied at once. As a present for the young bride, he sent 'Marianna Slocum, from an unknown friend' the little garnet cross set in a magnificent pearl necklace. This present, although very costly, did not ruin him: in the course of the thirty years which had passed since his first stay in Frankfurt, he had had time to amass a considerable fortune. In the early days of May he returned to St Petersburg – but hardly for long. They say that he is selling all his estates and is planning to move to America.

Notes

1. This song cannot be traced. It is most probable that Turgenev followed his practice of making it up and disguising it as a quotation. Cf. Notes to pp. 51 and 162.
2. *Taedium vitae* was not a frequent or usual Latin phrase. It is only known to occur once in literature – in the *Noctes Atticae* of Aulus Gellius, Book VI Section 18. Possibly Turgenev was led to the phrase by recalling lines 450–51 of Book IV of the *Aeneid*:

> *Tum vero infelix fatis exterrita Dido*
> *Mortem orat, taedet coeli convexa tueri.*

Book IV of the *Aeneid* forms a central element in Chapters XXXIX and XLII of *Spring Torrents;* and we know from his correspondence that Turgenev was rereading the *Aeneid* in the early years of the 1870s.

3. This description of life's 'ocean' is probably a reminiscence of Schopenhauer's *The World as Will and Idea*. The question of Schopenhauer's influence on Turgenev is discussed briefly on pp. 209–11 and 212–13.

CHAPTER 5

1. Pantaleone's equivalent for *Verfluchter Spitzbube,* 'confounded guttersnipe'.
2. 'Tuscan speech in a Roman mouth'.
3. Tuscan folk-songs.

CHAPTER 6

1. Vladimir Grigorievich Benediktov (1807–73) published a volume of poems in 1835 which met with almost universal success and acclamation among the young Russian intellectuals. Turgenev was among the admirers of these rather superficial and sentimental

poems at the time. The only severe note of dissent on Benediktov was struck by Belinsky, the critic, in an article in *The Telescope*.

2. The great Garcia was the father of Pauline Viardot, the object of Turgenev's lifelong adoration. Garcia was particularly noted as an interpreter of Rossini, as was indeed Pauline Viardot, who made her debuts both in London and in Paris as Desdemona in his *Otello*. Turgenev was presumably quoting from memory because the libretto of the duet is not quite as he gives it:

> Otello: *L'ira d'avverso fato*
> *io più non temerò*
> *morrò, ma vendicato*
> *si – dopo lei morrò.*
>
> Iago: (*L'ira d'avverso fato*
> *Temer più non dovrò;*
> *Io son gia vendicato,*
> *Di lui triunferò.*)

3. 'The land of Dante where the sì is sounded.'
4. 'Abandon all hope.'

CHAPTER 12

1. Gemma evidently had in mind one of Hoffmann's late and particularly involved tales, in which the real and the fantastic are so intermingled as to be almost indistinguishable. The story in question is '*Die Irrungen. Fragment aus dem Leben eines Phantasten*', which was published in 1821. It is indeed concerned with the pursuit by the hero of a beautiful Greek girl who is in the power of a magician; and there is in fact a scene in a tea-room. But the story is very different from Gemma's simple, sentimental version; and ends with the hero in full flight from the girl.

CHAPTER 13

1. The reference is to one of the *Romanzen* (Romances) of Johann Ludwig Uhland (1787–1862) '*Das Schifflein*' ('The Little Ship').
2. *Tresette* is an ancient game of Neapolitan origin, played with a pack of forty cards – the three, the two, and the ace being the highest in value, in that order. Scoring is by tricks and by the

declaration of a hand – a 'neapolitan', for example, which consists of three, two and ace, scores three points if declared. There are penalties for such offences as revoking and wrong declarations (see Chapter 19). The rules of the game seem a good deal more complex to the translator than they appeared to Sanin and Turgenev – see *Enciclopedia Italiana*, Volume XVII, pp. 349–50.

CHAPTER 15

1. This extraordinary work actually exists: it was published in 1841 and went into three editions. It contained 250 'interesting anecdotes' according to the subtitle, and was edited by Fr Rabener.

CHAPTER 17

1. This doggerel also seems to have been Turgenev's own composition. He used it first (in slightly different form) in 1842 in a sketch entitled 'The Adventures of Second Lieutenant Bubnov'.

CHAPTER 22

1. This is the last line of Canto XXIX of Chapter Six of Pushkin's *Eugene Onegin*, when the duel between Onegin and Lensky, in which the romantic poet and lover Lensky is killed, is described.
2. '*Fuori*' is said to be the equivalent of '*fora*', which was the form of 'bravo' in customary use in Italy when Pantaleone was still on the stage. But it could also mean 'from force of habit' in the sense of performing Napoleon and Bernadotte with the poodle Tartaglia, which, it will be recalled, ended with the poodle's stern dismissal with the exclamation '*fuori!*'

CHAPTER 26

1. This is a quotation, somewhat inexact, from a poem by L. A. Mei, forming one of his cycle of 'Hebrew Songs', published in 1849.

CHAPTER 34

1. A very hackneyed quotation from Act II Scene I of Griboyedov's *Woe from Wit*.

CHAPTER 38

1. 'Prince Kovrizhkin' was Turgenev's name for Prince P. A. Vyazemsky, as indeed Vyazemsky knew. There is a further jibe at Prince Kovrizhkin in *Virgin Soil*, chapter XIV, where he calls him an 'enthusiastic lackey'. Turgenev's attacks on Vyazemsky, a friend of Pushkin, seem to have been based solely on the fact that he had abandoned the oppositional activities of his youth and accepted office in the government: the suggestion in this paragraph that he contributed to the reactionary and odious government paper *Northern Bee* is particularly wounding.

2. Natalia Naryshkina, the mother of Peter the Great, came from a relatively humble boyar family, but was certainly not of peasant origin, as Maria Nikolaevna implies.

CHAPTER 39

1. Turgenev's attack on the Wiesbaden Theatre of 1840 is to be explained by personal animosity. Actually, the old Wiesbaden Theatre (demolished in the 1890s) enjoyed a reputation for beauty, which contemporary photographs seem to confirm. However, Turgenev was obviously less concerned in this paragraph with the Wiesbaden Theatre than with seizing an opportunity to attack Philipp Eduard Devrient, who was the director of the Karlsruhe Theatre from 1852 until 1870. In this capacity he produced in January 1870 the operetta 'The Last Sorcerer', for which Pauline Viardot wrote the music and Turgenev the libretto, and in which Pauline sang the main part. The production was a failure, and Turgenev, rightly or wrongly, ascribed the blame for the failure to the ill will of Devrient – as we know from his letter to Ludwig Pietsch of 17 February 1870. What Turgenev resented was not so much criticism of his libretto, but disparagement of Pauline. It is perhaps fortunate that Turgenev did not know of the entry which Devrient made in his diary (which was published ninety-four years later) with reference to the production: 'the Viardot herself with her cracked voice was the only disturbing element in the production.' Devrient seems to have been a competent rather than an imaginative producer. As regards the Wiesbaden stage in 1840, since von Bose, the Director, was required to produce one new

full-scale opera, one drama, one vaudeville, as well as two comedies in the course of the six-week season, Turgenev's description of the play and the acting may not have been far off the mark.

2. Hired toady.

3. Although the author does not say so, Maria Nikolaevna's father must almost certainly have been a serf, and she would have spent her childhood among the serfs.

CHAPTER 41

1. 'To the mountains, where Freedom is enthroned.' All efforts by successive editors to trace this quotation have failed, which raises the suspicion that it was made up by the author. The suspicion is strengthened by the fact that in the first fair copy which he made Turgenev wrote '*In die Berge, wo die Freiheit wohnt*' (dwells) and altered the word to '*thront*' in the second or third fair copy (the second is lost).

CHAPTER 42

1. 'Splash hunting' is a country phrase meaning game shooting in the early spring when the snows first begin to melt.

2. *Lenore* was a very popular ballad, written by Gottfried August Buerger, and published in 1773. A whole literature on it exists – there are twenty-six items on it listed in the catalogue of the British Museum Library and there are several translations into English, including one by Dante Gabriele Rossetti. While Lenore is lamenting the failure of her Wilhelm to return from the wars, and decrying God's justice, Wilhelm appears at her doorstep on horseback. He declares his intention to take her to their bridal chamber. After a wild and terrifying ride they arrive in a graveyard and both Wilhelm and the horse turn into skeletons. The ballad ends with a moral homily about not questioning the ways of God.

3. The Russian word for 'good', '*liubo*', which she uses is a peasant expression, with undertones of folk tale, which cannot be reproduced in translation.

Critical Essay – Spring Torrents

Its Place and Significance in the Life and Work of Ivan Sergeyevich Turgenev

THE action of *Spring Torrents* takes place in the summer of 1840. The story is in the form of recollection of past events thirty years later by the hero, Sanin. As will become apparent in the course of this essay, Sanin in certain respects stands for Turgenev himself; and the story is in some degree autobiographical. It is therefore important to establish the exact time when *Spring Torrents* was being composed, so that the significance of both the years around 1840 and of the period when Turgenev was working on this short novel can be assessed in relation to the author's life, and to his intellectual and emotional development.

The first reference in Turgenev's correspondence to the 'nouvelle' which was to become *Spring Torrents* is in a letter dated 27 September 1870* to William Ralston, his English translator. He referred to a new book 'in hand' which he hoped to show Ralston in London in about a month's time. The letter was dated from Baden-Baden, where Turgenev had been living fairly constantly, though with long absences, mainly in Russia, since 1863. Of two quite short earlier stories, one (*King Lear of the Steppes*) was finished on 21 March 1870, and the other (*Knock, knock, knock*) was written during August and September 1870, and revised in the course of October. It would therefore seem reasonable to date the beginning of work on *Spring Torrents* around the middle of 1870 or perhaps

* The dates throughout are the Russian ones, which are twelve days behind those of Western Europe.

a little earlier – in other words, to assume that he embarked on it soon after completing the one story, and interrupted his work on it to write the second story.

Turgenev's forecast of the date of completion proved much too optimistic. On 4 December 1870, writing from London, he informs his editor, M. M. Stasiulevich, that he might be able to bring him a finished new work for publication in serial form when he reached St Petersburg in a month's time. But it took a whole year before the manuscript was made available for publication in the *European Herald*, having been dispatched in final form on 26 November 1871. Turgenev had meanwhile moved from Baden-Baden to London, along with the Viardot household – the outbreak of the Franco-Prussian War had made it impossible for Viardot to remain any longer in Germany.* The reason for the delay in completing the novel appears from Turgenev's correspondence – the meticulous care and effort which were lavished on the composition of this work. 'I have set about finishing my story in a positive frenzy – you shall have the manuscript in a month,' he writes to his friend and literary intermediary Annenkov on 12 April 1871, from London; but already by 27 May 'My cursed story is stretching like elastic. The devil only knows when I shall finish it!' Evidently the long short story was turning into a short novel (the Russian word '*povest*' can apply to either). 'An infinity of care has been lavished on this thing,' he writes to Annenkov, 'let us hope that all the effort will not prove to have been in vain.' And, for the first time, on 6 November 1871, he supplies the title, *Spring Torrents*. There are further references to the amount of effort which this work cost Turgenev; the best proof, however, lies in the evidence of the text, about which more will be said later.

*Turgenev remained in London (with absences) until August 1871, and much of *Spring Torrents* was written there, at 16 Beaumont Street. The house has since been demolished. The Viardots lived near by, at 30 Devonshire Place, which is still standing.

The long time spent on writing and re-writing *Spring Torrents* contrasts very strikingly with the time spent on writing *First Love* – completed and published within the first three months of the year 1860; or with the six months spent on writing and re-writing his first completed novel, *Rudin*, in 1855. It seems a fair supposition that this story, probably to a greater extent than any other of Turgenev's works, reflected some of his innermost thoughts and emotions. Most of what follows in this essay is devoted to a discussion of this aspect of *Spring Torrents*, and to speculation about its significance for the author. But first, a few words about the text.

The text which finally saw the light of day in the January 1872 issue of the *European Herald* was the result of intensive writing and re-writing. The original manuscript, which was finished by September 1871, is lost without trace – it is possible (though improbable) that it was destroyed. The author then proceeded to make a fair copy, which was intended for the use of the printer. This was completed by the end of October, and is preserved in the Bibliothèque Nationale. However, the fair copy did not satisfy him. 'The devil has prompted me to start transcribing my story for the second time,' he wrote to Annenkov on 28 October. 'And all this because of my desire to polish it, and from lack of confidence in my declining powers.' This second fair copy is lost – though it is possible that it was presented by Turgenev to the poet K. K. Sluchevsky, and that it may therefore yet see the light of day inside the Soviet Union. The third fair copy was completed by 26 November 1871 and sent to Annenkov for him to pass on to the editor for the printer. Subsequently Turgenev asked Annenkov to get this fair copy back from the printer. This was done, and the manuscript of the third fair copy is now also deposited in the Bibliothèque Nationale.

Owing to the long delay which had supervened in sending the manuscript to Russia, Turgenev did not read the printer's proof himself, but left this task to Annenkov. He did, however, receive a proof in time to make some belated corrections, which were printed after the text in issue Number 1 of the *European Herald* for 1872. At a subsequent date Turgenev made some further corrections of an offprint of his story, and this corrected offprint is deposited in the Central State Archives in the Soviet Union. *Spring Torrents* was reprinted in collected editions of Turgenev's works in 1874, in 1880 and in 1883 – the year of his death. All the volumes of the first two of these collected editions were seen through the press by Turgenev, but he does not appear to have made very significant changes. Some changes, five in all, again of no great significance, beyond effecting very minor improvements, were made in editing the edition of 1883 for the press. This work of revision was begun by Turgenev, in spite of the handicap of his illness, with the aid of his friend, A. V. Toporov, who carried out many literary assignments for him. At Turgenev's request, Toporov entered on the text of the 1880 edition of Turgenev's collected works all the errors which had been detected, and Turgenev prepared the final texts for the forthcoming (1883) edition on the basis of these annotated volumes. Although he only lived long enough to revise four of the volumes of the 1883 edition, *Spring Torrents* was in fact included in one of those (Volume VII). But only very minor revisions were made in the text of *Spring Torrents*.

It would seem therefore that the third fair copy can be taken to represent the text of which the author approved – subject to the minor subsequent emendations (such as correction of errors of fact, like the substitution, to be found on page 23 of this translation, of Parma for Padua). The text of this translation is, in the main, based on the text printed in Volume XI of the complete works of Turgenev, published by the Soviet Academy of Sciences between 1960 and 1968. This Russian text in turn is based on the text of 1883, which is substantially the text of the third fair copy, together with subsequent minor corrections by the author. However, the editors of the text published in Volume XI of the complete works have made twenty-six emendations of the 1883 text 'on the basis of other sources' which they do not specify.* In most cases these are mere corrections of errors which had survived throughout successive editions. I have therefore in the great majority of cases followed these minor emendations in my translation. In two cases, however, I think the editors are wrong, and since they do not cite any authority for their text I prefer to follow Turgenev's third fair copy. On page 167 the words 'home' and 'Aeneas' are followed respectively by two and one exclamation marks in Turgenev's third fair copy. This seems to me to be much more in character with Maria Nikolaevna than the question marks gratuitously substituted in both cases by the Soviet editors.

Since 'the devil' prompted Turgenev to start re-copying the (lost) second fair copy, it is only reasonable to assume that he had made so many changes in the second, as compared with the first, fair copy (which is a fairly clean text with few alterations) that it was unfit to send to the printer. The third fair copy is quite clean and uncorrected. It is therefore reasonable to suppose that the differences between the first fair copy and the third fair copy (both of which are available to us) represent Turgenev's basic re-working of the text. These differences between the two fair copies are often quite substantial. They afford insight into the working of the author's mind, and detailed glimpses of his craftsmanship, and they will therefore be later subjected to some analysis. But first let us turn to Turgenev's life; and, more particularly, to the significance in his life and work of the years around 1840 and 1870–71.

Ivan Sergeyevich Turgenev was born in his parents' town house in Orel, on Monday 28 October 1818 at twelve noon.

*See pp. 454–5 of Volume XI of the *Complete Works*.

His chequered, solitary and largely unhappy childhood was mostly spent at his mother's estate in Orel Province, Spasskoe-Lutovinovo. It was a large estate by Russian standards, with around five thousand 'souls', or serfs, superb park and grounds (often described by Turgenev, and especially in his *Faust*) and a fine house in traditional Russian style built of decorated timber. The estate was the family inheritance of the author's mother, Varvara Petrovna Lutovinova. This formidable lady ruled over her serfs, her household and her children with patriarchal severity, and the young Ivan was subjected to beatings almost daily. The relations of Ivan and of his elder brother (a third son, Sergei, died in 1837 at the age of sixteen) to their mother were never to be based on affection: the beatings of childhood were followed by humiliations and petty persecutions when the sons grew to manhood, manifested especially in money-matters – to such an extent, that, until his mother's death in 1850, Ivan Turgenev was often penniless. Yet, there was tragedy in the life of Varvara Petrovna. She adored her sons, and was incapable of showing it, or of making them feel it. Her own youth had been extremely unhappy. Brought up by a stepfather who humiliated her and treated her with brutality until she reached adolescence and then proceeded to make sexual demands upon her, she escaped and sought refuge with her uncle, the owner of Spasskoe-Lutovinovo. Life with her uncle, who was mean and bigoted, was little better than with the stepfather. By the time his death brought release and the rich inheritance, this plain and embittered young woman had been scarred for life: her sons and her serfs were made to pay for the youth and happiness which she had never known. The naturally affectionate Ivan, whose longing for a home which he was never to satisfy pursued him to the end of his days, treated his mother with filial respect, but could never feel love or tenderness for her. When she died he wrote of her to Pauline Viardot: 'Her last days were so sad. God preserve us all from such a death. Her only desire was to deafen herself . . . by her orders an orchestra played polkas in a neighbouring room. One owes pity and respect to the dead, so I will say no more . . . And yet – I know it – it would have been so easy for her to have made herself loved and missed by my brother and myself! . . . God grant her peace!'

When she was over thirty and a rich landowner, Varvara Petrovna had married Sergei Nikolaevich Turgenev, the author's father. This remarkable man, of ancient Russian lineage (who died when Ivan was sixteen), made an indelible impression on the boy and may well have influenced his character and outlook. He drew, as he records himself, a faithful portrait of his father in *First Love* – the only purely autobiographical story which *Turgenev* ever wrote, though there is scarcely any story or novel of his without some autobiographical detail. Sergei Nikolaevich was handsome, self-confident and penniless, and made no attempt to conceal the fact that he had married Varvara Petrovna for her money. Slightly cold and cynical, he seems to have possessed the kind of charm that carries all before it. He made many conquests among women, and did not trouble to conceal his love affairs from his wife: she appears to have accepted them with tolerance as inevitable, but the failure of her marriage in terms of human affection must surely have added to her embitterment.

Ivan's admiration for his father, who was in everything different from himself, must be seen as an integral part of the author's character; it is the homage paid by the weak to the strong, of the uncommitted to the resolute and determined, of the one who lets life happen to him for the one who seizes life by the throat. There is, indeed, something of Sergei Nikolaevich in Maria Nikolaevna Polozova: the charm, the cynicism, the ruthless satisfaction of sexual desire. We do not know that '*Cela ne tire pas à conséquence*' was Sergei Nikolaevich's favourite saying, but it could well have been. Certainly, he resembled Maria Nikolaevna in many important respects. 'Reflecting subsequently on the character of my father,' Turgenev recalled many years after Sergei Nikolaevich's death (in *First Love*), 'I reached the conclusion that he had little time for me or for family life: he loved something else, and had taken his fill of delight in it. "Take everything you can yourself and never let anyone get a hold of you. The whole trick of living is to belong to yourself," he once said to me. On another occasion I once started, in my capacity of a young democrat, a discussion on freedom in his presence (he was "kind" on that day as I used to call it: this meant that one could discuss anything one liked with him).

' "Freedom," he repeated, "and do you know what can give a man freedom?"

' "What?"

' "Will, his own will. This will give him power, which is better than freedom. If you know how to want things, you will be free, and you will be able to give orders."

'My father before all and above everything wanted to live – and he did live . . . It is possible that he had a premonition that he would not have the use of this "thing, life", as he called it, for long: he was forty-two when he died.' There are details in this passage which repeatedly recall Maria Nikolaevna – the thirst for life, the exaltation of will, the desire to give orders, belonging to oneself and not 'letting anyone else get a hold of one' – even the early death.

If life in Spasskoe was in many respects unhappy for the young Turgenev, it was also a formative influence which remained with him for the rest of his life. It gave him a love of the Russian countryside which in turn is reflected in some of the most beautiful prose in the Russian language. He was to spend much of his time in Spasskoe throughout his life. It gave him a passionate, almost obsessive love for shooting game – it was indeed strange that this gentle and tender-hearted man, who was occasionally violent in his language, but quite incapable of doing harm or hurt to anyone, should have spent so many hours killing so many hundreds of birds and hares. But Spasskoe and his shooting expeditions also taught Turgenev that the peasants were human beings. He got to know them in a way that few Russian authors of the period ever did. The ultimate result was to be the famous *A Sportsman's Notebook*, which brought the author renown (in 1847) and – in the eyes of the radical intelligentsia of the time, and later – made him into a champion of the emancipation that was eventually to come in 1861. This book won him a reputation for radical views which was in fact quite out of keeping with one whose views were always those of a Western European Liberal. But no one could have hated serfdom more than Turgenev. There were many Russians in the 1840s who, like the politically unaware and, indeed, unreflective Sanin, would have felt deep shame in the presence of foreigners at having to acknowledge that human beings were still being bought and sold in Russia. But Turgenev's hatred of serfdom went much further than that – in spite of some similarities, Turgenev is certainly not identical with Sanin. As early as 1842 Turgenev had written a memorandum on serfdom as part of a set exercise on apprenticeship in the civil service (where he did not remain for long). In this memorandum he argued, with remarkable skill and vigour for a man of twenty-four, that serfdom was not only repellent from a humanitarian point of view, but was degrading and socially debilitating for the serf-owner quite as much as for the serf. He had indeed seen enough of this degradation in the course of his life at Spasskoe – during which, on a number of occasions, he intervened forcibly with his mother to right some major injustice against the serfs. (There is a vivid and memorable picture of his mother's household, the life of the serfs under her stern jurisdiction, and the effect of it all on a young boy, in the story *Punin and Baburin*, written between the end of 1872 and the beginning of 1874.) But *A Sportsman's Notebook* was to make its impact less for its portrayal of the degradation of the serfs than for the remarkable understanding it showed for serfs as living, individual, distinct and varied human beings – an aspect of serfdom that, curiously enough, had struck few Russians before. It is therefore worth recalling that Maria Nikolaevna, with her Swiss tutor and her Latin lessons, was only at one remove from serfdom – and she is perhaps, for all her moral depravity, the real heroine of *Spring Torrents*. At any rate she gets what she wants from life – always a very important factor in Turgenev's eyes; and as he wrote to Pierre Jules Hetzel, his friend and French publisher, who had suggested an alternative ending for *Spring Torrents*, '*Cette diablesse de femme m'a séduit, comme elle a séduit ce nigaud de Sanine.*'

In 1840, the year which Turgenev, like Sanin, spent in Italy and in Germany, there was as yet little to suggest the literary fame that was to come. What remains of his juvenilia – a few poems and a play in verse in the manner of Byron – would scarcely have led anyone (let alone their author) to the view that it was the work of someone who was destined to become one of the major figures in all nineteenth-century literature. However, if not yet discernible as a literary genius, the young Turgenev was already, for his age, of a certain recognized intellectual stature – again unlike Sanin. He had completed his university education, concentrating on the classics and on Russian literature and philology, and had so far distinguished himself in the University of St Petersburg that a career in university teaching lay open to him, had he wished to pursue it. He had also been accepted in the company of some of the leading literary figures of the day.

In May 1838 he had left Russia for Germany, in order to study philosophy (which at that time meant mainly Hegel) and history at the University of Berlin. (His mother, who saw him off, remained prostrate with grief: she appeared thereafter to live only for his letters, which were few and far between.) His fellow students, with both of whom he spent much time and whose influence upon his intellectual development was very great, were Stankevich and Granovsky – perhaps the leading minds in Russian intellectual life of the 1830s and 1840s respectively. In company with Stankevich he frequented the literary salon of a Russian couple named Frolov, where he met such distinguished figures of German intellectual life as Alexander von Humboldt, Bettina von Arnim and K. A. Varnhagen von Ense. In 1840, after a short return to Russia, he left once again for abroad, this time for Rome and a tour of Italy, which made a profound and lasting impression upon him, as many of his works, including *Spring Torrents*, bear witness. Once again he returned for further study to Berlin. Stankevich had died in June 1840. But shortly thereafter he met the young Michael Bakunin. The two became intimate friends – Turgenev was later to paint an idealized portrait of Bakunin as the hero of *Rudin*, which appeared in 1855.*

Early in 1841, Turgenev returned to Russia to spend his time partly in Spasskoe and, so far as his mother's niggardly allowance made this possible, in Moscow or in St Petersburg. His career in the civil service was short-lived, and indeed one of his contemporaries may be right when he records that it was only from weakness of character that Turgenev was ever persuaded (by V. I. Dal', the lexicographer) to join a department of the Ministry of the Interior. When in Moscow or in the capital he led a full social life. Contemporary accounts of him at this time vary. To some he appeared vain, boastful,

---

*A few years later he was to feel bitterly disillusioned with Bakunin, though the two men remained friends ('Our only friend in the opposite camp', according to Bakunin). 'I painted a fairly true picture of Bakunin in *Rudin*,' Turgenev wrote to a friend on 16 September 1862. 'But now he, Bakunin, is Rudin who failed to die on the barricades. Between ourselves he is a ruin.'

clever but affected. Herzen, who met him at Belinsky's house in March 1844, ridiculed Belinsky's lack of judgement in admiring Turgenev: 'Let him [Belinsky] analyse books and avoid any attempt at assessing living humans. Here is a Khlestakov [the fraudulent impostor of Gogol's play *The Government Inspector*], educated and clever, with a superficial nature, a great desire to express himself and *fatuité sans bornes*, and these are the kind of people that Belinsky almost cracks up to be geniuses.' Others, perhaps more discerning than Herzen, were alive to the penetrating intellect and liberal judgement which lay behind the affectations of youth; while those who knew Turgenev intimately became aware of the generosity, the warmth and the charm which were obscured by the cynical pose which he often assumed. In appearance he was unusually tall, quite strikingly handsome, with thick chestnut hair and blue eyes and a fair moustache. He was a brilliant *raconteur* with an elegant charm of manner. But his voice was thin and rather high-pitched, and he spoke with a slight lisp. The year 1843 was to prove the decisive year of his life. It was in May of this year that his first important literary work was published – a narrative poem, somewhat in the manner of Pushkin, though a very long way behind him in quality, entitled *Parasha*. It won the high praise of the then leading arbiter of literary fashion among the intellectuals – the radical critic Belinsky. Ivan Turgenev had become a writer. And at the end of the year he met the singer Pauline Viardot. He is reported to have been introduced as a 'young Russian land-owner, a good shot, an agreeable companion and a writer of bad verses'.

At the age of twenty-five Turgenev was by now not unversed in the affairs of love: the pattern of his future rather sterile and traumatic relations with women was perhaps already dis-cernible in the experiences of the young man on the threshold of life. Turgenev's description of the adolescent fervours of first love is to be found in the story which bears that name. The lyrical qualities of that story are immense; but it is probably more illuminating on the subject of his relations with his father than explanatory of Turgenev as a lover. The boy in the story is shattered and desolated when he discovers that his father is the successful rival for the favour of Zinaida, who is the object of his own adolescent passion. The boy is a secret witness to a scene in which his father strikes Zinaida with a riding switch because the girl, already pregnant, demands that he should leave his wife for her. The girl kisses the mark which the switch has left on her arm. The boy, though torn by hatred, jealousy and resentment against a rival and horror at the scene which he has witnessed, is nevertheless completely fascinated by his father's success with women, and by his power of domination over them: the fascination in the end proves far stronger than any resentment or jealousy. Turgenev's first experience of physical passion seems to have been with a serf girl (in the manner then customary in the young men of his social position) who made the first advances to the adolescent boy. There may have been romances in Germany of which we know nothing. But we know of two love affairs after his return to Russia. The first, which began in the summer of 1841 with Michael Bakunin's sister, Tatiana, was the prototype of the relationship which in one form or another he would reproduce again and again in his fiction. On the one side the woman, loving, utterly devoted, ready to surrender her life and honour; on the other the man, accepting this love, wishing to but unable to return it in the same manner, losing the happiness that could be his because he cannot bring himself to grasp it, to commit himself, yet, no sooner lost than bitterly repenting his folly. Sometimes the theme appears on its own – in the story *Asia*, for example; at other times it appears in conjunction with the *femme fatale* like Maria Niko-laevna, or Irina in *Smoke*, who sweeps the hero off his balance by her sheer physical power of attraction over him, and destroys his chance of happiness with the gentle and simple girl with whom he thought himself in love. Some of Tatiana Bakunina's letters have survived: they are an amalgam of romantic, passionate love and sheer bewilderment, of veneration tinged with despair. On Turgenev's side, as his letters to her show, there appear a certain literary falsity and pretence, but also some hints of genuine despair. Tatiana was probably right when, after their relationship had come to an end, early in 1843, she wrote to Turgenev: 'You are still a child. You have not yet grown up sufficiently to face the serious and terrifying things in life, the things of major significance.' His real emotional experiences lay ahead.

Back in Spasskoe, in the grim atmosphere of his mother's household, he formed (also in 1841) an association with another serf girl, one of his mother's sempstresses. She was quiet, submissive, affectionate and treated the young master with veneration. Her gentleness and humility seem to have evoked a genuine response of affection on Turgenev's side but there was very little in common between the two. The stern Varvara Petrovna drove poor Avdotia Ermolaevna from the house when her pregnancy became apparent: she was settled in Moscow. Turgenev treated her with generosity for the rest of her life, but does not appear to have had much desire to see her. Their daughter, christened Pelageia, was born in May 1842. Turgenev's relations with his daughter form an often unhappy chapter in his life. Of his continuing support and paternal devotion there can be no doubt – a long string of letters between the two shows the father bestowing (with the aid of Pauline Viardot) the best education he could upon his child, making every endeavour to arrange a successful marriage for her and sustaining her amidst the troubles caused by the financial improvidence of her husband and the eventual breakdown of her marriage. Renamed Pauline, she was transferred from Moscow to Paris at the age of eight, to the care of

Pauline Viardot, and thereafter her father was never far from her or long separated from her. And yet the two remained a world apart. Little Pauline shared none of her father's interests and showed none of her father's inclinations or talents, let alone his genius. One has sympathy for Paulinette – it is hard enough to be the daughter of a genius at the best of times, and the situation is made harder by illegitimacy, even where paternity is openly acknowledged and the relationship socially accepted. His letters to her show concern, devotion, duty, indeed a worrying, almost nagging, concern for the progress of the child as she grows up: there is little sign of warm love. The sad truth was that father and daughter had nothing in common. Nor was the situation improved by the fact that Paulinette failed to hit it off with Madame Viardot. It was a constant refrain of Turgenev that he had failed to 'weave himself a nest' in life and had been forced to perch on the edge of strange nests. His failure as a father, of which he was always deeply conscious, was an added burden which he carried with him through his unhappy life.

The relationship of Ivan Turgenev and Pauline Viardot has been closely and deeply analysed in a book which forms a landmark of excellence in the vast and often mediocre literature which has grown up around the novelist.* He loved her deeply and all-absorbingly for forty years, literally until his death. He made no attempt to conceal his love for her, let alone his almost hyperbolic admiration for her musical genius – and this in spite of the ambiguous situation necessarily created by the fact that the object of his passion was a married woman. His manner of life and his places of residence depended on the movements of the Viardot family, and for long

*See April Fitzlyon, *The Price of Genius. A Life of Pauline Viardot* (London, 1964), to which I am much indebted for what follows. I am also beholden to Mrs Fitzlyon for much generous help and advice in the preparation of this Essay, and am pleased to acknowledge this debt with gratitude.

periods he lived either with the family or in the closest proximity to them. His love and friendship embraced not only Pauline but her husband Louis Viardot, her mother and her children – none of whom, in spite of much gossip, can on the available evidence reliably be believed to have been fathered by Turgenev. On one of the children especially, Claudie, he lavished the kind of affection which he was unable to give to his own daughter. Turgenev's Russian friends were always ready to blame his enslavement on Pauline Viardot but these accusations were unjust: she certainly had a power over him which he found irresistible, but the enslavement was not of her volition. When the breaches occurred in their relationship, it was she who brought them about: Turgenev, like Sanin, was incapable of breaking off the relationship, but waited for it 'to end' – in other words waited for her to end it – and resumed it, with his love for her as strong as ever, whenever she permitted him to do so.

The course of Turgenev's love for Pauline Viardot is of the most immediate relevance to any understanding of *Spring Torrents*. Not because, certainly not only because, the story deals with the triangle of wife, lover and complaisant husband. This theme was explored frequently by Turgenev – in *A Month in the Country*, for example (his most important play, completed in 1850) or in *Smoke*, on which he had finished work some three years before embarking on *Spring Torrents*. Moreover, there is no possible parallel to be drawn directly between Maria Nikolaevna and Pauline, or between Polozov and Louis Viardot; nor was Turgenev ever made to suffer the humiliations inflicted on the wretched Sanin. Louis Viardot was twenty years older than his wife, and she had never loved him. Whatever he may have suffered in the course of his married life from Turgenev (and some others), he behaved throughout with dignity and decorum, and it was perhaps to the credit of both men that their friendship survived whatever crises may have been caused by the relations between his wife and her Russian lover. In spite of the difference of age between the two men, they were bound together by their two dominant passions – shooting and literature. If *Spring Torrents* is auto-biographical on the subject of lover and husband, it can at most reflect the frustration which such a situation must necessarily produce. But, as I hope to show later on, *Spring Torrents* is a synthesis, or perhaps symphony is the better word, of the four themes which dominated Turgenev's life and work: the destructive force of the sexual passion: the unattainable illusion or ideal of happy lasting mutual love; the homage paid by the uncommitted to the committed, by the weakling to the strong; and the fear of enthusiasm. And it is for the understanding of these themes, in their relationship to the most important thing that ever happened to Turgenev, his love for Pauline Viardot, that the outlines of this complex love story become relevant.

When they met in November 1843, Pauline, making her operatic début in Russia, was twenty-two and famous, Turgenev twenty-five, and undistinguished. It was 'love at first sight' in his case – ebullient, unrestrained and uninhibited adoration, which irritated and embarrassed his friends. On her side, she at first accepted him as one of her many admirers. But the relationship changed before long to the mutual one of love accepted and love returned. There are many open questions which still remain about this period of their love, which lasted until June 1850; but what is quite clear is that the character of their relationship was determined by Pauline. It was she who decided the course and extent: it was she who decided when the end was to come. On his side there was the patient admiration of a man who was prepared to accept what he was offered, and who apparently made no demands.

The break in June 1850 may have been a combination of a new emotional involvement by Pauline, of her determination to put an end to a situation which she found embarrassing and no longer tolerable, and of a desire for a reconciliation with her husband. At all events, the birth of her daughter, Claudie, on 21 May 1852, may well (in the light of Mrs Fitzlyon's imaginative analysis) have been the result of her desire to effect a reconciliation with her husband.

The subsequent course of their love story suggests that Pauline maintained her determination to see that relations between her and Turgenev remained distant and that the former intimacy would not be allowed to recur.* On his side there was no change of feeling, no abandonment of hope: but, except for two occasions (in Moscow, secretly, in 1850, and later in Courtavenel, the Viardots' country house, much beloved by Turgenev) there was no resumption of the former relations. Indeed between 1857 and 1859 relations between them virtually ceased, though 'the coldness was entirely on her side'.† For Turgenev it was a period of deep suffering – and, be it noted, the most intense period of creativity in his life. *Asia*, *A Nest of the Landed Gentry*, and *On the Eve* were all written in rapid succession between June 1857 and October 1859, mainly in Russia. In contrast, *Fathers and Sons* was begun in August 1860 and only finished, and with great effort at that, some eighteen months later.

In 1863 the Viardots decided to settle in Baden-Baden. She was only forty-two, but her voice was already deteriorating, and she planned to retire – although in fact she was to continue to sing in public for some years. Some kind of relations between her and Turgenev had been resumed a few years before, but without the one-time intimacy. Turgenev's love remained unchanged, and his hope and resignation persisted as they had in the darkest hours of his relations with Pauline.

*My summary follows Mrs Fitzlyon's detailed analysis, which was made on the basis of all existing evidence, but necessarily limited by the fact that not a single letter from Pauline to Turgenev has ever been published. But it is possible to hope now that some of her letters will see the light of day. Some twenty letters from Pauline to Turgenev were published in Paris in 1971 and 1972.

† *The Price of Genius*, p. 321.

He too moved to Baden-Baden, where he was to remain for seven years – all the time the Viardots lived there, until driven from it by the Franco-Prussian War. Although only forty-five, Turgenev already saw himself on the decline. He was never very much absorbed by the physical side of love. His sexual needs were (it would seem from his letters) still occasionally satisfied in casual encounters. His emotional needs, which were much stronger, were to find a partial outlet in several of those erotic friendships with women, devoid of sexual involvement, which the French call *amitiés amoureuses*, and which were a necessity for Turgenev almost to the end of his life. But his main emotional need was always Pauline Viardot. Once settled in Baden, his life became completely absorbed in that of the Viardot family. (As Herzen wrote of Turgenev during the Baden-Baden period, 'he is in love with the Viardot like an eighteen year old'.) Pauline's musical salon, her composition, the libretti which he wrote for a number of operettas which she composed, their public performance, her children and shooting with Louis Viardot were soon occupying a large part of his time. It was a new relationship in many ways, with the storm and stress of earlier years no longer forming a part of it. For Turgenev it was the home 'on the edge of someone else's nest', as he often described it; it was the life that he was to pursue in Germany and then in France until his death in 1883. 'Turgenev's relationship with Pauline had by now acquired an almost official character: both Pauline herself and, apparently, Louis Viardot, had accepted it at last ... Viardot ... had abdicated ... He had clearly made his peace with a situation which he knew he could no longer influence in any way.'* For Turgenev it seems to have been a full and relatively happy life, apart from his illness: but it marked the end of the intense creative period which separation from Pauline seems to have evoked. *Smoke* was published in 1867. It was the last major work until 1876,

*ibid., p. 389.

when *Virgin Soil* appeared. The number of minor works in between included *Spring Torrents*.

By the time he wrote *Spring Torrents* Turgenev had changed considerably, not only in appearance but in temperament, when compared with the young dandy who had so much irritated Herzen on first acquaintance. Guy de Maupassant, who met him at Flaubert's in the early 1870s, has left a vivid description of him in an obituary. 'The door opened. A giant appeared. A giant with a head of silver, as one would say in a fairy tale. He had long, white hair, large white eyebrows and a large white beard – but, truly silver-white, all shining, all illuminated by reflections. Amidst all this whiteness, a good, serene face, with rather strong features – a real head of the River God, "pouring forth his waves", or better still, the head of the Eternal Father.

'He was very tall and broad, with a large frame, but without appearing corpulent. But this colossus had the gestures of a child, timid and restrained. He spoke in a very gentle voice, rather slurred, as if his tongue were too thick for him to move it around his palate with ease. At times he hesitated, searching for the exact French word which he needed to express his thought. He found the word every time; and with astonishing aptness at that; but these slight hesitations gave a most peculiar charm to his speech.

'He could recount in an enchanting manner, imparting artistic significance and a diverting character to the most trifling facts. Yet he was loved less for the acuteness of his intelligence than for his naïveté – always kindly and always a little surprised. For he was quite incredibly innocent, this novelist genius who had travelled far and wide, had known all the great men of his age, had read everything that it is possible for a human being to read, and who spoke all European languages as well as he spoke his own. He showed surprise, stupefaction even, when confronted with things which would have appeared simple to a Paris schoolboy . . .

'He was simple, good, and straight almost to a fault, ready to do a favour as none before him, dedicated – to an extent which is almost unknown – and loyal to his friends, both living and dead.'

I suggested earlier that *Spring Torrents* is a symphony of the four themes which mainly dominate both Turgenev's life and his work. Perhaps just because it was written during a period of low creativity, a period of reminiscence almost, it became for that reason a vehicle for expressing thoughts and emotions with which he had been living all his adult life. By the time he was fifty-two or fifty-three (when *Spring Torrents* was being written), indeed long before then, Turgenev genuinely saw himself as an old man declining towards his death. (Sanin, at the same age, is also a man who believes that his life is all behind him.) 'Nearly the whole of my life is behind me,' Turgenev had written soon after his forty-second birthday to Countess Lambert, with whom he maintained until 1863 one of his '*amitiés amoureuses*'. 'I am not afraid of looking at the future. Only I am conscious of the fact that I am subject to certain eternal and unalterable, but deaf and dumb laws . . . and the small squeak of my consciousness means as little in this life as if I were to babble "I, I, I" on the shore of the ocean that flows without return. The fly still buzzes, but in another instant – and thirty, forty years is also an instant – it will buzz no more.' This deep pessimism had become an integral part of Turgenev's being by the time he settled in Baden-Baden (this letter was written a year before that). The marasmic depression and disgust which Sanin experiences before he recollects the events of thirty years before is Turgenev's own experience. Was it perhaps his reaction to the passions of sex, after they were over, the cloying of the emotions sated or disappointed? Did he perhaps always feel sexual passion as a degradation, as an enslavement to a dominant female? Was there perhaps some hatred and contempt for himself for the subjugation which he suffered from Pauline – even if Pauline was no Maria Niko-laevna in character? But dominant she certainly was, and it was the dominant woman by whom Turgenev was usually aroused. 'A terrible woman, worse than Lady Macbeth' he had called her a few months before his death, in a delirium induced by the morphia which the doctors gave him. Of course his love for her was genuine – almost the last words which he spoke were of love for her: 'The queen of queens, how much good she has done.' But yet, this love is not incompatible with self-contempt, or (like Sanin) with the rage of the weak which unconsciously reflects the injury to dignity and integrity that an enslaving passion brings about. Like Sanin, Turgenev, a few months before his death, saw the hideous and shapeless monsters on the sea bed and told his old friend Annenkov about them. 'I was on the sea bottom, and I saw monsters and concatenations of most hideous organisms, which no one has yet described because no one has ever come back to life after seeing such a spectacle.' But the early pages of *Spring Torrents* suggest that the nausea, the helplessness, the disgust which these monsters symbolized were present within him for many years before the end.

This is conjecture. Nevertheless the conjecture that *Spring Torrents* was in some ways related to deeply felt, and secret, emotions connected with the relationship between Turgenev and Pauline Viardot is supported by one remarkable fact: he never read the manuscript of this story to Pauline before sending it off for publication, even though, as he says himself, it had been his practice for years to submit everything he wrote to her judgement before publication (translated orally into French for her benefit). Nor do we have any evidence of her opinion of *Spring Torrents* after publication; yet she must be presumed to have read it when it appeared in (poor) French translation in the summer of 1873. What is certain beyond doubt is Turgenev's attitude to passion between man and woman which is one of the four themes to which I have referred as forming the symphony of *Spring Torrents*. Fear, almost hatred, of the enslavement to love or desire runs like a thread of scarlet throughout Turgenev's life work, from the earliest to the latest. 'My son,' Ivan Turgenev's father had written when the son was aged fifteen, on the morning of the very day when he himself was to suffer a fatal stroke, 'fear the love of woman, fear this happiness, this poison . . .' (Turgenev recalls these words in the autobiographical *First Love*, written in 1860.) But the theme of love as a poison, love as a disease, love as madness had appeared much earlier in his work. In *A Correspondence*, which he started to write as early as 1844, the theme is fully developed – in fact this story is in many respects a foreshadowing (though a much weaker shadow) of *Spring Torrents*. Told in fifteen letters, it shows the development, by correspondence, of what appears to be deep and lasting love between the man and the woman. The last letter is written with a gap of nearly a year: it reveals the infatuation of the man with a dancer whom he despises, but whose power over him is irresistible.

'Do you remember,' the letter ends, 'how you and I, both in conversation and in correspondence, used to discuss love? Do you remember all the subtleties we used to indulge in? But when it is put to the test it then appears that real love is an emotion which is quite unlike the kind we used to imagine. In fact, love is not an emotion at all: it is a disease, a certain condition of mind and body. It does not develop gradually. It is in no way open to doubt, and certainly cannot be fooled – even though it does not manifest itself everywhere in the same way. Most usually it takes possession of a person unbidden, suddenly, and against his will – to all intents and purposes like cholera or a fever . . . There is no equality in love, there is none of the so-called free union of souls and all the other idealistic notions invented by German professors when they have nothing better to do . . . No, in love one party is a slave and the other master, and it is not for nothing that the poets talk of the chains which love imposes ... What a fate mine has been, when you think of it! In my first youth I was quite determined to conquer the heavens ... then I began to have dreams about the happiness of all mankind, about the well-being of my country. Then that too passed. I thought of nothing else but how to organize for myself somehow domestic family life ... and then I tripped over an ant hill, and crashed to the ground and to my grave ... What past masters we are, we Russians, at finishing up in this manner!'

A Correspondence was completed in 1854, when his relations with Pauline were at their lowest ebb. But the pessimism, cynicism almost, which it voices was not the result of temporary depression: the theme was too constant in Turgenev's writing for such an inference. For example, *Petushkov*, written in 1847, when the course of his love for Pauline was at its happiest, is even more sombre on the same theme than *A Correspondence*. Written in the style of Gogol, it is a simple story of a retired lieutenant, aged forty, who becomes enslaved by his passion for a peasant girl, Vasilisa, the niece of the local baker, and ends in total subjection to her, relieved by occasional drunkenness, occupying a small corner in the bakery which is now owned by Vasilisa and her rich and flashy husband. It is a story which is difficult to read unmoved if one recalls the author and his personal life. This was in 1847. Twenty years later the theme recurs in *Smoke*, where it is developed to the full, much as it was to be three or four years later in *Spring Torrents*, in the form of the hero, Litvinov, and the two contrasting women. On the one hand the quiet, domestic Tania, to whom the hero is engaged to be married, on the other Irina, the first love of his youth, the tigress who appears just in time to destroy his romance with Tania, to enslave him once more in a passion for which he despises himself, but which is beyond his control. There is, it is true, an unwonted note of optimism in *Smoke*, a suggestion towards the end that

Litvinov will eventually find that domestic bliss, which always escapes Turgenev's heroes, in the arms of the forgiving Tania, to whom in the end he returns – as Sanin did not return to Gemma. But I have never found the ending of *Smoke* very convincing, and I doubt if Turgenev did – perhaps the weak-willed Sanin was wiser after all to realize that his romantic whirlwind passion for Gemma was an illusion which could not have lasted.

The last treatment of the theme is to be found in *The Song of Love Triumphant*, written in 1881, one of the last things he wrote. But this work is so closely related to the question of Arthur Schopenhauer's influence on Turgenev, and especially of his treatment of the relations between the sexes, that this question must first be briefly examined. Schopenhauer's most influential work, *The World as Will and Idea*, was first published in 1818, but made little impact. It was only some years after it had been republished in 1844 that it began to attract some attention. Turgenev appears to have read Schopenhauer soon after 1860 – at any rate there is no evidence of his acquaintance with him before 1861. That it made a profound impression upon him appears both from direct assertions, and from the indirect evidence of several of his works. As Bertrand Russell observes, the appeal of Schopenhauer 'has always been less to professional philosophers than to artistic and literary people in search of a philosophy that they could believe.' Turgenev seems to have found in Schopenhauer a justification of the profound pessimism and sense of the impotence of the individual which characterized his outlook at many periods of his life. He also, no doubt, found in Schopenhauer's emphasis on the primacy of will an echo of his own tendency to exalt will above all other human attributes. For Schopenhauer will is paramount and is the only reality behind appearances – not separate, individual acts of will, but one vast will, appearing in the whole course of nature both animate and inanimate. But Schopenhauer's cosmic will is nothing like a divine will, in conformity with which happiness or virtue is to be found. On the contrary, the universal, cosmic will is the source of all our endless suffering. Will has no fixed end which would bring contentment if fulfilled: hence Schopenhauer's profound and unredeemed pessimism, from which he offers no escape (except in the form of extinction, or Nirvana). And so, although death must conquer in the end, we pursue our futile purposes, 'as we blow out a soap-bubble as long and as large as possible, although we know perfectly well it will burst'. Happiness does not exist: a wish causes pain if it is unfulfilled, and satiety, and hence disgust, if once it is attained. There is no escape even in suicide, since transmigration is effectively, if not literally, true.

There are a number of reflections of this gloom of despair in Turgenev – I have cited one instance in a quotation from a letter written in 1862 to Countess Lambert. The most complete exposition of Schopenhauer's pessimism in Turgenev's interpretation also dates from 1862, at any rate so far as the first draft was concerned. This is a short piece entitled *Enough*, written in the form of a diary, and sub-titled *A fragment from the notes of a deceased painter*. It is a cry of unredeemed despair, a rejection of human effort, of human ideals, of love, in the face of an inexorable, eternal power of fate, or nature, or time. Nature is 'unconsciously and inflexibly obedient to its laws, it knows neither art nor freedom nor the good'. The individual has the illusion that he creates but ... 'it is strange and terrifying to utter it, we are creators for a single hour ... as they say there once was a caliph for an hour ...' Although this despair did not recur in this stark form in Turgenev's works, there are many echoes of Schopenhauer in his work after 1862, and especially in *Spring Torrents*. For example, Sanin's state of *taedium vitae* seems to me to reflect the following passage from Book II of *The World as Will and Idea*: '... Human endeavours and desires ... always delude us by presenting their satisfaction as the final end of will. As soon as we attain to them they no longer appear the same, and therefore they soon grow stale . . . We are fortunate enough if there still remains something to wish for and strive after, that the game may be kept up of constant transition from desire to satisfaction, and from satisfaction to a new desire, the rapid course of which is called happiness, and the slow course sorrow, and does not sink into that stagnation that shows itself in fearful ennui that paralyses life, vain yearning without a definite object, deadening languor.' Or again, the following passage from Book IV recalls Sanin's image of the boat and the monsters (see p. 14): 'Life itself is a sea, full of rocks and whirlpools, which man avoids with the greatest care and solicitude, although he knows that even if he succeeds in getting through with all his efforts and skill, he yet by doing so comes nearer at every step to the greatest, the total, inevitable and irremediable shipwreck, death; nay even steers right upon it: this is the final goal of the laborious voyage, and worse for him than all the rocks from which he has escaped.' Or, finally, the following passage from Chapter XX of the Second Volume, should be compared with Sanin's reactions on page 15: 'Upon what depends the identity of the person? Not upon the matter of the body; it is different after a few years. Not upon its form, which changes as a whole and in all parts; all but the expression of the glance by which, therefore, we still know a man after many years; which proves that in spite of all changes time produces in him something in him remains quite untouched by it. It is just this by which we recognize him even after the longest intervals of time, and find the former man entire.'*

It is, however, mainly in his treatment of the nature and function of the sexual impulse that the influence of Schopenhauer is discernible in Turgenev's work, and especially in *Spring Torrents* and in *The Song of Love Triumphant*. Brought up as we are in an age which is under the influence of Freud, it

---

*The quotations from Schopenhauer are taken from the English translation by R. B. Haldane and J. Kemp.

is difficult for us to imagine either the impact or the originality of Schopenhauer's treatment of sex – in a book first published in 1818. So far as Turgenev was concerned, in view of his preoccupation with the sexual passion, Schopenhauer must have come as a revelation; and his analysis of the unconscious cosmic will that lies behind love between the sexes the source of an entirely novel idea. Hartmann's *Philosophy of the Unconscious*, from which Freud derived the germ of his doctrine, was not published until 1869, and there is no evidence that Turgenev ever read it. But in Schopenhauer he would have found an explanation of the blind destructive sexual passion which he had been writing about from his youth: *Spring Torrents* is the most complete exposition of this theme in all his works.

Schopenhauer's exposition of his views (in the Third Volume of *The World as Will and Idea*, which is in effect a series of supplements to the main text) seems commonplace enough today: to Turgenev in 1862 it must have seemed an illumination. The argument of this supplementary chapter, entitled 'The Metaphysics of the Love of the Sexes', is simple enough. What appears to the individuals concerned as an essentially personal choice is nothing of the kind; it is the cosmic force of Nature which is interested in nothing but the perpetuation of the human species, and is quite indifferent to the concerns of individuals. The individuals are no more than instruments of this force of which they are not aware: this is the Will. And, since the individual counts for nothing in the work which the Will seeks to accomplish, 'every lover, after the ultimate consummation of the great work (that is to say of the Cosmic Will) finds himself cheated: for the illusion has vanished by means of which the individual was here the dupe of the species.' The Cosmic Will sweeps the poor mortals involved with it into the maelstrom of passion in which they are blind pawns, unable to resist and deprived of the power to decide. This is surely the predicament of Sanin. For Turgenev,

Schopenhauer may well have provided the answer to the human predicament which had so long absorbed him – the enslaving and degrading nature of the state of being in love.

The Song of Love Triumphant, written almost at the very end of Turgenev's creative life, sets the seal on this aspect of Turgenev's thoughts about human passion in an imaginative and largely symbolic way. It is a fairy-tale, written in the manner of Hoffmann, in which the real and the fantastic are intermingled, and an air of mystery, almost of Grand Guignol, is wrapped around an essentially simple tale of marital infidelity. The story is cast in sixteenth-century Ferrara. Two friends, Mucius and Fabius, both handsome, rich, well-bred and talented (the one in music, the other in painting) fall in love with the beautiful and accomplished Valeria. They vow to accept her choice: the loser will leave Ferrara and only return when he is certain that his passion is subdued. Valeria (on her mother's advice) chooses Fabius, and Mucius departs. The young couple live for five years in complete happiness, marred only by their failure to have children. Then Mucius returns: he is welcomed and installed in a pavilion in the garden. Accompanied by a mysterious Malay servant, he is laden with exotic Eastern objects and lore – including an Indian violin, on which he plays a stirring, triumphant melody, which he describes as a song of satisfied love, a song from Ceylon. The effect on Valeria is disastrous. Mucius comes to her by night in a dream, and haunts her by day. One scene, when Fabius finds Valeria in the garden, seems to typify Turgenev's poetic interpretation of the intrusion of sexual passion, seen almost as a desecration: 'Fabius ran into the garden, and there, in one of the most distant alleys, he saw Valeria. She was sitting on a bench. Her head had sunk to her breast, her hands were crossed on her lap. Behind her, emerging from the dark green of the cypresses, appeared a marble satyr, his face distorted by a smile of malicious contempt, his outstretched lips laid close to the pan pipes ...' There follow nocturnal encounters, which are discovered by Fabius (it is never made quite clear whether these encounters are real or merely imagined). Fabius stabs Mucius to death, as he believes. But Mucius is revived by the magic art of the Malay servant and leaves the house of Fabius: Valeria appears as much relieved by his departure as she was oppressed by his presence, even though she could not free herself of the influence of Mucius upon her. (There is no suggestion at any time that she was in love with him.) Life returns to normal. Then, one day, Valeria sits idly by the organ, her fingers gliding over the keys. Suddenly, without her willing it, the sounds of the song of triumphant, satisfied love burst from the organ. At the same time she feels, for the first time since her marriage, the stirring of a new life within her womb. The story ends abruptly at this point.

It seems, then, that in Schopenhauer Turgenev found an interpretation of the sexual passion which explained, or illuminated, for him the fear, even horror, which he seems to have felt for it, and which he had portrayed long before he became acquainted with *The World as Will and Idea*. Sex as the cosmic will, in action, quite indifferent to the individual, sweeping him up in a whirlwind of which the sole purpose is procreation, the future of the race, the eugenics of the coupling, leaving the individual humiliated and bewildered – this is the theme that Turgenev pursued again and again in his work throughout his whole life. In *The Song of Love Triumphant* at the end of his life, he would portray this cosmic will symbolically – it is the satyr grinning behind Valeria plunged in her reflections on the garden seat. In *Spring Torrents* it appears in the more familiar and less fantastic guise of the weak Sanin drawn first into an impossible and quite unpractical romantic attachment, and then, equally swiftly, swept out of it into another as irresistible as the first, but more degrading and destructive, the seductive power of Maria Nikolaevna. But even here the symbolism is not absent. The falling in love of Sanin and Gemma is portrayed as a sudden squall or whirlwind, which sweeps over and past them, like a flock of great birds. The capture of Sanin by Maria Nikolaevna is in turn shown as a wild bacchanalia enacted in the placid wooded country of the Taunus foothills. But whereas both Gemma and Sanin are shown as victims of the cosmic will, quite unable to resist or control it, Maria Nikolaevna is in full control of it; she may almost be said to invoke and exploit it for her own end. She alone of all the three characters is free, and she alone has will and strength, the ability to live life to the full and to get what she wants from it. It is in this respect that Turgenev parts company with Schopenhauer in his conception of the cosmic will. For Schopenhauer this is a blind and ineluctable force – the individual cannot even achieve his freedom by recognizing and adapting himself to this force, as he can, according to Hegel or Marx, by the recognition of 'necessity'. Free will and the cosmic will are for Schopenhauer one and the same. 'Spinoza (Epist. 62) says that if a stone which has been projected through the air had consciousness, it would believe that it was moving of its own will. I add to this only that the stone would be right.' But for Turgenev the man, or woman, of will is really free, indeed enjoys a freedom which, however morally reprehensible (his father, Maria Nikolaevna), nevertheless confers a dimension of human quality which the weak man lacks.*

The revulsion which Turgenev often shows in his works for the sexual passion reminds one of Hamlet, weary of 'this too, too sullied flesh', trailing the theme of morbid, physical disgust with sexual passion throughout the play. The apparent resemblance of Turgenev to Hamlet is no coincidence, since, as will appear later, Turgenev in many respects saw himself as a weak and indecisive Hamlet, letting circumstances control him rather than controlling them himself. But such an

*For a fuller (and different) discussion of the influence of Schopenhauer on Turgenev see A. Walicki, 'Turgenev and Schopenhauer', *Oxford Slavonic Papers*, Vol. X, 1962, pp. 1–17.

obsessive attitude to sex is often a sign of impotence, and could conceivably have been in this respect a symptom of Turgenev's disturbed psychology as well. Not that he was impotent in the physical sense. Although we can only guess at the actual course of his relationship with Pauline Viardot (in the absence of any evidence from her side) we do know of a number of physical associations of a casual nature throughout nearly all of Turgenev's life. But even if physical impotence can be ruled out, there could well have been frustration and failure in his relations with women so far as the sexual link was concerned: unlike his father, he was certainly no Don Juan.

Although some hints which he dropped could be cited in support of this view, it is nevertheless conjectural. What is certain, however, is that he sought throughout his life associations of a quasi-erotic nature with women in which physical relations played no part. There were to be at least two such affairs, of great charm and pathos, in his later years, after the time with which we are at present concerned, when *Spring Torrents* was being written – with Baroness Julia Vrevskaia between 1873 and 1877; and, towards the end of his life, in 1880 and 1881, with the actress Savina. In the case of Vrevskaia, at any rate, his letters show quite plainly that had Vrevskaia taken the initiative the romance could have become more than the passionate, but platonic, one which it remained. 'Since I met you,' he wrote to her on 26 January 1877 (not very long before her death as a nurse in the Russo-Turkish war), 'I grew to love you as a friend – and at the same time had the constant desire to possess you. This desire was not however so uncontrollable (I was in any case not so young) as to ask you to marry me – and there were other reasons which prevented me from doing this too. On the other hand I knew quite well that you would never agree to what the French call *une passade* ... There you have the explanation of my behaviour. You are anxious to assure me that you never nurtured any "ulterior wishes" with regard to me – alas! I was only too well aware of that. You say that your time *as a woman* is over: when my male time is over too – and there is not very long to wait for that – then, I have no doubt, we shall be great friends, because nothing will disturb us any longer. But meanwhile I still turn a little hot and somewhat frightened at the thought: what if she were to press me to her heart, *not as a brother*? And I want to ask you then, just like my Maria Nikolaevna in *Spring Torrents*, "Sanin, do you know how to forget?" Well, there is my confession for you. It is frank enough, is it not?' It should be noted that here, as in most of the love affairs described by Turgenev, it is the woman who takes the initiative: even Gemma is the first to suggest marriage, not Sanin – for all the nobility of motives and intentions of which he persuades himself. It is a fair inference that this is how Turgenev usually saw his own relations with women.

But there was also another alternative to the bond of sex which Turgenev sought and found – the bond of past sexual desire, overcome and superseded, the quiet haven of age which supervenes when the restless passions of youth no longer trouble one. Such, at any rate, was the nature of the relationship with Pauline Viardot that Turgenev was building up, with apparent success, in Baden-Baden and in London, while he was writing *Spring Torrents*. (The constant stress in his correspondence on age, on the fact that life was already behind him when he was still in his early fifties, is in tune with the mood of the new life which he had taken up with the Viardot family.) Was this, perhaps, for Turgenev the one attainable haven in life where all others necessarily ended in shipwreck? Perhaps one clue to the deep meaning which *Spring Torrents* obviously had for him is to be found in the last line: 'They say that he (Sanin) is selling all his estates and is planning to move to America.' One can see it all. The luxurious Slocum household on Broadway. Gemma, now middle-aged and rather broad in the beam, but still retaining much of her beauty, ruling the household and her husband, organizing the marriage of her daughter Marianna, occupying herself with the affairs of her married children and their families. Then Mr Jeremiah Slocum, the successful man of business, who worships her. And lastly, on the fringes, lodging near by, perhaps, or in a wing of the spacious house on Broadway, is Sanin – prematurely aged, living in harmony and happiness with both Gemma and her husband, with no suggestion of passion on his side, or of jealousy on the husband's side, adored by the grandchildren and becoming an indispensable part of Gemma's life – if only because she is slightly bored with the worshipping Mr Slocum (though she would never admit it) and is delighted to have somebody new around the place whose life she can run. Such, perhaps, was the way in which Turgenev's imagination pictured the future for Sanin. If so, it was a reflection of his own experience; and of the resignation with which he had sought, and welcomed, quiet happiness in which passion played no part, in the vicinity and company of the woman he loved.

The second theme of *Spring Torrents*, which constantly recurs in Turgenev's writing, is the unattainable, almost illusory, nature of complete and harmonious love between the sexes: where it is harmonious, it is incomplete, as, for example, in his first published work, the long poem *Parasha*, where the price of marital harmony is seen to be a dull, commonplace, trite and infinitely boring life. Of course, the variations on unhappy love are without end. One would not expect a writer so rich in imagination, sympathy and understanding of the human predicament to confine himself to one theme alone, and Turgenev's portrayals of love show every kind of situation – except that happiness and fulfilment in love are very rare, as they were rare in Turgenev's own life. The three great tragic love stories – of Liza in *A Nest of the Landed Gentry*, of Elena and Insarov in *On the Eve* and of Bazarov in *Fathers and Sons* –

are in a class by themselves: they do not belong to those works in which Turgenev's own predicament appears to be the dominant theme. But there are several treatments of love throughout Turgenev's creative life in which, in one form or another, the happiness that could perhaps have been – and there is always a big 'perhaps' in Turgenev's treatment of satisfied love – is snatched away, or is lost through indecision, when it is not overwhelmed and wiped out by a sudden onslaught of the 'cosmic will' in the shape of some irresistible rival physical magnet. This is what happens in *Smoke*, and again in *Spring Torrents*. But, even without the intervention of the Polozov affair, Sanin's romantic infatuation for Gemma remains, to me at any rate, very unconvincing, and I think Turgenev meant it to be unconvincing. How long, one may ask, would a spoilt Russian *barchuk*, or son of the gentry, have been content to run a dingy café in Frankfurt along with the slightly ridiculous and very bourgeois Signora Roselli? Even Gemma, for all the transports of first love, must have known that this was nonsense, as Sanin in his heart knew it was. There is a constant irony in the telling of the story which suggests that Turgenev wanted us to know that it was all largely make-believe. (However, the descriptions of the ardours of love seem serious enough in intent. They are not typical of Turgenev's style and are not very convincing outside nineteenth-century convention. They are the most dated passages in the book.) Presumably, a stronger man than Sanin would have insisted on carrying Gemma off to Russia, away from the Patisserie Roselli. But Sanin would not be Sanin if one could ever imagine him doing anything so courageous as standing up to the formidable and temperamental lady who presided over it, and over her daughter.

Sanin is, in short, the embodiment of weakness – the man without a will of his own. Weakness of will is the third recurrent theme in Turgenev's creative work. That Turgenev to some extent identified himself with Sanin is evident, as instances already quoted have shown – though it was an identification with a caricature, since obviously Sanin had neither the powerful intellect nor the broad education nor the perceptiveness of Turgenev at Sanin's age. But the identification lay in the weakness, in Sanin's inability by an act of will to mould life to his own desire, and in the inability in his relations with women to impose his will upon them, or indeed to take any initiative at all in the affair. 'He had not a particle of vanity . . .,' Henry James, who loved Turgenev, recalled after his death. 'His humour exercised itself as freely upon himself as upon other subjects, and he told stories at his own expense with a sweetness of hilarity which made his peculiarities really sacred in the eyes of a friend. I remember vividly the smile and tone of voice with which he once repeated to me a figurative epithet which Gustave Flaubert (of whom he was extremely fond) had applied to him – an epithet intended to characterize a certain expansive softness, a comprehensive indecision, which pervaded his nature, just as it pervades so many of the characters he has painted. He enjoyed Flaubert's use of this term, good-naturedly opprobrious, more even than Flaubert himself, and recognized perfectly the element of truth in it.'

'Softness' was indeed the epithet that above all applied to Sanin, according to his creator. ('A soft pear' was the expression used by Flaubert – though Henry James does not record this.) The attraction of the strong-willed and determined character who seizes upon life and forces out of it what he desires and wills dominates all of Turgenev's life: in part it explains the enormous influence exercised over him by the strong-willed, Pauline Viardot. His father had been just such a man of will and force. And this man of will, the committed man – the man with the qualities which Turgenev so markedly lacked – remained as an ideal in the author's mind, and finds a clear reflection in many of his works, including *Spring Torrents*.

There is indeed ample evidence that Turgenev despised himself for cowardice and lack of will. His enemies and critics were not slow to accuse him of political cowardice, often with less than justice: the radical friends of his youth, like Herzen, could never forgive him for avoiding political commitment to extreme causes, and trying to remain on the fringes of political debate. He was cautious in his relations with revolutionaries living in exile, because he was anxious not to compromise his position with the Russian authorities. Politics apart, there were also some seemingly discreditable incidents in his personal life which ill-wishers have also no doubt distorted in the telling – Turgenev had many enemies. To discuss the justice of the many accusations and insults levelled at him by his compatriots throughout his life would take us too far away from the present theme, although it will be necessary later to touch on the question of Turgenev's attitude to the Russian radicals. But what is certain is that he often believed the accusations to be true and suffered accordingly. His close friend Ya. P. Polonsky, who could not conceivably have invented the story, recounts the following conversation with Turgenev towards the end of his life, in the summer of 1881, in Spasskoe:

Turgenev as usual was unwell. Before his departure he lay down on the divan ... crossed his arms and after a long, long silence, said to me:
'Can you describe my character in five letters?'
I said I could not.
'Well try, describe the whole of me in five letters.'
However, I simply had no idea what to reply to him.
'Say coward* and that will be just.'
Turgenev insisted that he was a coward, and that he had not got a pennyworth of will.

The man, or woman, of will and commitment (and the two are not always clearly separable) figures in nearly every work of importance that Turgenev produced and it is quite clear that the subject obsessed him. *Spring Torrents* reproduces the

* The Russian word for 'coward', *trus* (as spelt with the hard sign in 1881), contains five letters.

theme of the strong will versus the weak in the relatively crude contrast of Maria Nikolaevna and Sanin – it is the third of the themes which I have suggested recur constantly in Turgenev's work. But there is also the closely linked theme, which in Turgenev's mind seemed to be inseparable from the notion of weakness – the lack of commitment, the failure to dedicate oneself to the single purpose, whatever that might be, the lack of the all-absorbing enthusiasm. Lack of commitment is not directly expounded in *Spring Torrents*. The easy-going Sanin is, naturally enough, quite unpolitical – but then so were most of his contemporaries. For the more alert consciences, like Stankevich, Granovsky and Turgenev (who, it will be recalled, were close companions in Berlin in 1838 and 1839), the many problems which Russia faced indeed formed a constant preoccupation. Sanin, in contrast, 'knew little of the disturbing emotions which had raised a storm in the breasts of the best of the younger generation of that epoch.'

The 'committed' man had figured repeatedly as a hero in Turgenev's works – Rudin was the first, inspired by Bakunin in those student days in Berlin; then followed Insarov, the Bulgarian patriot, the hero of *On the Eve*. Some of the Russian intelligentsia had criticized the fact that this liberator–patriot was a Bulgarian and not a Russian; but Russia in early 1860 was still 'on the eve' of her true political awakening. Turgenev's committed hero of the period of political awakening during the years after the emancipation of the serfs in 1861 was Bazarov, the hero of *Fathers and Sons*, which appeared in 1862. To Bazarov, probably Turgenev's favourite hero, it will be necessary to return. But the whole problem of 'commitment' had been fully expounded by Turgenev in an essay on *Hamlet and Don Quixote* which, after a very long period of incubation, had seen the light of day two years before Bazarov in *Fathers and Sons*.

The very length of time that Turgenev spent reflecting and working on *Hamlet and Don Quixote* shows the extent to which its theme was central to his thought. It was first referred to by him in conversation around the time of the revolutionary events of 1848, and discussed soon after, in 1850, when he spoke of an article which he had in mind, dealing with the theme of the two contrasting types of personality symbolized by these two characters in literature. But it was not until the beginning of 1857 that he actually started work on the article. In spite of repeated urging by his publisher and repeated assurances by Turgenev that he was working on the essay, it was in fact only completed at the end of 1859. As he noted on the covering sheet of the manuscript, it was 'written with long interruptions'. He gave a public reading of his essay in St Petersburg on 10 January 1860, when it was greeted with wild enthusiasm.

The audience, at the time when the emancipation of the serfs was imminent, seems to have drawn its own, over-simplified, conclusion that Turgenev intended above all to exalt the Don Quixotes, whom they identified with the radicals, as against the reflective philosophers, incapable of action, the Hamlets. (Probably rightly. In one of the early drafts of *Hamlet and Don Quixote* the Knight is described as 'a democrat', the usual term then in use for a revolutionary radical.) Following a much-read essay by Belinsky, they identified Hamlet with the intellectuals of the Russian 1840s and 1850s, the men and women who talked and talked of Russia's predicament but did nothing about it, the so-called 'superfluous people'. In fact, Turgenev's analysis is a good deal subtler than this simple black and white picture, which many among his audience drew from a hearing of his words. Turgenev is not primarily concerned to exalt one type above the other: his aim is to show the values and defects of each, while leaving little doubt that emotionally he is on the side of the Don Quixotes, the men of indomitable will and un-quenchable enthusiasm.

Turgenev begins by stressing the coincidence that both

Hamlet and the First Part of *Don Quixote* were published in the same year: this fact symbolizes the two opposite poles of human nature, since men can be divided into one type or the other – although (he says) there are many more Hamlets around. Everyone has an ideal in life which determines its course: but the Don Quixotes find this ideal outside themselves in some eternal truth, the Hamlets within themselves, in their own self-analysis. Don Quixote is far from being the traditional figure of ridicule. (Turgenev was here attacking a popular Russian tradition: even in popular speech in Russian 'Don Quixotry' has none of the meaning of our 'Quixotic', but rather that of 'playing the fool'.) He is the symbol of faith in an eternal truth, a truth which demands sacrifice and devotion, and which becomes an ideal to which everything in life must be subordinated. This truth is often distorted in Cervantes' novel by the Knight's disordered imagination: but the purity of the ideal is not thereby in any way sullied, since it draws its inspiration from something outside Don Quixote's deranged mind. Since he is devoid of egotism, he is fearless and has no vanity: he is an enthusiast, the servant of an ideal. Hamlet, in contrast, has no faith: he is all 'I', and a man who is completely preoccupied with himself can have no faith. Hamlet, with all the advantages of his social position, hesitates, tricks himself, consoles himself by strong language (like Sanin!) – but does nothing to carry out his father's injunction: Don Quixote, poor, old and without influence, joins battle with all the evil forces of the whole world.

At this point Turgenev introduces an argument which is central to the whole of his lifelong attitude to the enthusiast, to the committed, to the man of strong will. It does not matter, he says, that Don Quixote's efforts to redress a wrong end up by making things worse – as in the scene where he rescues a boy from a beating, but only to leave him the victim of a beating ten times worse as soon as the Knight has departed. The self-sacrifice, the enthusiasm, the commitment is all . . .

'The main thing lies in the sincerity and strength of the conviction . . . the result is in the hands of the fates.' (Turgenev's argument that the purity of motive is all, and that consequences are in the lap of the gods, recalls very vividly the views of the friend of his student years, the historian Granovsky.)

The contrast between the two types (Turgenev continues) is further revealed by the relations between each of them and the human mass, the 'crowd' – exemplified in the two works respectively by Polonius and by Sancho Panza. Polonius humours Hamlet, but does not believe him for a moment: 'Hamlets, indeed, are useless for the masses: they can give them nothing, they can lead them nowhere, because they are going nowhere themselves.' In contrast, the mass will deride, persecute and curse Don Quixote but will follow him blindly to the end of the earth (as Sancho follows the Knight), drawn irresistibly by his unswerving faith in his ideal. The contrast is also exemplified by the attitude of each type to women. Don Quixote loves his ideal: the real Dulcinea, when he meets her, is quite irrelevant to his love for the ideal, which is devoid of any physical passion. Hamlet, on the other hand, is a sensualist, and his love for Ophelia is largely play-acting and pretence, and the reflection of his preoccupation with himself.

So far, the advantages would all seem to be on the side of Don Quixote – 'When such men as Don Quixote cease to exist, let the book of history be closed forever!' says Turgenev half-way through his analysis. But he then turns to the positive side of Hamlet. Hamlet's scepticism and doubt are valuable qualities so long as they do not have the effect of paralysing all will for action, which happens all too easily. Can it really be the case, asks Turgenev, 'that one has to be a madman in order to have faith in truth?' No, this cannot be so, since the two principles symbolized by the two types, Hamlet and Don Quixote, are fundamental to human life, which consists eternally of their struggle and their coming together, of the struggle between inertia and movement, between progress and conservatism. Besides, the pure types of Don Quixote and of Hamlet are not in fact to be found in their extreme form in nature. Usually we encounter only approximations to them, and in life the contemplative Hamlet is an essential counterpart to the inventive and imaginative Don Quixote. The essay ends on a note which is rare in Turgenev, a note in which the Christian ethic is sounded, if only in muted form. He stresses the moving and beautiful death-bed scene in each work: Don Quixote claiming, for the very first time in the work, the title of Alonso the Good; and Hamlet's injunction to Horatio – 'the rest is silence'. For Turgenev, Hamlet is much redeemed by the love which Horatio bears him: it is the great merit of the Hamlets that they engender such love, and consequently 'educate and develop men like Horatio', in whose hearts the seeds of their reflection are sown and thus carried throughout the world. Kindness indeed is all, Turgenev concludes; all vanishes like smoke, save good deeds alone. 'All passes,' said the apostle. 'Love alone will remain.'*

I have dealt at length on this essay because it is essential for the understanding of Turgenev's mood during the period to which the writing of *Spring Torrents* belongs, and which is reflected, if only indirectly, in the novel. *Spring Torrents* formed one of a series of excursions into the past of which Turgenev's writing for some years after 1867 consisted. Turgenev felt strongly that the very fact of publishing a simple love story in 1872, after a series of demonstrably political novels, was a denial,

*This is presumably Turgenev's version of the First Epistle of Saint Paul to the Corinthians, Chapter 13, verse 8: 'Charity never faileth; but whether there be prophecies, they shall fail; whether there be tongues, they shall cease; whether there be knowledge, it shall vanish away.' The Greek Testament word for 'charity' is '*agape*' which in Russian is rendered by '*liubov*', 'love'. There is no Russian equivalent for the contrasting Greek '*eros*'.

even a criticism, of all commitment, and it was seemingly intended as such. As he wrote to his close friend Ya. P. Polonsky on 18 December 1871: 'My tale (between ourselves) will hardly find many admirers: it is a love story told in considerable detail which contains no reflections on social or political questions, and no hint at any contemporary problem. So much the better – unless I am very much mistaken.' The generally hostile reception accorded to the novel by the Russian radical intelligentsia showed that the forecast he had made of their reaction was not very far wrong. Indeed, between 1867, when *Smoke* appeared, and 1877, when he published *Virgin Soil*, everything he wrote was scrupulously devoid of all political content, and consisted for the most part of fairly short stories which bore the character of reminiscences or of pictures of past life in Russia. *Spring Torrents* is far and away the longest and most significant work of this period of his life and of a much more personal nature than any of the other stories. Its importance seems to me to lie in the fact that, apart from reflecting Turgenev's attitude to love and passion, it also directly illustrates, in the stark contrast between Maria Nikolaevna and Sanin, something of his preoccupation with the contrast between the strong-willed character who makes what he wants of life, and the weak man who waits for things to happen; and indirectly, if only because of the period when it was written, recalls the theme of *Hamlet and Don Quixote*: the hankering of the reflective, indecisive and un-committed for the certainty of the enthusiast and the fully committed.

So far as his personal life was concerned, Turgenev had sought happiness in love in passive submission to a dominant partner: it had brought him to the point where he could look for happiness only in the calmer relationship which supervenes when the time for passion is past. But so far as his public life was in question, it had led him, after 1867, almost to the point of rupture with the radical intelligentsia, by whom his failure to commit himself to their cause was seen as cowardice, even treason. Herein lay Turgenev's tragedy. His emotional sympathy lay with the revolutionary radicals. He often voiced his antipathy for the régime of Nicholas I, though, understandably and reasonably, less so for that of Alexander II, under whom hope for peaceful reform always remained alive. But his reason and his reflection – his 'Hamlet' temperament, as he would have put it – made him unable to accept the radicals uncritically, let alone commit himself to their uncompromising struggle against Alexander II and the existing order in Russia. The radicals wanted commitment or nothing: Turgenev's emotional support meant nothing to them, indeed exasperated them, without the all-out, uncritical taking of sides which they demanded. (To use the language of contemporary Communism, they wanted 'positive heroes', portrayed in terms of 'socialist realism': for this Turgenev was always too much of an artist, although he was to get perilously near the radicals' standard in his last novel, *Virgin Soil*, which from a literary point of view was a failure.) In order to understand this relationship of Turgenev to 'the committed', and the consequent reaction from which he was suffering during this non-political period of 1867–77, it is necessary to look at the reception accorded to *Fathers and Sons* and to *Smoke* inside Russia.

Of course, one must not look at the nineteenth century through the eyes of the twentieth. Today's readers of *Fathers and Sons* will find it difficult to see why its hero, Bazarov, aroused such fury among the Russian radicals when it appeared in 1862. One would have thought that Turgenev's admiration, love and sympathy for Bazarov were so self-evident as to be beyond question. This, however, was not the point that appeared most important to the radicals of the past century (with the notable exception of Pisarev, who, rightly, saw in Bazarov a reflection of his own views. But Pisarev was hardly a revolutionary, and was a lone thinker among his contemporaries.) But why should Bazarov, the 'nihilist', the man who accepts nothing on trust that his own intellect has not approved, the hard man, the cynic, the convinced materialist, the man for whom everything in the world has to be reshaped and the old destroyed by the man of the people, have aroused the anger of the 'democrats'? I think the answer is to be sought in Turgenev's failure to make him into the Soviet-type 'positive hero', instead of a human being. After all, Bazarov falls in love, for all his efforts to resist it, and his last thoughts are for the woman whom he loves. Bazarov dies a useless premature death, caused by negligence and by the insanitary conditions of Russian life: no 'positive hero' dies before his time! Bazarov has many more human failings – enough of them to make one wonder whether perhaps some of the brash nihilism will not rub off, along with the exuberance of youth, and make of him a sensible, valuable scientist or doctor who knows that revolutions, like operations, often cause more ills than they cure, and should therefore, if possible, be avoided. Perhaps some of Turgenev's more materialistic readers inside Russia were also put off by the last lines of *Fathers and Sons* which suggest, rather like the free paraphrase of Saint Paul in *Hamlet and Don Quixote*, that nothing endures for all time but human love and kindness. (In order to understand the reactions of the radical intelligentsia to Bazarov, one has only to contrast him with the revolutionary hero, Rakhmetov the Superman, of Chernyshevsky's novel *What is to be Done*, published a year after *Fathers and Sons*: unlike Bazarov, the improbable Rakhmetov, who is almost a caricature of revolutionary virtue, became the darling of the 'democrats' at the time, and the favourite hero of the young Lenin twenty-five years later.) The fiasco of *Fathers and Sons* was a shock to Turgenev which he did not expect; and which, as he saw it, he had done nothing to deserve. (In fairness to the revolutionaries, it should perhaps be recorded that when Turgenev died in 1883 the few remaining members of the revolutionary organization, 'The

Peoples' Will', paid a generous tribute to him for his faithful portrayal of the Russian revolutionary over several generations.)

Turgenev's reaction was, however, not only one of bitterness: he also sought in the years that followed to explain to himself why it was that his outlook seemed to be so far out of harmony with the younger generation of 'democrats'. One of the results of this reflection was the novel *Smoke*, published in 1867. It could scarcely have been intended to endear Turgenev to the radicals: its purpose rather was to set down in the form of a novel (which, like *Spring Torrents*, from the literary point of view, was one of the most perfect of all Turgenev's works) what he believed about the all-absorbing themes of Russia, Western Europe and radicalism. Set in Baden-Baden, *Smoke* is predominantly a love story, exploring one of Turgenev's favourite contrasts in types of women – the gentle, domestic, virtuous and compassionate Tania, and the elemental, cynical, strong-willed, sensual and dominant Irina. The weak hero, Litvinov, is swept away from Tania by Irina – the first love of his youth, who threw him over for life in high society: as I have suggested earlier, the story ends with a somewhat unconvincing return to Tania and forgiveness, of the kind which Sanin, more realistically, never attempted, and which I do not think the author believed in either. (Perhaps that is why Turgenev, on reflection, refused to alter the ending of *Spring Torrents*, though much pressed to do so; and in spite of the fact that he himself in his correspondence had expressed the intention of providing an altered ending for the French translation.)

But it was not as a love story that *Smoke* aroused passionate resentment inside Russia. 'It appears,' Turgenev reflected in 1880, 'that I equally offended both the right and the left sides of our reading public – though from different points of view. I began to have some doubts about myself and remained silent for some time.' Although the political passages of *Smoke* are incidental to the love story, they are quite sufficient to explain the hostility which they aroused at all points of the Russian political spectrum. For in a number of incidental, quite brilliantly portrayed, scenes in the course of the main narrative, Turgenev satirizes both the radicals and the ultra-reactionaries among his compatriots – a group of Russian radicals living in exile, and the fashionable society visitors to Baden-Baden who form part of Irina's entourage. Turgenev's dislike of serf-owners and their mentality (ex-serf-owners as they had become since 1861) was nothing new: but *Smoke* was the first occasion on which he had publicly attacked the revolutionary radicals. Perhaps even more hostility, and from such opposite ends of the political scale as Herzen and Dostoyevsky, was aroused by Turgenev's views on Russia and Europe, expressed in the conversations between Litvinov and an incidental character in the story, Potugin. Potugin is a Westerner, an enemy of Russian chauvinism, a man who, for all his love of his country, refuses to blind himself either to its faults or to its backwardness in relation to the rest of Europe. Such indeed was Turgenev himself, as his controversy with Herzen in correspondence earlier in the decade showed clearly.*

Spring Torrents therefore belongs to a period when Turgenev, under the impact of the reaction provoked by his political novels, devoted himself in his writing (of which there was, in truth, very little during the period with which we are concerned) to reminiscences, to story-telling and to craftsmanship for its own sake. His considered statement on commitment to a political cause lay ahead – it was to be made in his last novel, *Virgin Soil*, published in 1877. But the idea of a novel, which was to be wholly devoted to the Russian revolutionaries, occurred to him as early as 1870: during the years which followed he reflected deeply on the theme which he had con-

*I have discussed this controversy in my *Rationalism and Nationalism in Russian Nineteenth-Century Political Thought* (New Haven, 1967), pp. 102–6.

ceived, and studied in great detail accounts of revolutionary activity. *Virgin Soil* is not relevant to *Spring Torrents*. But it may be observed that it represents a modification of Turgenev's almost uncritical worship of commitment for its own sake which is suggested by *Hamlet and Don Quixote*. For it is not the all-out revolutionaries who emerge as the heroes in Turgenev's work, but rather those who by patient, daily service to the people set about the long, laborious task of educating and preparing them for the rôle which they must one day play. And yet – perhaps this was the real message of *Hamlet and Don Quixote* already present in Turgenev's mind, and even hinted at in the words, ' "All passes," said the apostle. "Love alone will remain" '. Maturer reflection was to wean Turgenev from the overwhelming and uncritical worship of will and enthusiasm towards which, because he himself lacked these qualities, he was for so much of his life drawn. *Spring Torrents* perhaps marks the beginning of this process. Hamlet and Don Quixote have become Sanin and Maria Nikolaevna Polozova. But each has by now already become a caricature of the type: he of weakness and vacillation, she of will, dominance and selfishness of purpose.

And so, as Turgenev had anticipated, *Spring Torrents* was roundly abused by the Russian intelligentsia. A number of cruel and vicious satires upon it, aimed at Turgenev himself and his relations with Pauline Viardot, appeared before long. Among those readers whose concern was more for literature than for politics, its exquisite craftsmanship won the highest praise – although even some friendly critics were disturbed by the excesses of humiliation which were heaped on the unhappy Sanin after his enslavement to Madame Polozov. (Turgenev's most sympathetic critic, his friend Annenkov, was particularly appalled by the pear which Sanin peels for Polozov, sitting on the uncomfortable front seat of the carriage which is bearing them all to Paris!) As the story became known in translation, it won the most extravagant praise from fellow-writers, including Flaubert, Georg Brandes, and many more. The first translation to appear, the German (the Germans were very affronted by some of the satire on Germans in general and on Herr Klueber in particular!), was in 1872, and in the following year *Spring Torrents* appeared in French. The first English translation, by Sophie Michell, appeared serially in the United States, in the *Eclectic Review* in 1873 and 1874. There have been numerous translations into English since, and, of course, into a number of other languages.

The form in which the story is cast – the reminiscence many years later – was one of Turgenev's favourite devices. What is at first sight curious in so meticulous a craftsman is the way in which the conventions of this form of narrative are departed from: there are numerous occasions where the author takes over from Sanin, indeed the author is never far in the background. He describes Sanin for us, he interposes his own reflections on Germans, on young love, on the Wiesbaden Theatre, and the like. Nevertheless this is never in the slightest distracting. The convention of the reminiscence is in this case more than a mere literary device: it is an integral part of the story, because it leads on to the pilgrimage to Frankfurt thirty years later and to the projected departure for America. Hence the interposition by the author of his own comments never jars, as it might if the form of reminiscence were no more than a story-teller's device. It is no doubt for this reason that Turgenev was not concerned about the two passages in which the convention is most flagrantly violated by the description of important events in the narrative, which form an integral part of the story, but which Sanin could not possibly have 'remembered'. Such is the scene between Gemma and her mother which concludes Chapter 24. Such too is the symbolic, and prophetic, threatening gesture with which Pantaleone speeds the departing Sanin after he has taken leave of Gemma, in Chapter 32: yet we are specifically told that Sanin never noticed this, so how could he have remembered it thirty years later? It is obvious that these passages could not have escaped the notice of Turgenev: the inference is that he saw no need to change them. Indeed, so natural do they seem within the framework of the lightly worn convention of the reminiscence that I wonder how many readers of this translation have even noticed the inconsistency of the two passages to which I have drawn attention, let alone been disturbed by them?

Turgenev's art derived from images, not from ideas, as he explained himself, and as has been so often analysed and expounded in literary criticism, notably by Henry James who recalls Turgenev's own words in the Preface to *Portrait of a Lady*. 'It began for him,' says James, 'almost always with the vision of some person or persons who hovered before him, soliciting him as the active or passive figure, interesting him and appealing to him just as they were and by what they were . . . He . . . then had to find for them the right relations, those that would most bring them out . . .' Henry James then introduces Turgenev's own words: 'The result is that I'm often accused of not having "story" enough. I seem to myself to have as much as I need – to show my people, to exhibit their relations with each other; for that is all my measure. If I watch them long enough, I see them come together, I see them *placed*, I see them engaged in this or that act and in this or that difficulty . . .' Turgenev's characters were almost invariably drawn from life, but naturally more than one living model might go to the making of a fictional person. Moreover, once the process of writing had been embarked on, the characters would develop an impetus and a life of their own, and would grow and change in the process of writing, sometimes in a manner not originally intended by the author.

In some instances the evidence enables us to determine

exactly the original sources which inspired Turgenev's fiction. (Bakunin for Rudin, for example; or almost all the main characters of *Virgin Soil*.) In the case of *Spring Torrents* this is not possible to the same extent; nonetheless, certain conversations with Turgenev about this novel, recorded in the memoirs of his contemporaries, tell us a little about the sources from which the germ of the idea for the novel, and for some of its main characters, sprang – even if we have no means of testing the accuracy of the records which have come down to us. When he was in Frankfurt in 1840 a young girl of extraordinary beauty suddenly emerged from a tea-room to plead for his help in reviving her brother, who had fainted. The girl was a Jewess, not an Italian; and the susceptible Turgenev, unlike Sanin, had the sense to leave Frankfurt the same night. But the image of Gemma was to grow out of this memory thirty years later. From another source we learn that Maria Nikolaevna was inspired by a certain Princess Trubetskaia whom Turgenev knew in Paris, and Pantaleone by someone who occupied the position halfway between that of friend and servant in her household. No models have ever been suggested for Polozov, Klueber or Signora Roselli: but it is very likely that all of them (and no doubt that poodle Tartaglia), crossed Turgenev's path at one time or another. And what of Doenhof? The model for him (and for Sanin's encounter with him) could have been one of the two young German officers with whom Turgenev was involved in a scene in Switzerland in 1864. A large company, including Turgenev and the officers, was seated around the luncheon table of the *pension* where Turgenev was staying. A fellow-Russian, an émigré who had lost his fortune as a consequence of exile, and who was frequently invited to a meal by one or other of the many Russian guests who lived in the *pension*, came into the dining-room for a moment, stood at the door as if in search of someone, and not seeing him there, left. At this point one of the two officers observed aloud in German to his companion, that 'this Russian émigré is always hungry. He is just like his country from which he fled. It too is always on the look-out for one of its trusting and simple-hearted neighbours in order to devour and swallow it.' Turgenev, white with rage, addressed a most dignified speech to the officer concerned. His country, he said, needed no protection from ill-bred bounders. But, since his compatriot who had suffered misfortune was absent, he, Turgenev took his defence upon himself. He demanded (he said) neither an apology nor a withdrawal of the words spoken. 'But I request you to rise from the table and leave our presence. A man who permits himself, without any provocation, such ill-mannered conduct cannot be tolerated in the company of decent people.' The officers appeared at first to be about to reply with further insolence; but they then thought better of it, left the table, and departed from the *pension* the same day.

Comparison of the third and first fair copies of *Spring Torrents* (which, as suggested earlier, reveals Turgenev's re-working of his text in the second fair copy, which necessitated a third fair copy) enables us to see something of the meticulous care with which the characters were developed and delineated. A full analysis of the differences between the two manuscripts can obviously not be undertaken here. But a selection of examples of Turgenev's workmanship must be cited in order to illustrate some of its aspects. First, let me give a few examples of the way in which, by removing a word or two in the course of revision, Turgenev succeeds in concentrating and thus heightening the visual image by the greater economy of description. Thus, originally Emil's necktie was not only 'tight' but also 'brightly coloured': the omission is much more consistent with Sanin's worried concern for the boy and for the fact that he is being stifled by his clothing (p. 17) to which the colour bears little relevance. Pantaleone's feet (on p. 18) were originally not only flat and gouty but 'diseased' as well – a plainly redundant and distracting adjective, which adds nothing to the picture evoked by 'gouty'. There are many more instances of such pruning by the removal of superfluous adjectives especially, so that in the end result every word in the sentence is essential for the completion of the picture, and no redundant words are there to distract attention from the picture. Perhaps the best illustration of this concentration on the terse, vivid picture is the omission of a passage which was apparently originally intended to follow after the words 'these abstractions are exceedingly useful as a start, as a point of departure . . .' (on p. 156): 'The soft and strong rings of the "beautiful snake", quietly, without a sound, but irresistibly, were settling themselves and becoming entwined around the rabbit? Is that right? Oh no! [it is impossible] one cannot use such a [word] expression . . . around the inexperienced victim, if only such a word [is suitable] can be used . . . in such a context.' One has only to read this somewhat laboured draft to see how much better the text is without it – and indeed, how much better anything it attempts to say is in the end implicit in the narrative which has come down to us.

To take a second type of variant – where the change is required less in the interests of style than because it is desirable for the clearer delineation of a particular aspect of a character or a situation. Tartaglia (on p. 19) makes his first appearance. He is a dog of a very distinctive character – his main trait, indeed, will later be shown to be intense interest and participation in all that happens in the household and to its members, and an enormous enjoyment of life. The insertion in the first fair copy of the word 'inquisitively' seems to me to underline this aspect of the dog's character most felicitously. More striking is the change made in the physical description of Gemma (on p. 30). Originally her black curls were made to cascade about her neck 'like snakes'. But how right Turgenev was to omit this word which is later to become associated with Maria Nikolaevna, and therefore quite out of place in a description of Gemma. There are two more such instances where the omission of a word or two in the final text is designed to show Gemma's disciplined propriety and chastity, no doubt the better to underline the contrast when we meet Maria Nikolaevna. When Sanin returns Gemma her rose, after the painful journey back from Soden (p. 54), she 'pressed his hand'. Originally she had been made to press his hand 'tightly'. Again, when Sanin returns to the patisserie after the discussion with Herr Richter about the forthcoming duel (p. 63), Gemma no longer, in the final version, 'seizes Sanin's hand in both of her own'. Evidently on second thoughts Turgenev decided, and I think rightly, that this was too forward a gesture for Gemma to have made. And lastly, an example of a change in the final version which adds most colourfully to our picture of Maria Nikolaevna. When she is recounting to Sanin her early passion for Monsieur Gaston, the Swiss tutor, the words 'or some other feeling' in the sentence where she relates how she lay in bed listening to his footsteps overhead, seems to add a whole dimension to this woman's sensuality: they were inserted in the course of the revision of the first fair copy (p. 149).

And finally, a few examples must be quoted from comparison of the manuscripts which illustrate the skill with which Turgenev could depict a small scene. In the cases which follow the addition of a few words in the final version prepared for the printer often makes the picture more vivid and true to character. Take Pantaleone, mocking Gemma's reading of Maltz (p. 132), 'poking his face forward and splaying his fingers': the last four words, added in revision, gives us a more living picture of the old Italian opera singer by the use of this additional, typically Latin, gesture. Again, no one who has ever seen a somewhat confused yokel will be in much doubt that the addition (on p. 40) of the words 'against his stomach' greatly adds to the scene of the astonished customer whom Sanin serves in the shop. Herr Klueber is depicted with a studied hatred and total lack of charity which are rare in

Turgenev: he seems to have unloaded in this portrait all his detestation of the commonplace, of vulgarity, of that petty meanness of character which the Russians call – in a word that defies translation – *poshlost'*. It was a good idea, I think, when describing Herr Klueber's proposal of a game of skittles before the fateful luncheon party in Soden (p. 49) to underline the character of this pompous Germanic ass with the words 'adding that this was very good for the appetite, hee, hee, hee!' There are several more such brilliant additions. The windows of the houses in Frankfurt sparkling in the morning sun 'like silver foil' (p. 69); or Polozov helping himself to 'about eight spoonfuls of jam', and not, as originally, to 'an enormous quantity of jam' (p. 128): obviously so meticulous a feeder as Polozov would have his habits fixed on a certain, definite ration of post-prandial jam in order to make sure of keeping body and soul together! Or Gemma in the garden with Sanin, after the duel when he modestly disclaims any heroic action on his own part: 'Gemma moved a finger to the right and to the left in front of her eyes. Another Italian gesture' (p. 83). Again, these words, which appear in the final revision, add to our picture of Gemma's vigorous Latin vitality and reveal Turgenev's close observation of the gestures typical of Italians in conversation. There are many more such examples, too many to quote. The comparison of these manuscripts is an enriching experience, since it enables one to see Turgenev's mind at work.

Is there any point in the kind of analysis to which I have tried to subject *Spring Torrents*? Those who have read and enjoyed the story, and skipped the reflections with which I have burdened it, have probably remained much closer to Turgenev's purpose in writing it – to entertain. It is primarily, after all, a light love story. Neither Sanin nor Maria Nikolaevna is really cast as a great tragic figure, while the practical and sensible

Gemma does not in the end take very long to get over the affair, and does incidentally shed the odious Klueber in the process. She is really a very tough girl. As for Maria Niko-laevna, her life is barren, pointless and short: but she willed it that way. It would perhaps be too much to read into her a suggestion that she is the victim of the corrupting influence of serfdom, from which she was one of the few (in 1840) to have escaped. But the type is a familiar one in Russian literature and life – Lopakhin in the *Cherry Orchard* is a reminder that the rise of the peasant to a position of nominal social equality with the gentry was not an easy process. Perhaps, like Sanin, but for very different reasons, Maria Nikolaevna should be allowed her small measure of tragedy.

And what is one to say of Sanin, '*ce nigaud de Sanine*', as his begetter calls him? The fascinating aspect that I find in him derives from the fact that he both is, and is not, Turgenev. He is Turgenev caricatured by Turgenev, perhaps; a kind of paradigm of weakness and fecklessness, perhaps, which Turgenev never was, but which in moods of depression he believed himself to be. As such Sanin serves his purpose: he reveals to us much of Turgenev's own suffering and predica-ment, even though the circumstances of the two men are so very different in every respect. We catch a glimpse through him of Turgenev around 1840 – the young man with the world before him, thrown into a passionate and romantic fever of love. '*Je me suis laissé entrainer par des souvenirs,*' Turgenev told a correspondent, referring to *Spring Torrents*. These distant events must have looked very different some thirty years later. But *Spring Torrents* is an attempt to recapture past moods and emotions and relive them with the benefit of the mellowness and maturity which experience brings. Small wonder that Sanin's raptures are interspersed with almost cynical comments by the author as the story progresses. Sanin is not Turgenev, but he, as it were, stands in for him: he reveals to us as much about Turgenev as Turgenev wishes us to know. He too has his small measure of tragedy, since he reflects the tragedy in the life of a much greater and much more spiritually developed man – his creator, the author.

So, whatever tragedy there may be in the story it is probably of minor consequence. Naturally, like every great writer, Turgenev wrote to entertain, in the sense that every great artist creates in order to entertain. I use 'entertain' in the broad sense – to delight by craftsmanship, as a Vermeer interior or a fourteenth-century French ivory mirror-back delights us by its craftsmanship, and therefore entertains. But, in the process of entertaining us the writer of genius reveals himself, the greatness of his spirit, the depth of his own tragedy, the shapes and images and ideas which have gone to the making of his rich mind. I have tried as best I could to catch a few glimpses of Turgenev's spirit and experience as they are reflected at different points from the many facets which *Spring Torrents* presents. For me the search for these reflections has enormously heightened my appreciation of *Spring Torrents* and of Turgenev's greatness. I can only hope that others too may feel that my search has not been entirely in vain.